the ocean
between
us
MICHELLE HEARD

Cover Designer: Sybil Wilson, PopKitty Design
Cover Model: Drew Truckle
Photographer Credit: <u>Eric David Battershell.</u>

WARNING

Please note that The Ocean Between Us
contains graphically violent scenes that may be
upsetting to some readers.

Previously published as Wake Me Up.
Scenes have been changed and edited.
It's basically a new book!
Happy Reading.

Goodbye, my almost lover
Goodbye, my hopeless dream
I'm trying not to think about you
Can't you just let me be?
So long, my luckless romance
my back is turned on you
Should've known you'd bring me heartache
Almost lovers always do

I cannot go to the ocean
I cannot drive the streets at night
I cannot wake up in the morning
Without you on my mind
So you're gone, and I'm haunted
and I bet you are just fine
Did I make it that easy to walk right in and out
of my life?

'Almost Lover' ~ Alison Sudol.

If I had wings, I'd fly.
I'd soar high where only eagles dare.
I'd let them rip.
I'd let them tear.
Until all that remained was me bare.

PROLOGUE

EMMA

Sitting across from my mother, I keep my eyes lowered while she tells me once again what a colossal failure I am.

This has become my life.

I'm so bloody tired of it.

She never has anything good to say about me. I try so damn hard, but nothing I do is good enough.

I feel her hate-filled eyes on me while the stench of wine fills the air, making it hard to breathe.

"Say it," she hisses, her voice heavy with loathing.

Knowing what she wants to hear, my insides quiver with defiance, but years of conditioning keep me from standing up for myself.

Instead, I say, "I'll be like Mom."

6

It makes me sick to my stomach to say the words.

My mother is a master at playing mind games. She's perfected the art of emotional abuse to get what she wants. Thinking back on my past, I can honestly say I can't remember a time where she showed me an ounce of kindness. What makes it so unbearable is that I know she can be a loving mother.

She hates me but loves my older brother. I don't know what I did to make her despise me so much. She abuses me every chance she gets but gives Byron the world. Where he can do no wrong in my mother's eyes, I can do nothing right.

My mother is an alcoholic. Sometimes I think she has more wine in her system than blood. My grandfather was a drunk too. My soul shudders at the thought of becoming anything like them.

I want to fight back and scream at her, "*Stop, Mom! Can't you see what it's doing to you? What it's making you do to me?*"

But I can't. I don't dare as it will only make things worse.

Instead, I keep my eyes lowered, praying this night won't get any worse while years of being subjected to this torture and fear keep me frozen to the spot.

It wasn't always this bad. We were never close, but after my fourteenth birthday, things got worse. As I grew older, the calculated words got sharper, and by the time I reached my eighteenth birthday, it had escalated to beatings.

I can still handle the physical abuse. Scars fade. It's the emotional abuse that's the real killer. Words never heal. They become an endless echo in your mind, a living nightmare. Never losing their potency, they grow stronger over time until you believe them.

"You just read those books. That's all you do," Mom snarls.

She takes another sip of wine, and I hear the ice jingling in the glass. I wish she would stop drinking.

"You're throwing your life away. There's no silver lining, no happily ever after. There's no such thing as a fairy tale. Life is hard, babes."

Leaning closer to me, she hisses. "And without me, you won't make it." Her stinking breath wafts over me, sticking to my skin.

Every day it gets harder to remain submissive. Unable to stop myself, my eyes dart up. I watch as she leans back in the chair. Her eyes look like they've been carved from stone as they rest on me.

My mother used to be beautiful with her raven-black hair and huge brown eyes. But hatred and alcohol have ruined her, leaving her with oily hair and cruel eyes.

"You think you're better than me?" she growls which makes me quickly lower my gaze from hers.

Crap, I shouldn't have looked up.

"You're nothing!" she snarls.

There's a familiar sinking feeling in my stomach, knowing what's coming.

She wants me to tell her how grateful I am for her, how amazing she is. They're just empty words, but still, she gets high on hearing them.

You have to, Emma. It will only escalate if you don't boost her ego. Your back is still raw from the last beating.

Rising to my feet, I take a step toward her, while it feels as if my body is being weighed down.

Kneeling at her feet, I take hold of her free hand while focusing with all my might to not show any emotion on my face. Contempt rises in my throat as I lift my eyes to hers, praying that I look like a loving daughter.

Hatred slithers through me, threatening to squeeze the last bit of life from my heart.

The clamminess of her alcohol-drenched skin sticks to my hand, and I struggle not to yank it back. I swallow hard on the bile rising in my throat as I force the words out.

"I'm so lucky to have, Mom."

Her eyes gleam with satisfaction as she pulls her hand free from mine. Holding the empty wine glass out to me, she orders, "Fill my glass. Half ice, half wine."

"Yes, Mom."

Taking the glass, I scramble to my feet and rush to the kitchen. I hate pouring wine for my mother. It feels as if I'm enabling her addiction. But I need the few minutes of reprieve before I have to go back to her.

While I keep busy with the task, I tell myself that it's only two more days.

On my twenty-first birthday, I got access to the trust fund left by my grandfather. Even though my mother has to approve all the transactions until I'm twenty-five, I at least get a monthly allowance. It's given me the freedom to leave this place and make a life for myself somewhere far away.

Staying here in this house is no longer an option, knowing that I won't survive it.

Chloe, my best friend, helped me get a passport and study visa so I can escape to America. While we were studying, she drove me wherever I needed to go so I could get all the paperwork done. Without her, I'm not sure I would've held out for as long as I have. She's been my saving grace from the first moment we met in high school.

I would've loved to get a job and move into my own place but living in South Africa makes that hard. Jobs aren't easy to come by, and not having a car makes it near impossible. If this country had decent public transport, it would've solved the problem of getting to work and back.

It's one of the reasons I'm going to America. I'll be there on a study visa, but with a little luck, I hope to get a job. The main reason is to get as far as possible away from my mother.

"What's taking so long?" Mom yells from the living room, yanking me out of my thoughts.

Picking up the glass, I rush back to her.

"Sorry, Mom," I whisper as I place the wine down on the table beside her chair.

"When are we eating?" Dad asks, coming out of their bedroom, wearing a pair of shorts. His big stomach wobbles with every step he takes.

He spends his days off in the sunroom at the back of the house with his nose buried in newspapers. He chooses to ignore the abuse, which is ironic actually, seeing that he's a policeman. He protects others but never me. He's too weak to stand up to my mother.

Life has taught me that the people who are supposed to protect you are the ones who will hurt you the most. It doesn't help that South Africa's policemen are all corrupted, so I can't even go to them.

"The food should be ready, my love. Take a seat at the table," Mom says sweetly. As she gets up, she grabs the glass of wine and makes her way to the kitchen.

I follow behind her so I can help carry the dishes to the dining room.

Placing the glass of wine on the kitchen table, Mom grabs a dishcloth then opens the oven door. I pick up the oven mittens, and as I'm about to offer them to her, she takes hold of the bowl of rice.

"Shit," she cries as she drops it.

I watch in horror as glass shatters and rice spills all over the floor.

For a moment there's only silence as fear slithers down my spine.

No!

I fall to my knees and start to scoop up as much rice and broken glass as I can. A shard of glass stabs into my palm, but I ignore it. I have to clean up this mess.

"Look what you've made me do," Mom snarls, throwing the cloth at me.

"I'm sorry, Mom," I whisper, dread creeping into my voice.

Knowing what's about to happen, I should get up and run.

I want to rise to my feet, so I can at least defend myself, but self-preservation wars against years of psychological manipulation.

I hate myself most in moments like these.

"You're so pathetic. I've been slaving over a nice meal all day long, and this how you thank me?"

"I'm sorry, Mom," I whisper again. Saying anything else would only make things worse.

Grabbing hold of my hair, and yanking me to my feet, her fingers claw at my scalp. I drop the rice and pieces of glass I've managed to gather, and my hands fly to the back of my head, grabbing hold of hers.

The words *I'm sorry* get stuck on the tip of my tongue as she starts to walk toward my room, pulling me along. My scalp stings where strands of hair are being ripped out. The saliva in my mouth thickens with trepidation, and my heart begins to beat faster in my chest.

She shoves me into my room, and I pray that she'll only deny me food, locking me inside the room. But my prayers are once again ignored as she storms down the hallway. Trembling, I stand beside my bed, with wide eyes glued to the door.

Hearing her footsteps coming back toward me, my breaths speed up as hopeless tears sting my eyes. Grinding my teeth, I swallow the tears down, knowing it will only make her angrier if I cry.

You're leaving soon, Emma. This won't be your life forever.

You can endure this for forty-eight hours. Then you'll finally get to escape this hell.

Storming into the room, she raises her arm, and I quickly turn my body sideways as the belt lashes over my shoulder. The stinging pain is fleeting.

15

"Spare the rod, spoil the child," she hisses.

When she strikes at me again, the urge to grab the belt from her almost overwhelms me.

I want to fight back with every ounce of my body, but instead remind myself of how disastrous that will be.

The last time I grabbed the belt from her, she lost her shit, and after beating me unconscious, I had to stay home from school for two weeks to hide the bruises from the world.

It was the worst two weeks of my life.

Another blow to my back forces me to my knees, and I grab hold of the side of my bed to keep myself from sprawling over the floor.

An agonizing blow almost rips a scream from me, but I press my mouth against the back of my hands to smother it. When she finally stops, my back feels flayed to the bone.

As she drops the belt next to me on the floor, I cringe closer to the bed. Her hand brushes gently over my hair, making my body shudder violently with revulsion.

16

"This is for your own good, babes. If I don't keep you in line, who knows what will become of you."

I've grown accustomed to the hateful words, and the angry beatings, but it kills my soul when she touches me while justifying why I deserved to be punished.

I keep still until she leaves, and hearing the door shut behind her, I let out a shaky breath. Once I'm able to climb to my feet, I gingerly pull my shirt over my head. Turning my back to the mirror against the wall, I look over my shoulder at the new slashes that have been added to my skin.

A numb feeling settles in my heart, and I know I won't last two more days. I have to leave as soon as they're asleep. I'll stay at the airport until my flight.

I switch off the light and crawl onto my stomach on the bed so nothing will touch my aching back.

An hour later, when the door opens, I quickly shut my eyes and pretend to be asleep. As she switches on the light, she lets out a heavy sigh before coming closer and placing something down next to the bed.

She leaves, not bothering to switch the light off.

I wait a few minutes before I turn my head to the side so I can see what she's placed on the floor.

Feeling degraded and broken down, I swallow the useless tears back as I stare at the plate of chicken bones. It's supposed to be my supper.

What have I done to deserve this? Why does my own mother get so much pleasure from torturing me?

Instead of finding any answers, I bury my face in the pillow and countdown the minutes until I can safely escape this hell.

CHAPTER 1

EMMA

The last three days have been exhausting. Sneaking away from the house in the middle of the night like some criminal was the most daring thing I've ever done. While sitting at the airport, I chewed my nails to the nerve out of fear that I'd be caught and dragged back to that hellish prison.

I unlock the door to the flat which will be my new home for the next six months. Not knowing whether my roommate is home, I slowly walk inside.

Closing the door behind me, I leave my bags at the entrance. "Hello, is anyone here?"

Silence greets me, and I let out a sigh of relief. It will give me time to get settled before whoever I'm sharing the flat with gets back.

19

Crap, I should've asked Miss Jessie, the landlord, about my roommate. For a moment I contemplate going back to her but decide to put it off until I go out to explore a little of the town.

Opening the door to the first bedroom, and glancing inside, I see a pair of men's sneakers beside the bed. It's clear I'll be sharing with a guy unless the girl has big feet, which I doubt.

Actually, I hope it's a guy. I don't think I can handle living with another woman so soon after all I've been through with my mother.

The second door opens to a bathroom, and I'm glad to see that it has a shower.

Grabbing my luggage, I walk to the last room, which I assume will be mine. Pushing the door open, my eyes greedily take in all the space.

There's a closet against the wall, and a big bed stands opposite it. I've never slept in such a massive bed. I just want to face-plant onto it and sleep all my worries away.

"Wow," I whisper. "This flat is amazing."

Even though my parents live in a mansion in Clifton, one of Cape Town's wealthiest neighborhoods, my bedroom at the back of the house was small and only held a bed. There wasn't even space for a dresser, and I had to keep my clothes in the closet of one of the guest bedrooms. It was just another way for my mother to make me feel like an unwanted burden.

For the first time since I left home, a smile forms around my lips and excitement starts to bloom in my chest.

I hate my parents for doing this to me, for making me run to North Carolina, the other side of the bloody world. But I've had enough. A person can only take so much abuse.

I have to prove to myself that I can survive without them. The trust fund isn't huge, and with the exchange rate being so bad, it doesn't leave me with much of a monthly allowance once it's converted to dollars. I'll only have enough for rent, one meal a day, and paying for my studies.

THE OCEAN BETWEEN US – Michelle Heard

Even though my finances aren't the best, I feel hopeful, and for the first time, I don't dread what tomorrow might bring.

Lifting my bag onto the bed, I start to unpack. It only takes a minute to transfer my clothes over to the spacious closet. The few items look lost in all the space, but still, a warm feeling settles in my heart.

I might not have much, but I have my freedom.

"You've done it, Emma," I whisper. I grab clean clothes and the only towel I have, then walk back to the bathroom so I can shower. "You have six months to find a way so you can stay here."

After I've taken a quick shower, I get dressed in a pair of jeans and a t-shirt.

Back in my room, I place the dirty clothes in my backpack. I'll have to find a laundromat where I can wash them.

I turn on my phone, and immediately it starts to vibrate with messages and missed calls. I choose to ignore them for now and search for Chloe's number.

Holding the phone to my ear, a smile spreads across my face the second I hear her voice.

"I've been going insane! Did you land in one piece? Is the place you're staying at nice? What is your roommate like? Have your parents cont –"

"Chloe, slow down. One question at a time," I stop her interrogation with a burst of laughter. "I'm safely here. The flat is very nice. It's a two bedroom, and it has an open plan kitchen and small lounge. The bedroom is huge, Chloe. It has so much closet space, and the window looks out over a beautiful courtyard. It's nothing like the room at home. It's easily twice as big. Don't even get me started on how comfy the bed looks."

A sense of freedom washes over me as I take in my new home.

I'm really free.

"I'm so happy you like it, Em. You sound better too. You did the right thing by leaving. Have you met your roommate?"

"I haven't met the person I'm sharing the flat with. I'm a little nervous about that. I saw a pair of men's sneakers, so I'm sure it's a guy. Miss Jessie, the owner, let me in. She seems nice, but she was surprised to see

THE OCEAN BETWEEN US – Michelle Heard

me. My application got mixed up with some other guy's. After explaining that I can't afford to live on my own and how important it is that I share a flat, she relented and gave me the keys."

"Oh hell. I'm just glad you got it all sorted. Anyway, I'm glad you've settled in. After everything we had to go through to get you there," she sighs. "Just don't answer your phone if that bitch tries to call you. Don't reply to her texts. Don't let her intimidate you. Remember, she's on the other side of the world now. You're safe in America."

"Thank you for helping me," I say, thanking my lucky stars again that I have such an incredible friend.

"You know I'd ride a porcupine butt naked for you," she laughs. I don't know where she heard that, but since she did, she hasn't stopped saying it.

"You're the best," I whisper. It's the best I can do to tell Chloe that I care about her.

I can't say the words *I love you*. My mother has made them lose all meaning, and now they're just empty words I hear after a beating.

"Now, go on! Go out and have some fun," she says, her voice laced with excitement for me.

"I'm a little scared, to be honest, but I'm not going to let it hold me back," I admit.

"Yes, don't hide in your room. Go out and experience new things. You'll see not everyone is as evil as that insane mother of yours."

I want to experience everything this world has to offer. I've never gone out before and have no idea how to socialize. Being out and between people is the only way I'm going to learn.

"Take your phone with you and call if you need me. Or text me. I'm on standby," Chloe says, offering her support like she always does.

"You're the best. You know that, right?" I say again.

"No, you're the best," she laughs.

"I'll let you know how it goes."

My phone beeps just as I cut the call. One glance tells me I can't run from the inevitable. Chloe would kill me if she knew I was answering them, but I can't just ignore my parents. They are my family, after all. I'll just let them know I'm safe.

Dad: *Where are you? We can't reach you. Your mother's worried.*

Me: *I'm taking a break from it all. I'm safe.*

I bite my bottom lip as I watch the message go through. Even though an ocean separates me from them, I can't help but feel scared.

My heartbeat starts to speed up as a panic attack threatens to engulf me.

Closing my eyes, I picture an eagle taking flight, and I let all my feelings soar away with it. It's something I started doing two years ago after I saw an eagle soaring above our house. I had just finished gathering all the dead leaves from the swimming pool when I heard the sharp cry. I must've watched it for an hour before it flew away. What I remember most from that day was the peaceful feeling which filled my heart.

Sucking in a deep breath, I slowly open my eyes. "You're going to be fine, Emma. You can do this."

CHAPTER 2

EMMA

I lock the flat behind me and make my way down the stairs. Chloe and I picked this place because it's close to town, and I won't have to worry about transport.

I don't get to see much of Chapel Hill on my quest to find a place where students hang out. I spot a group of girls around my age walking into a place called *Strikers Bar* and decide to go inside.

Stopping in the entrance first, I take in the people and surroundings while I force myself to not turn around and run away. My nerves feel shredded, but I know if I turn around now I'll never try again. I have to do this for myself.

An upbeat song fills the air. To my right is a weathered, overused dance floor. There's a really old bar counter to my left. Seeing the students sitting around tables while laughing and having drinks, makes excitement grow inside of me.

Not wanting to sit alone at a table, I walk over to the bar. I find a seat in the far corner, so I can watch everyone around me and hopefully not look like a creep while doing it.

When I glance at the men to my right, my nerves almost get the better of me. A couple of them look my way, and my mouth dries right up. I feel my cheeks flush and quickly look straight ahead of me.

I watch the bartender serve some patrons, his hands working fast to get the glasses filled. A door behind the bar opens, and another bartender places some clean glasses on the counter before he looks up. He smiles at me, and I have to admit, he's not too bad looking.

"What can I get you?" he asks, and hearing his heavy Southern accent makes my stomach flutter.

Wanting to know what all the fuss is about when it comes to alcohol, I ask, "What would you suggest?"

"Start her off on tequila," the guy to my right says with a creepy sounding laugh.

Yuck, I wouldn't touch him if my life depended on it.

"Just not wine," I quickly add as the bartender glares darkly at the man before getting busy fixing my drink. Seconds later, he places a frosted glass in front of me. There's even a strawberry wedged on the side.

"Strawberry Daiquiri," he says, winking at me.

"Thanks," I say as my eyes drop back to the drink.

Taking a sip, I'm surprised by how pleasant it tastes. It's sweet and actually refreshing and not all what I expected.

After another sip, I glance around. I haven't even dated back home. How am I going to handle dating American guys?

It's during moments like this when I realize just how much my mother has held me back. Finally being free, I have an urgent need to experience everything all at once.

I want to face all my fears and rise above them, and coming to this bar tonight is hopefully a step in the right direction. With a little luck, I'll have enough courage to talk to a few people tonight, and maybe even meet a guy. I have to start somewhere, right?

I hate feeling broken, and want to prove to myself that I'm the same as any other girl. I'd like to experience sex for the first time. I'm not looking for romance, because that will only lead to having to tell someone about my horrible past, and I'm not sure I can do that.

Knowing I might never get another chance like this, I want to live life to the fullest, just in case I have to go home.

Halfway through the drink, which is really only seconds later, a loud roar of cheers erupts from the entrance, and just like everyone else, my curiosity gets the better of me. Glancing over my shoulder, I see a group of guys greeting people. They must be the 'in' crowd because most of the girls are staring at them.

It gets even louder as more students start to arrive. For a few minutes I sit and watch as guys hit on girls, friends talk and laugh, and couples dance.

It's just like the books I've read.

A sharp burst of laughter draws my attention, and my eyes go back to the group of guys. They're slowly making their way in my direction but stop at every other table to talk to someone.

I notice that there's only one girl with the testosterone brigade. I've never seen a girl move with so much confidence before, and it makes me stare.

Her black hair shimmers in the dim light, and the sparkly top and short skirt doesn't cover much. But then again, if I had legs like hers, I'd walk on my hands to show them off.

The men are built like rugby players. They give off a vibe that says, 'screw with us, and you're dead'.

Before I can turn my attention back to my drink, the girl glances around, and her eyes meet mine. Instantly a cold shiver runs down my spine, making my stomach pull into a tight knot. Even with the distance between us, I can see she's bad news.

Then she smiles at me, and no matter how I try to force my lips to curve up, I can't make myself return the smile. She reminds me too much of my mother.

Don't judge every woman you meet just because your mother is a monster!

I take big gulps of my drink while berating myself for being so judgmental.

Placing the empty glass back on the counter, I have to admit that I feel less nervous than when I walked in here.

Glancing at the bartender, I'm just about to ask him for another drink when I hear, "Hey, sweet thing."

Crap.

I freeze, and for a second, I hope that the person isn't talking to me.

"Why's a pretty little thing like you all alone?"

Please, please, please don't let it be her.

Even as I send up the silent prayer, I know it's going to go unanswered. My first night out, and the first person to take an interest in me has to be the woman I was staring at.

Just my bloody luck.

I take a deep breath before I glance over my shoulder. Bugger! Her eyes are so cold, they look like they've been carved from ice.

"Ah… Hi," I whisper lamely, not sure how I should respond.

I'm willing her to go away, but she doesn't. Instead, she squeezes in beside me, way too close, and I'm starting to wonder if I read her wrong. Is she a lesbian? Did I give her the impression that I am?

"Rob, the usual. Add one for my new friend," she practically purrs at the bartender before turning her sapphire eyes back to me. "Come on. You're too pretty to be sittin' here between the uglies. We'll take care of you."

She's not asking, but instead, demanding I join them, and I can't begin to imagine why. If I looked like Chloe, then I'd understand. Chloe has brown curls I'd kill for, and brown eyes to match them, along with a body that would fit in with this group.

Me? With my blond hair, green eyes and pale skin, I look anemic. I'm utterly dull in comparison to this girl's beauty.

I'm just about to decline her invitation when a guy catches my attention from over her shoulder. I didn't notice him at first, but he's all I see now.

33

Damn, he's hot.

I've read a lot of books, and this guy is definitely book boyfriend material. He's not built as bulky as his friends even though his shirt sits tight enough for me to see that there's plenty of hard muscle hidden beneath it. His brown hair is a little longer on top than at the sides.

He gives off an intense vibe which draws me in like a moth to a flame.

For the first time in my life, I have an urge to touch someone. I want to see if the tingling sensation I'm feeling can possibly get any more intense. That's saying a lot coming from me, seeing as I don't do the touching thing, at all.

While staring at the guy, I wonder if I'll be able to let him touch me. Just thinking about it, I don't feel the familiar wave of disgust well up in my stomach, and without another thought, the word slips over my lips, "Sure."

I follow her, all because of him and the distracting tingling feeling growing in the region of my stomach. Which is so much better than the bad case of nerves I had earlier.

"Look what I found all alone by the bar," the girl drawls when we join her group of friends. They've moved a table closer to the booth in the corner, so there's enough space for everyone to sit.

"What's your name, sweet thing?" She throws her arm around my shoulders which instantly makes me cringe. I take a step closer to the booth and out from under her arm.

"Emma," I answer.

I have to force myself to not look at the guy who caught my attention. The last thing I want to do is embarrass myself in front of him.

"Well, Emma..." She says my name as if she's tasting it. "This is Colton. He's mine."

Colton has shaggy, blonde hair and sharp brown eyes. His smile doesn't soften his face at all but instead makes him look downright scary. I'll make sure I stay away from him.

My attention is drawn away from Colton as the girl keeps introducing everyone.

"Paul, Harper, Aiden," My eyes stop on Aiden, and I can't help but eye-stalk.

Even his name… *holy hotness.*

I'm going to drool just saying it.

Aiden finally looks at me, and the bar starts to spin around me. I've never seen grey eyes like his before. It looks like there's a storm brewing in them. His eyes sweep over me, and suddenly, I wish I'd dressed better. I feel like the dullest girl here.

"And Joe, and Dave." She finishes. I don't bother looking at them because I'm still admiring the work of art that's Aiden.

Aiden's mouth curves at the corner, just slightly, but enough for me to notice. The tingles are back in full force, making it feel as if hundreds of eagles have taken flight in my stomach. The slight smile makes him look devastatingly good looking.

Stop gawking, Emma. Now! Jeez, stalker much?

I manage to tear my eyes away from his and look back at the woman. She's waiting for something, and then I realize she hasn't introduced herself.

"Oh… and you are?" I ask so she will feel important. I'm very good at making people feel important. I've done it all my life.

"Katia," she says, a slow smile spreading over her perfect face. "Slide in," she orders pointing to the booth.

Hesitating, I dare another glance in Aiden's direction. He catches me glancing at him, and a tidal wave of heat spreads through my body, before pooling in my cheeks.

Feeling flustered, I slide in, and when Katia follows behind me, I realize I'm going to be pinned in by them.

I glance under the table, looking for the fastest way to escape should I need to make a quick exit.

"Or you can just climb over it," a deep voice says close to my ear.

I glance up, and everything around me fades away as my eyes meet Aiden's.

You're gawking again, Emma.

I square my shoulders as I lift my chin, trying to look braver than I feel. I don't want these people to see how nervous I am.

"Why would I climb over it?" I feign ignorance.

"You look a little nervous," he says.

So much for trying to be brave. It probably took Aiden a second to see right through my act.

"Great," I whisper as I shove my hands into my lap.

"Some people here might bite," he says. His gaze sweeps over his friends before they settle back on me. "But I don't."

He tilts his head slightly, and the corner of his mouth lifts in that sexy way again.

Aaand my hormones start to play table tennis with my ovaries.

From the way my body reacts to being near Aiden, I start to think that I might just be able to be intimate with him. The thought of getting naked with a stranger is daunting, and I'll need another drink to gather up some courage to go through it.

Hell, at this point it's hard just talking to him, never mind trying to have some fun with him.

I now understand the meaning of liquid courage, and damn do I need some desperately. I'd really like to see how far I can take it with Aiden, even if just to prove to myself that I'm normal.

I finally manage to force my eyes to the bar, but they have a mind of their own because they pop right back to Aiden. He smiles, and my ovaries are suddenly in the Wimbledon final.

CHAPTER 3

AIDEN

She stands out like a sore thumb. Don't get me wrong. I see why Katia zeroed in on her. She's pretty and all, but she doesn't belong here. Every other girl is smothered in make-up, some sinus-killing perfume, too tight underwear, and too little of everything else.

Then there's her.

With her blonde hair up in a ponytail and those wide green eyes, she looks way too innocent to be in a bar.

I wonder if she's even old enough to drink. I hope Rob asked for ID.

This girl should be home, safely away from all of this, and that's why Katia went for her. Katia loves to play with the innocent type girls. She feeds on them.

Seeing that she looks flustered, I try to put her at ease with a smile. Her cheeks flush a soft pink, and that tells me just how right I am about her being innocent. I'd love to know what she's doing here, though.

"What brings you to a place like this, Emma?"

She leans in. I'd like to think it's to get away from Katia and closer to me, but the music's been turned up so she's only doing it so I can hear her answer.

I haven't dated in a while; I mean a long while. Saying that I've been too busy will only be fooling myself. The thing with Laurie, my sister, hit hard. It's just been Zac and me ever since.

The second she gets close, I get a dose of her faint scent. Something flowery.

You're working, dude. You don't have time for this.

She glances up at me, and the lecture I was about to give myself takes a hike. Okay, maybe I can make time for a little flirting. Having some fun won't be so bad.

41

Zac's been on my case about dating, and there's no harm in flirting.

"Experiences. I promised myself new experiences," Emma answers, way too honest.

"Aiden, don't keep her all to yourself," Katia purrs behind Emma.

"I can't help she likes good company," I say, adding a smile to take the sting out of my words.

I know some of them have been frowning at the lack of women at my side. For some reason, it's important to them to show what effect they have on the female population of Chapel Hill. I don't want to bring someone into this group, not while I'm working.

Then again, I didn't bring Emma in. Katia did.

I rest my arm on the seat behind Emma. "You should be happy, Katia." I wait for her to take the bait, but instead, Colton does.

"Why's that, bud?" He leans forward, his eyes moving slowly from Emma to me.

"I finally have a woman sittin' at my side."

I lean closer to Emma, and I'm surprised when she doesn't make a run for the exit. She's letting me come

THE OCEAN BETWEEN US – Michelle Heard

onto her, and it makes my blood pump faster through my veins.

I only pull back once the waitress arrives with our drinks.

Reaching for two shots of tequila, I hand Emma one. I see the question in her eyes. Whether it's about the comments or the drink, I don't know. She has the most expressive face I've ever seen.

"So, is everythin' organized for tomorrow night?" I ask Katia.

I have to remember I'm working. It's imperative that I blend in as a student.

"Yes, we have six new guys lined up. We'll see if they're stupid enough to show. Maybe we'll find some new talent. We found you a few months back," she says all possessively. Her eyes roam hungrily over Emma, and I have to admit that I don't like it one bit.

Emma takes the shot and throws her head back, swallowing the liquid. She grabs at her throat and gasps for air. Yeah, she's obviously not used to drinking.

"Have some salt and lime." I hand her a slice of lime, so she can at least get rid of the aftertaste.

43

Our fingers touch lightly as she takes the slice, and her eyes jump back to mine. I'm sure she felt the same spark I just did. Her eyes are huge as she looks from the slice to me. When I see the confusion on her face, I realize she has no idea what to do.

Just how innocent is this girl?

I lean in, placing my arm behind her again. "You need to suck it," I say, and as soon as the words are out, I realize just how bad they sound.

She nods, cheeks flaming bright red. When she brings the slice to her mouth, I freeze. Pulling back is no longer an option as I watch her lips part and a perfect line of white teeth bite into the soft flesh of the lime. I have to remind myself to breathe because damn, that's the hottest thing I've ever seen.

My eyes lock on Katia's finger as she reaches to touch Emma's flushed cheek. Emma flinches away from Katia's hand, and it puts her face inches from my shoulder, while the side of her body brushes against my chest.

I have to force myself to sit still. I can't make a move yet. As much as I hate it, I have to wait for this

44

thing to play out. If Emma makes a move, then only can I do something. But right now, I can't interfere with Katia.

"Not used to drinkin', are you, princess?" Katia leans into Emma, and as her eyes focus on her target, I know for a fact that she's going to try something.

Emma will either freak out and run or play into Katia's hands. For some reason, I don't want to see either of the two happen.

But then Emma surprises the hell out me as she turns right into me. Her hand clasps my thigh, her fingers digging into the muscle. The heat rushing through my body is all the encouragement I need. When she brings her other hand up to my neck, it sends streaks of lightning down south.

I have to remind myself that Emma's only coming onto me to get away from Katia. That is until her hot breath skims over my ear.

"Aiden, dance with me, please," she whispers. Her voice is laced with panic, and it's all it takes for me to stake my claim.

45

Grabbing her hand, we slip out of the booth. I can feel Katia glaring after us as we walk to the dance floor. I pray that I'm not flushing all our hard work to get closer to Katia down the drain by pissing her off.

As I pull Emma into my arms, she takes hold of my sides.

Damn, how can a stranger feel this good in my arms?

I'm a Southern boy, but Emma has an accent which makes me wonder where she's from.

I lean down, and with my mouth close to her ear, I ask, "Where are you from?"

She turns her face closer to mine as she answers, "South Africa."

"You're far away from home," I say more to myself than to her.

Never in my life did I think I'd like a foreign girl. Maybe it's because of the mystery of something new, something you have to have, and once you've had it, your world settles again.

The air tightens between us, and I feel every muscle in my body tense as her body keeps brushing against mine.

Needing to touch more of her, I slide my free hand from her back to her neck. Fuck, her skin is as soft as it looks. She moves her hips with mine, and her breath warms my shirt.

Emma's hand starts to tremble lightly in mine, and I press it to my chest. Brushing my thumb over her skin, I try to put her at ease.

"Aiden," she says. Glancing down, the look on her face slams hard into my gut and other places I shouldn't be thinking with. She looks really anxious, vulnerable even, and it makes my protective side flare to full capacity. "Sorry I grabbed hold of you back there."

I smile. "I don't mind. I know Katia can be a bit overwhelmin'. I'd rather be dancin' with you than sittin' over there."

Her eyes leave mine, jumping to my chest. Another nervous action. And then it hits me – she's not anxious about Katia – it's me, which only confirms that the attraction between us is mutual. I struggle to keep from smiling now that I know she's all flustered because of me.

"I want to ask you something," she says standing on her toes, so she can get closer to my ear. I lean down as she continues, "I was wondering... you look like a pretty decent guy, and I'd like to have fun without Medusa over there."

Medusa, ha! Good one.

"Would you be interested in... uhm... a one-night stand? No strings attached, of course."

Fuck me.

Did I hear her right?

I stop moving, and people start to bump into us. It's the last question I expected from her. Right now my mama would smack me upside the head. My brother, Wyatt, would high-five me, and Zac would sigh with relief.

Without thinking, I grab her hand and drag her out of the bar. Once we're outside and I'm sure we're alone, I turn to face her.

"Do you have a death wish, Emma?" I snap. The detective in me takes over because, shit, I care about what happens to people. I've seen too many women assaulted and murdered to just walk away and not care. "What if I'm some psycho?"

"You..." She actually looks shocked. "You're not," she says, and then glances away from me. She can't even look at me. She sighs, a miserable sound, and I hear it catch in her throat. Then she just starts to walk away.

"Hold on one damn minute." I take hold of her arm. "Why ask the first guy you see to go to bed with you?" She flushes a deeper shade of red.

I can't be wrong about her which only makes this all the more confusing.

"You're not the first guy I saw. There were some creepy ones before you got to the bar. I really like you and thought it was something we could do."

She still won't look at me. Is this all about that stupid "wanting to experience things" for her?

I shove my hands through my hair. I can't just let Emma go. I'll worry myself to death whether her face will pop up on my screen tomorrow as one of the missing ones.

"You're being damn near stupid, woman," I snap. I wish I could just talk some sense into her, but I'll blow my cover, and I can't risk that. Damn it all to hell.

I should be angry at her for being so careless with something as precious as her life, but I'm not. I'm just damn-well frustrated. I have to pretend I'm some careless fucking student which means turning Emma down will only raise suspicions if Katia finds out.

"Why?"

"I just want to have some fun, Aiden. Isn't it normal for people to sleep together without any strings attached?"

The look in her eyes makes me take a step closer. It's not pain or heartache, it's something else.

"I'm not looking for a big brother. I have one of those," she continues. "Tonight is all I'm giving myself. Drinking, dancing, sex, all of it. Once I start school, there won't be time for any of that." Her eyes pin mine back for the first time. "Are you in, or are you leaving?"

Dammit! I can hear it now. *Hey, Mama, I just wanted to let you know I did the noble thing and got a girl drunk. Then, I slept with her so no other guy would.*

It just doesn't sound right. Maybe I can still change Emma's mind.

"Fuck... okay," I agree. "I'm in."

When she smiles brightly, I start to worry that she might just change my mind.

Back in the bar, I order us drinks before pulling out a chair for Emma on the opposite side of the table from where Katia is sitting.

When we're settled with our drinks, I lean into her and ask, "You're old enough to drink, right?"

She lets out a burst of laughter. "I'm twenty-one. I've been legal for three years."

"It might be legal for you to drink at the age of eighteen in South Africa, but here the legal age is twenty-one." Needing to make sure she's not lying to me, I ask, "Do you have your passport on you? I've never seen a South African one."

51

Luckily, she falls for my white lie, and she reaches into her pocket. She opens it on the back page before holding it out to me so I can see.

I check her date of birth and hold back the sigh of relief when I see that she's telling the truth. Before I can see any more information, she pulls the document away.

We alternate between dancing and sitting at the table, so I can at least still do my job.

Getting up to go to the restroom, Emma staggers into my chair. Fuck, she's drunk. I shouldn't have gotten her that last drink.

I watch her until she pushes through the door which leads to the restroom, before paying attention to the conversations around me.

Just as Emma gets back to the table, Katia takes the seat next to me.

"Looks like you're havin' fun," Katia says as she watches Emma.

Getting up, I reach for Emma to help her keep her balance. Emma ignores Katia, and grabbing my hand, she drags me outside. I was hoping to have more time to convince her to change her mind, but those drinks seemed to have hit her hard. I should've stopped her after the first one.

In the parking area, Emma swings around, slamming hard into my chest before she pushes up on her toes. I feel every curve of her body rub against mine and my pulse speeds up, easily racing a mile a minute.

She presses her lips to the corner of my mouth.

"Let's get you to a bed," I say, taking hold of her shoulders and turning her in the direction of my car.

My new roommate is only arriving on Sunday. I'll let Emma crash in his room for the night. I help her into the car and make sure her seat belt is on before I close the door.

Parking the car outside the apartment, I watch her tug at her seat belt as if it will just spring loose on her command.

"Let me get that for you."

I reach over and unsnap the belt, but before I can pull back, her fingers slip into my hair, and she pulls me down.

THE OCEAN BETWEEN US – Michelle Heard

"Wow, they do get more intense when I touch your face," she murmurs against my mouth.

"What?"

"The tingles," she admits with her new-found drunken bravery.

I meant to be a gentleman and to put her to bed, but there's only so much a man can take.

Her hot mouth presses against mine, and she teases me with those full lips I've been staring at all night long. I grab hold of her hips and pull her to my side of the car. As she straddles me, I tell myself that I'm only having a little taste of her.

Her lips part on a moan which makes it feel like I'm standing on the edge of the unknown, and the moment our tongues touch, I free-fall.

Digging my fingers into her hips, I tug her closer which makes another moan drift over her lips as her pussy rubs over my cock.

I should thank Katia. If it weren't for her unwanted attention, Emma wouldn't be sitting on my lap right now.

The thought makes me hold her tighter, and her softness feels perfect against every hard inch of me.

She hums her approval as my fingers trail up her arm towards her neck.

Fuck, she feels so good.

I should take her up and put her in bed. I shouldn't touch or kiss her.

She pulls away and takes hold of my hand resting on her hip. Now there's a lot I should and shouldn't be doing, but when she slips my hand under her shirt and presses it against her breast, it's practically game over for me.

Feeling the warmth of her skin through the lace of her bra, along with her pussy grinding against my cock is unbelievably erotic.

"Dammit, you're hot," I growl, before crushing my mouth against hers again.

She kisses me back with the same maddening frenzy which only makes me take hold of her ponytail so I can pull her head back for better access. Her soft moans vibrate against my lips.

When she grinds down hard on my cock, my vision blurs for a second.

Fuck, that feels so good.

I'm definitely not going to be able to keep control of anything if she keeps riding me like this.

Her mouth brushes against my ear, making my body ache for her.

"Do you want me to beg?" she whispers, and it's just about the hottest thing I've ever heard.

"Hell no," I groan.

It takes me mere seconds to get us out of the car and up the stairs.

It only takes one second to cool us both down as Miss Jessie, my landlord comes walking down the passage.

"Aiden. Oh, good, you found Emma. I wanted to hear if she's happy with the place."

Damn, it feels like I've just been caught red-handed by my grandma.

"You know Emma?" I ask. Right then Emma's whole body stiffens, and her hand flies to her mouth.

Shit, she's going to be sick.

"Of course, she's your roommate. She came early, and I let-" Miss Jessie's eyes widen as Emma makes a run for my apartment.

I see her take the key from her pocket, and my eyebrows dart into my hairline when she lets herself inside.

My roommate?

Miss Jessie continues talking. "I went and got the applications mixed up. You see, Emma applied to share an apartment. You don't mind, right?"

Emma's my new roommate? "What happened to the guy I would've shared with?"

"He applied for a one bedroom apartment. You don't mind?" Miss Jessie asks again.

"We'll make it work," I answer while trying to process the new information.

Emma's my roommate.

Fuck me.

CHAPTER 4

EMMA

Kill me.

Shit, it feels like I'm dying.

I heave, over and over again until it feels like my stomach is about to come out. If only the world would turn back on its axis so I won't feel this sick any more, I swear I'll never touch alcohol again.

Minutes later, it still feels like I'm dying. How can Mom drink so much and never feel this sick?

No wonder she's such a bitch to me all the time.

Ugh, I feel horrible. The one night I have a few drinks, and I gather enough guts to throw myself at a guy, it ends in disaster. And he's my bloody roommate. Can it get any worse?

I heave again as beads of cold sweat erupt over my skin, making me shiver.

It took everything I had to ask Aiden to have sex with me. The only reason I went through with it was that it felt unbelievably good being touched by him.

Aww crap.

After tonight I'll have to find a new place to stay. I have to phone Chloe and tell her what a massive failure the night was. She'll help me figure things out. The thought should make me feel better, but instead, it makes me feel even more miserable.

Why did I go out? I made a mess of what was supposed to be a fresh start for me. What am I going to do now?

"Emma." Aiden's voice sounds far too kind for what I did. He should be disgusted with me, especially seeing as I'm hanging onto a germ-infested toilet for the little my life is still worth.

"Go away," I groan as my empty stomach spasms.

I don't want him seeing me like this. If I look like I feel, then they can use me for a scarecrow somewhere.

I shouldn't have talked because my body starts heaving again. Luckily nothing comes out. I'm not sure I'll ever survive this humiliating night.

After I flush the toilet, I grab hold of the basin to pull myself up. I stand still for a few minutes, hoping the awful spinning will stop.

Feeling hot, I grab hold of my shirt and drag it over my head. I'm in desperate need of a cold shower. I'm sure I'll feel better then.

The basin jumps and wobbles in front of me as I reach for my toothbrush. My stomach rolls and I freeze, waiting to see what my stomach decides.

"You're gonna fall and hurt yourself."

He's still here? Fuck my life.

Aiden slips his arm around my waist which makes the world stop tipping to the side.

"It feels soooo good when you touch me," I admit in my drunken state.

I never knew it could feel this amazing being touched by someone. I only knew what it felt like to be abused by my mother. Just thinking of her makes my stomach roll with nausea.

"I need to brush my teeth."

I want to cry because I feel so bloody awful, but first I need to get rid of the taste of alcohol and clean myself up. I'll deal with the embarrassment once I feel human again.

"Let's do that then."

I feel his chest pressing against my back as his arms come around me. Damn, that feels good. I want to lean back and close my eyes for a second.

"No, Emma." My eyes snap open, and I blink a couple of times. "Brush your teeth," he whispers right by my ear.

I reach for the jumping items. The basin rushes toward me as I grab for it, and it makes my stomach lurch. When I try to squirt some toothpaste on the brush, I get it all over my hand.

"Crap, it won't stay still," I mutter. I shake my hand to get the toothpaste off.

"Let me get that for you," he says. With his arms caging me in, he takes hold of my hands to steady them.

"You're so nice," I whisper.

I'm *so* not making a great first impression. I think I've done just about everything possible to put off Aiden for good.

Finally, I get the toothbrush in my mouth and scrub and spit for a full minute before I rinse. I repeat the action another two times, but I can't get rid of the bitter taste on my tongue.

As I reach for the mouthwash, I feel Aiden's fingers brush down the length of my back.

"Fuck, Emma. What happened to you?"

Opening the bottle of mouthwash, I mumble, "I got drunk. Alcohol is poison from the lowest level of hell."

I rinse a few times, and I'm about to start drinking the rest when Aiden takes the bottle from me.

"You're minty enough. Let's get you in bed."

"Can I shower first?" I pull a face as I fight the urge to lie down right where I'm standing so I can sleep.

Leaning back against Aiden, I close my eyes until the smell of alcohol wafts up my nostrils again.

I stink like Mom.

"I need to shower. I need to get her off me," I whisper as I move towards the shower. I manage to open the taps and then stumble under the cold spray, clothes and all.

I rest my forehead against the tiles while I unzip my jeans. Struggling to shove them down my legs, the wet fabric gets stuck around my knees, and I almost lose my balance.

Strong hands take hold of my hips, and then I hear, "You can't even stand, babe."

I close my eyes as my chest tightens. It sounds nothing like when my mother calls me *babes*.

He turns me around and helps me to step out of the jeans. Opening my eyes, I watch as drops run down his face. His eyes have darkened to charcoal as they start at my legs and travel back up to my face.

The tingles are back, spreading through my body, and it feels intoxicating.

I want to feel the way he made me feel in the car. I don't want to think. I want to lose myself again until there's only that maddening rush inside me. I've never felt as alive as I did at that moment while we were kissing.

I take in his wet clothes. Damn, he looks delicious. I reach for the hem of his shirt and tug it up.

"You're wet, Aiden."

Duh… like he didn't know that already.

It's all my alcohol-drenched mind can come up with as an excuse to get under his clothes. He feels hot and silky wet beneath my fingertips. I get lost as I take in the ink covering his skin. As I glance up, he pins me with those penetrating grays of his.

I still want tonight to happen so very badly, but I'll have to leave if I go through with it. There's no way I can share a flat with him. I swallow hard as I try to gather my thoughts so the words won't come out all jumbled.

Aiden leans closer and presses me lightly back against the tiles. The words get lost in my throat as I tighten my hold on his shirt. I've never wanted a man so much before. I want his touch everywhere on my body. I just want to lose myself in him and feel good for one night.

"Be careful what you ask of me, Emma. I'm tryin' really hard here."

He moves in even closer to me until I can feel the heat from his body against my cooling skin. Heart pounding, I push his shirt up, until he has no other choice but to let it slip over his head.

Holy crap.

This man is a work of art. He's all hard muscle and ink. My abdomen clenches until I feel it in my core. I bite my cheek to keep myself from saying something embarrassing.

My eyes zero in on his right arm and chest, both inked with some sort of tribal design. I follow the pattern from his shoulder over his chest, and woven into the design is the head of an eagle. I swallow and reach for him - for the eagle as my lips pull into a smile.

Tracing the outline of the tattoo, I know there's no way I can just use Aiden for one night.

The water stops, and as my body starts to shiver, Aiden wraps a towel around me. Somehow, the bed appears before me, and I watch it for a second as the world spins around me.

Damn, never in my life has a bed looked so good. Dropping the towel, I struggle out of the wet

THE OCEAN BETWEEN US – Michelle Heard

underwear. Once I'm in my pajamas, I climb under the covers and lie as still as I can. The world continues to whirl around me which only makes the nausea worse.

"Drink this."

Peeling my eyes open, I see Aiden holding a glass out to me. With shaky hands, I take the water and tablets from him and quickly swallow it down.

"Why are you so nice to me? I haven't been nice to you," I groan as he places the glass next to the bed.

When Aiden sits down next to me, I rest my head against his chest. It's a shame he's not the one. Got all drunk, but I didn't manage to lose my virginity. So much for killing two birds with one stone.

"I'm sorry I got drunk. I think you would've liked the sober me," I whisper as I snuggle closer to him. "Why is it such a hard thing to lose? I'm going to die one. I'm going to be the only one left on the bloody planet," I ramble drowsily.

"Sleep now." That's all he says while his fingers softly caress my back.

CHAPTER 5

EMMA

With every second that ticks by, I just know I'm going to be in more trouble, but I can't bring myself to leave the safety of my room. She started drinking earlier than usual which means nothing good for me.

People define abuse as being physical violence, and nine out of ten times it is by a man. Abuse. *Few people would call what Mom does to me abuse. Dad sure doesn't care.*

She sees herself as the head of the house, and Dad is too much of a wimp to stand up to her. You do everything she says or else she'll make you pay with her cruel words. Her tongue is sharper than any double-edged sword.

Some days she'll just make you pay because she's had too much to drink. That's usually Fridays,

Saturdays, and Sundays. I stay in my room on those days. I only leave it when I really have to. And I have to now. I need to pee so badly.

I open the door enough to listen. I can't hear her, so I make my run for the toilet. It's on my way back that she catches me.

"Emma." She never slurs. She doesn't get slurry when she's had too much to drink. She doesn't pass out. She's not one of those drunks.

With a sense of dread washing over me, I walk to the living room. I just need to be quick. Do what she wants and get back to my room. Don't make eye contact.

She's sitting in her favorite chair between the two couches. Light from the TV breaks the darkness. She looks like a nasty old hag perched on her throne.

"Babes."

My stomach drops at hearing the word. When she calls me that, it means there's a speech coming.

"Fill my drink. Half ice, half wine."

Like she has to remind me after all these years, but she does, every single day. She kids herself into thinking the ice thins out the wine.

I do as she says and fill her glass, hating myself for doing it. I'm enabling her addiction. If I don't, I'll be in more trouble. According to Mom, she doesn't have a problem.

I place the glass down on the table next to her, so I don't have to hand it to her. Touching her is something I try to avoid at all costs. It makes me feel dirty. It disgusts me just to think about touching her hand.

"Sit, babes," she starts, and my insides knot up with fear. "Sit with Mommy."

She's not my bloody Mommy! I want to scream the words at her red, drunken, glazed-over eyes. But instead, I sit and look down at my folded hands. I look down so she won't see the repulsed look on my face.

"You're going to be a failure, babes."

I sigh. Really slow of course. It's more like a deep breath. If she catches me being disrespectful in any way, it will undoubtedly be the end of my pitiful existence.

"You're so beautiful, but if you don't study harder, you'll fail. Look at how well your brother is doing. He got the brains, and you got the beauty. You both got my fancy genes."

I don't feel beautiful. I feel stupid, and it's all because of her. She is common, and no amount of money can change that fact. She looks down on others, but behind closed doors, she is nothing but common rubbish. It saddens me to think this of my own mother, but it's the awful truth.

"You're mine, and you're beautiful."

There's the reason I don't feel beautiful. To me, she is the ugliest person alive. Alcohol has made her ugly. I can see it eating away at her skin, the wrinkles starting early, the darkness in her eyes.

"You're going to fail. You can't go around wasting your time on things like friends, dating, and those pathetic books you read." *This is her way of telling me not to even dare bring a friend home. Not that I would. I'd be too embarrassed.*

Her voice starts to grow angry, and this is where she doesn't make sense anymore. She always falls off the bus.

"I was so pretty when I was your age."

My heart starts to thump faster in my chest, and I say what I know she wants to hear. Anything to make her stop. "Mom's still pretty. None of the other kids have such a pretty mom."

I hear her sigh and then the rattle of ice as she takes a sip.

"You're so lucky," she says, and dread starts to spin its web around me. "You have me. It was hard growing up with your grandfather. He used to beat the shit out of your grandmother. Blood all over the walls."

I don't know if this is the truth. My gran never says anything bad about my grandfather. He died when I was thirteen. All I know of him was that he drank – brandy, straight from the bottle.

"Oh, those were good times. He'd bring food home from the restaurant-" She stops, and I know she's waiting for me to look up. Her beady eyes stare hard at me, dropping to my waist, then back up to my face.

71

"You must be careful what you eat, babes. You don't want to go getting all chunky like your dad's side. They're all hips and bum." Then she smiles, a watery smile, as she refers to my biological father whom I have no memory of.

"You're so beautiful, just like me." She reaches for my hand and I know I must keep still.

I swallow hard as I watch her hand creep closer, but horrified, I watch my own move to avoid her touch.

Crap! Crap! Crap!

What have I done? Why did I move?

Terror washes hot through my body. She's going to flay me with that tongue of hers.

Her eyes harden as her mouth sets in a grim line. "You don't want me to touch you?" Her voice drips with rage.

Fear ripples over me, tightening its hold on my chest, and I dare a glance at her. Her eyes are usually brown, but when she gets like this, they go black. Black and hard and hateful.

She hates me. I know she does because no mother that loves her daughter would do this to her. She's

72

spiteful and malicious because she only puts me down, never my brother. Never the perfect one.

"No, Mom... I mean, yes... I mean... Mom can touch me," I ramble as panic sets hard in the pit of my stomach.

"Do I repulse you?" Her voice dips even lower, and her eyes start to gleam as they become little slits.

"No, Mom." I'll have to work hard to defuse her, or I'm going to sit here until tomorrow morning, listening to her wail on about what a horrible daughter I am.

"I love Mom." I try to avoid saying the word 'you.' She really tears into me then. It's disrespectful to her. She comes from an Afrikaans family where you're taught that you don't 'you' and 'your' your parents and elders.

"Please, hold my hand." I reach for her with a trembling hand, trying not to show disgust on my face.

She yanks away and downs half her glass of wine.

"I can't believe this!" she wails. "My own daughter finds me repulsive. I sacrifice my life for you. I give you a roof over your head. I give you food, and..." I cringe

73

back, *"this is how you repay me? I only want the best for you."*

"I'm sorry, Mom." That's all I can do now until she stops.

"You're selfish!"

"I am. I'll do better. I'm sorry, Mom," I say the empty words which mean nothing to me.

Dad comes around the corner and looks from Mom to me. If only he'll stop her, but he never does. He just goes back into the room to go watch his stupid TV shows in there, choosing to ignore what's happening in his own home.

"You're going to be just like your father if you don't get your act together."

Again, she means my biological father. The one who left us before I could walk. The one who didn't want me either. This one, my stepfather, adopted us, and he's not much more of a man than my biological father was.

"No, I won't." I swallow the bile down. "I'll be like Mom."

"You just read those books, that's all you do," she goes on. "You're throwing your life away. Life is hard,

babes." She leans over and hisses in my face. Her stinking breath wafts over me, sticking to my skin. "And without me, you won't make it. Ever."

She sits back, her chin wobbling. Crap, not the tears.

I have to hold her. It's the only way to calm her down. I get up and move to her, my body feeling rigid. It feels as if every muscle is fighting me, wanting to run the other way. I reach out to her, my arms like rubber. I hug her to my chest, and another wave of disgust wells up in me, threatening to squeeze the last bit of life from my body. The smell of her greasy hair makes my stomach turn. The clamminess of her alcohol-drenched skin sticks to my hands.

I go numb.

No, I'm lying. I do feel something. I feel sick. To. My. Stomach. Sick.

"I'm nothing without Mom. I won't make it without Mom. Ever. Please hold me, Mom. Don't let me go."

I hate myself the most. I hate myself so much.

I can still taste the horrid words on my tongue.

75

Arms tighten around me, and I stiffen. A voice whispers right next to my ear, and it's not Mom's voice. *She's not here.*

"It's okay, Emma. It's just a dream."

Opening my eyes, I'm afraid I'll see my mother, and it won't just be a nightmare but my reality.

The first thing I see is a swirl of black ink. I pull back slightly so I can follow the trail of ink down from Aiden's shoulder to his chest.

"An eagle," I whisper as I reach out to touch him. I expect to wake up any second, but instead, he feels warm beneath my fingers. I trace the outline of the eagle until my eyes drift shut again.

I wake up with a heavy weight on top of my chest, and I feel... Hell, I'm not so sure how I feel.

I try to move and freeze, my eyes snapping open. My heart rate shoots through the ceiling, right out of the flat, leaving me to deal with the guy draped over me.

Every time I breathe, his head lifts, and I feel him brushing against my breast. I stop breathing until eventually, I can't hold my breath any longer, and it rushes from me, making a mortifyingly loud whooshing sound.

I struggle to piece last night together, but it's all a bit of a blur. Slowly, I remember going to a bar, the weird Amazonian woman whose name I can't remember, and the drinks.

Oh hell, the drinks.

It all comes back like a tidal wave.

My face turns furnace hot, remembering how I grabbed Aiden, kissed him, and then practically begged him to sleep with me.

The vomiting.

The shower. Ugh... the shower. I want to die all over again.

The memories keep coming. They're merciless in their assault. The ones of how I tried to undress the poor guy have me dying of embarrassment all over again. He must think I'm some cheap skank.

When he pulls me closer to him, and his breath warms my nipple through the thin material of my top, I can't stop the words from bursting over my dry lips.

"Bloody hell!"

77

He sits up as I dart off the bed. The first thing I see as my feet touch the floor is my wet underwear.

"Oh, bloody hell!"

I have no words for what I've done. I didn't think I'd feel this bad the next morning.

I dare a glance in his direction, and it's the worst thing I could've done because he looks devastatingly hot where he's sitting on my bed with his tousled hair and chiseled bare chest.

"We didn't have sex if that is the reason for all the bloody hells," he says, his voice gruff with sleep, which only makes him sound downright inferno hot.

He moves to get up, and I all but run to grab the wet underwear off the floor. I can feel my cheeks flaming up again.

"I'm so sorry." I don't know how to apologize for my behavior. "Just give me an hour, and I'll be gone."

"What? Why?" He moves fast around the bed. It's quicker than I can move with the left-over grogginess from the alcohol.

He shouldn't have gotten up. With no drunken stupor to obscure my vision, I see every rippling

78

muscle, every piece of ink-covered skin, each one of his perfectly sculpted abs.

Holly freaking moly!

My. Hands. Touched. All. Of. That.

I want to touch it all again. The angels were in a hell of a good mood when they made him.

"Why would you want to leave?" he repeats when I take too long to answer.

"I can't even face *myself* right now, so I can only imagine how you must feel." I stand frozen holding my wet underwear to my chest, and I know I must look awful. Still, he keeps coming, until there's only an inch separating us and the air thins out, making it difficult to breathe.

"You're not leavin'. If I'm not mistaken, you paid for six months in advance. You have classes startin' on Monday. Besides, Miss Jessie will have my ass if you leave." He takes a breath and tucks some of my wild bed hair behind my ear.

His bare chest and Southern accent melt me on the spot.

Crap. That's not good. How will I share a flat with Aiden when I'm crushing on him? That will only make things awkward.

"Things happened. We're adults. We'll deal. You, Emma Bowen, are stayin'," he says.

I can only nod like an idiot. Oh, and drool.

Ha! So much for leaving.

He reaches in and hugs me as if we've known each other for ages. My body responds by doing some more melting, wanting desperately to become one with his.

"By the way, welcome. As you know by now, I'm your roommate, Aiden Holden. Please make yourself at home. Unpack."

I watch as Aiden leaves, pulling the door closed behind him – my roommate for the next six months.

Things happened. He has that part right.

I stand, staring at myself in the mirror, horrified by my appearance. I look like a bloody panda with mascara streaked under my eyes.

Needing to talk to Chloe, I quickly dial her number.

Not waiting for her to say hello, I launch right into my problem. "I have to move. I can't stay here with him," I give voice to my panic.

"Hold on, Sunshine. Who? Why? What are you on about?" she asks, clearly confused.

"My roommate. I went to a bar last night. Out of all the bloody guys there, I asked my roommate to have a one-night stand with me. Then I got drunk. Then I got sick." I feel a little faint just thinking about how bad the night before was. "Ugh, I puked in front of him. It doesn't help that he's the hottest guy I've ever seen. Oh, you should hear his accent. I could listen to him reciting the damn alphabet all day long," I try to explain everything that happened in one breath.

"So what's the problem, then?" she says, clearly not understanding my predicament.

"Huh?"

"Sunshine, it sounds like you had a normal night out."

"What's normal about what I just told you? The guy saw me puking my guts out. I freaking got undressed in front of him," I snap.

81

I hear her take a sharp breath. "What was his reaction?"

"He helped me get in bed."

"Oooh… what happened then?

"Nothing. I fell asleep," I say, feeling disappointed that I missed my one chance at having sex with Aiden because of bloody alcohol. I'm never touching that poison again.

"Could've been worse. You said he's hot?" Trust Chloe to latch onto that part. "Send me a photo. I want to see what he looks like," she teases.

"I'll just go and ask him to strike a pose for me quickly," I tease her back, then blurt out, "I like him. I already like him too much."

"That's a bonus. Just don't carry your heart on your sleeve. Be yourself, Sunshine. You're a stunning person."

"You know you're the best, right?"

"No, you're the best. I want all the details. Email me."

"I will," I say before cutting the call.

I'm worth it. I'm a stunning person.

Then I catch sight of myself in the mirror, and I cringe. Yeah, let's shower first before we try that speech again.

CHAPTER 6

AIDEN

I didn't mean to fall asleep. It's just... Emma felt so damn good.

First, she half-stripped in the shower. That sight took just about every ounce of gentleman I had in my body, not to shove her up against the wall and finish what we started in the car.

And then in the room. Fuck, I had to go take a cold shower, and that was just because Emma reached for the clasp of her bra.

I'm thankful she passed out. She was drunk, and that's a line I'll never cross.

Like I said, I didn't mean to fall asleep there, but she took the aspirin and slumped right down against me. It felt good holding her.

84

The second she grabbed me, I woke up. Now, I've had nightmares, and I've seen Zac have them after Laurie, my sister died, but this was something else.

She whimpered. I've never heard a person make a sound like that. She groaned the same thing over and over.

"I'm nothing without, Mom. I won't make it without, Mom. Ever."

Along with the whimpering, trembling, and the look in her eyes I've been trying to place the whole damn night, I'm not so sure she meant those words in the way most people would take them.

And the scars on her back? I was shocked when I saw them. My gut is telling me this girl is running from something.

I've only heard of the 'boy meets girl' and then BANG, scenario. I never believed in insta-love until Zac and Laurie happened. They got married three weeks after they met; they damn near gave Mama a heart attack, eloping like they did. But they stayed in love until Laurie died four years later.

I was dating Megan at the time but broke it off because I knew she wasn't the one, and there was just no point in wasting her time or mine.

But now this?

Emma Bowen.

I've never had such a strong reaction to a woman before. The second I laid eyes on her I knew my life was about to change.

My phone starts vibrating on the kitchen counter, and I leap for it.

"Please let it be Zac," I whisper as I quickly look at the screen. "Fuck yes!"

I need my brother-in-law's advice.

"You're a godsend," I answer the call.

I sink down onto one of the couches in the living room.

"I am? You haven't sounded this happy to report back in some time. Did you find out when the main event is?"

He sounds tired. Not that I blame him. We've been on this case for far too long, and I'm sure he's in a hurry to head back home. I know I am. I miss my own bed and house.

"Actually, I need your advice with women," I start, but then I hear something fall in the background.

"Hold on. I just dropped my coffee," Zac mumbles. I hear him shuffle some things around. "Say that again. You, Aiden Holden, need advice? From me? On women? You do realize I'm the one stuck between four walls the whole day? You're the one out there, livin' with them." I can hear the laughter in his voice. The fucker is never going to let me forget this.

"Being surrounded by them and takin' an interest in one are two different things," I say, a little too sharp as I glance at Emma's closed door. "We're workin' a case. I'm not even a real damn student. But... she's..."

I stop to think how I'm going to word this.

"She makes me want to fall. Did you feel that way about Laurie?"

There's silence on the other end, and I worry that it's too soon for Zac to talk about Laurie.

"Yeah, she made me fall so hard that I'm still fallin'."

I take a breath, regretting that I brought it up.

"Sorry, Zac. I shouldn't have –"

"No, if you can't talk to me, who you gonna talk to? Besides, I'll be fallin' until the day I see her again. She's the love of my life. The day I saw Laurie come up those stairs and I stopped her, tellin' her I was gonna marry her before I even knew her name, I meant it. I meant it because the second I saw her, everyone else faded away. That's when you know, Aiden – when everyone else fades away. Your soulmate wakes you up, rattles your cage and makes you fall all at once."

Zac sounds lost in his own words, but I know what he means.

"I have a fight tonight." I change the subject back to our case. "It's gettin' close to the end of the year, so things should start heatin' up. I've gotten closer to Katia and Colton as well. They've let me into the inner circle."

"Good, we need to bust this open and wrap it up. Your roommate is comin' tomorrow, right?"

I glance at Emma's closed door again, thinking what a surprise it was when I learned that she's my new roommate.

"She arrived yesterday," I say, keeping my voice neutral.

"She? What happened to the guy? I remember you clearly sayin' a guy was movin' in with you."

"He turned out to be a smokin' hot woman." I take a deep breath and lean back against the couch.

"Is this where all the questions are comin' from?" he asks, and I nod.

He can't see me nodding like a dumbass, so I answer quickly, "Afraid so. Things also got more complicated, Zac. Katia saw me leavin' the bar with Emma last night. I'm worried that I won't be able to keep Emma away from Katia's claws."

"Could Emma help the case? If you played this right, she could make your cover more solid."

"Katia already showed an interest in Emma. We'll be riskin' her life."

There's a moments silence before Zac says, "Katia is responsible for fourteen missin' girls. She's dealin' in sex traffickin'. We've come too far to let her slip through our fingers now."

"I can't just ask Emma to play along. Hell no, I'm not draggin' her in deeper."

As I say the words, I close my eyes, because I know Katia, and what Katia wants, she goes after, unless…

"Then my advice to you is simple. Get a new roommate," he states.

As if it will solve the problem.

"Don't be a dumbass," I snap. "I can protect her better if she's here. Let's see what Katia and Colton do. If they go for her, I'll consider it. Let's just wait and see what happens first. Maybe I'll strike it lucky, and Katia moves onto a new target."

"It's your call. Let me know how tonight goes down. I've been in touch with Wyatt. He says everythin' is still on track with Cole and Troy. Their covers are solid with the other fightin' ring back home. It's time to bust this case wide open and put Katia where she belongs, behind bars."

"Thanks, bro. I'll catch you later."

"Good luck."

THE OCEAN BETWEEN US – Michelle Heard

Ending the call, I get up from the couch to make coffee. My thoughts turn to my cousin who's helping us back in Lyman. I'm fucking worried about Cole and Troy. They might be trained Marines, but one wrong move from either one of us and this thing can go sour.

Zac and my brother Wyatt are working behind the scenes to make sure everything runs smoothly. I know I can fight, but I've never seen Cole and Troy fight before. At least, not since school. Wyatt's the one who brought them in.

I take a deep breath to clear my head and glance at Emma's closed door. Why did she have to come here now? Too many girls have gone missing.

I'll have to make sure Katia doesn't get her hands on Emma.

Wanting to offer Emma some coffee, I knock on her door.

"Come in," she calls.

Easing the door open, I step inside. Emma's sitting on the bed with a laptop open in front of her.

"Give me a sec. I'm just finishing this email," she says, not looking up.

"Sure," I reply as I glance at the phone that's buzzing on the bed. I watch as it goes to voicemail. My eyebrows pop up when I see that she already has eight missed calls. A little envelope pops up showing that she has nineteen messages.

Damn, someone really wants to talk to her.

The phone starts to buzz again, flashing *Mom*.

"Aiden?"

My head snaps up, and I smile as I ask, "Would you like some coffee?"

The phone starts buzzing again, and I glance down. It's her mother again.

"You should take that call. It might be urgent."

"I'll check it later. Coffee will be nice." She sounds tense, and I hope I didn't overstep by telling her to answer the call.

Deciding to let it go, for now, I ask, "How do you take it?"

"One sugar, and milk, or none... depending on what you have here. I'll run to the shop later... uhm, the store." She looks uncomfortable, and I'm not sure why.

"Great, come have it in the kitchen with me," I say as I turn to leave.

Emma follows me out and watches while I get our coffee ready. As I turn to hand her a mug, my eyes sweep over the t-shirt and shorts she's wearing.

Da-yumn, the girl has legs that go on for miles.

"Here you go." I place a mug a few inches from me, so she has to come closer to get it.

"I'll take you shoppin'," I offer as she takes a sip. "It will save you from tryin' to figure out where to go."

"Thanks." She smiles, looking relieved. "I'm sure I'll get to know the town and where everything is once school starts. It's actually funny. I Googled Chapel Hill and the way people talk so I can just blend in, but now that I'm here I can't remember any of it."

"It's not like you're speakin' another language," I chuckle. "If you get stuck just let me know, and I'll help out."

A soft smile forms around her lips as she glances up at me. "I didn't expect people to be so friendly here."

Damn, she's breathtakingly beautiful when she smiles.

Realizing that she said something, I clear my throat before I say, "Aren't people friendly in South Africa?"

"To be honest, I'm not sure." She draws her bottom lip between her teeth, looking a little nervous. "It's not like I got out much."

The second the words leave her mouth her eyes widen slightly. She turns her body half away from me, taking big gulps of her coffee.

"Now you have to explain because you're makin' it sound like you're from a convent."

The night before she was intoxicated, but now, it's a different story. If last night is anything to go by, then she's definitely feeling the attraction between us. It is something I'd like to explore, but I need to know just how inexperienced she is. The last thing I want to do is ruin my chances by coming on too strong.

I lean back against the counter, so I'm facing her, and it places me inches away from her body.

Shaking her head, she says, "I just didn't get out much. I had my studies which kept me busy."

"What did you study?"

"Nursing." She doesn't offer anything more on the subject. I can see it's not going to be easy getting to know her.

"You mentioned school. What are you going to study while you're here?"

"Creative writing."

For a moment I watch as she swallows the rest of her coffee down. She's so different from last night, and I have to admit it's a little frustrating.

"Relax, Emma," I say, hating that she's so on edge around me. "Hell, we almost had sex last night. We slept in the same bed. If I were goin' to hurt you, I would've done it by now."

"I'm sorry," the words rush from her. "I didn't mean to make things awkward. Last night I practically threw myself at you... twice. I'm just a little embarrassed right now."

Finally, she seems to relax a little.

"I wouldn't say you threw yourself at me. Judgin' by the kiss we shared in the car, it's safe to say the attraction is mutual."

I lean even closer to her until my shirt brushes against her knuckles. Emma's eyes dart to my chest before coming back to my face.

"Mutual?" she whispers, looking torn between embarrassment and desire.

Thank fuck, we're back on track. I was worried there for a moment.

"Yeah," I say, as a smile pulls at the corner of my mouth. My eyes jump between her mouth and darkened green eyes.

Fuck, I want to kiss her again.

She's without a doubt on the same page as me. But I want to make the sexual tension between us last, so I ask, "You said you wanted to experience things? What kind of things?"

"Normal stuff," she says as she places her empty mug on the counter. "See new places. Meet people. Just normal fun stuff."

"Was last night fun for you?" I ask, not able to resist teasing her.

She quickly looks down but not before I see her smile. As she starts to turn away from me, I reach for her, preventing her from escaping.

Her tongue darts out and as she licks her lips, I struggle to suppress the groan building in my chest.

I pull her toward me, bringing her body right up against mine until I can feel her heart racing against my chest.

This barefoot, wet hair, green-eyed girl might just be my undoing.

She's not as relaxed as last night. "Don't go all tight on me now, Emma. We kissed. It was good. We might even do it again when I get you drunk enough," I tease her again, hoping to lighten the air.

She glares up at me, but there's no potency in her eyes. Not with the shy smile playing around her lips. All her drunken bravery is gone, and now it's just Emma, the one she said I'd really like.

I brush my fingers down the side of her face, taking in the feel of her soft skin.

"I'm never touching that poison again," she says with a laugh.

She's so fucking beautiful, I could stare at her all day long and not get tired.

Her breaths begin to come faster, and I'd be lying if I said it's not a turn-on.

"You're not denyin' we'll kiss again," I whisper as I tighten my hold on her.

I should stop, but kissing her was really good, and it's all I can think about right now.

That… and her naked on my bed.

Her eyes settle on my mouth, and because I want it, I ignore the warning bells that I should take it slower. Instead, I start to remind myself of how good she tasted.

As I lean down, there's a spark in her eyes the second she realizes that I'm going to kiss her.

I crush my mouth against hers, and when her lips part and I finally get to taste her again, a groan rumbles up my throat. She throws herself into the kiss, making it so much hotter.

I move my hands down to her ass and take hold, lifting her onto the counter. Once I have her in front of me, I slide my hands to her hips. Pressing against her knees with my body, she opens for me so I can move closer.

Damn, it's not close enough.

I dig my fingers into her skin between her shirt and shorts and tug hard. She gasps as we collide, and I know she can feel how much I want her right now.

Her arms slide around my neck, and I inch my hands up beneath her shirt. I should take it slower, but then she shudders in my embrace, and I kiss her harder, our tongues twisting greedily.

Feeling her hot skin beneath my hands makes my cock strain against the zipper. When a soft moan slips past her lips, I push her shirt up and over her head.

Her eyes are glazed with lust, just the way I want them. I reach behind her with one hand and unclasp her bra. Then I dip to her neck, pressing soft kisses all along her creamy skin, over her collarbone, all the way down to her cleavage. I slip the straps off and duck lower, taking her nipple into my mouth.

Fucking heaven.

With her hands fisting my shirt, she almost comes off the counter as she tries to press closer to me.

Damn, she's sensitive.

I pull her legs around my waist and lift her from the counter. As I walk her to my room, I keep kissing her neck, not wanting to break this moment between us.

After placing her on my bed, I quickly rip my shirt over my head, needing to get back to her.

The way she looks at me is intoxicating. It makes me feel damn near invincible.

I unsnap her shorts and hook my fingers into the sides of her panties, tugging them both down. Sucking in a deep breath of air, I ease my hands up her quivering legs as I crawl over her body. I slide an arm in under her and move her up to the middle of the bed.

She's got her bottom lip trapped between her teeth, and her eyes are on my chest. Leaning down, I free her bottom lip, only to bite down on it myself. Only then does she place her hands lightly on my arms.

She's very nervous.

I kiss her slowly, nipping at her mouth while I move my hand down, cupping her. She gasps into my mouth, which only encourages me to slip a finger inside her hot pussy.

"Dammit, Emma," I groan with need when I feel how tight she is.

Her body quivers beneath mine as I press my thumb against her clit which makes a sweet moan escape her lips.

I let go of her for the second I need to get my pants off before I'm back on top of her. Her eyes are wide, and it looks like she's switched over to the highest gear of nervousness, and I'm no rocket scientist but ...

"Are you okay with this?"

She nods, fast, and that's just not good enough for me.

Framing her head with my arms, I look into her wide eyes.

"Babe, is this your first time?"

She swallows hard, and after a few seconds, she nods. I've been many things in my life, but an ass is not one of them. I may want her badly, but not like this.

I smile gently so I don't hurt her feelings when I say, "Then it should be special."

But I'm also not leaving her unsatisfied.

I kiss her tenderly and move my hand back down, cupping her pussy. Pinning her right leg with one of my own, I slip a finger back inside her. Her lashes lower as her lips part with desire.

I could orgasm just from watching her.

She lifts her hips from the bed as her hands fist in the covers. Ducking my head low, I take her nipple in my mouth and suck hard until she's writhing underneath me. I move faster as I listen to her breaths escape in short, sweet gasps.

Wanting to feel her touch me, I take hold of her hand and press her palm to my abs.

"Touch me, Emma," I growl, letting her hear how much I need her right now.

As she wraps her fingers around my cock, my hips jerk forward, a deep growl rippling from my chest. She starts to move her slender fingers up and down my cock, speeding up until she matches me thrust for thrust. I'm not going to last long.

Our eyes lock as she groans, "Aiden."

"That's it, baby. Come for me."

Rubbing my palm hard against her clit, I curl my finger inside her.

"Oh…" Whatever she was going to say trails away as I find her sweet spot. She arches up, pressing her body hard into mine, her fist tightening around my cock. I can't keep from groaning as I feel her orgasm start, and my own starts to ripple through me.

"Aiden," she whimpers while her muscles clench around my finger. It's the hottest thing I've ever experienced. With I growl I find my release.

I drop my forehead to hers as she lets go of my cock. When she brings her hand up between us, I catch it and lace our fingers together.

She curls into me, small and trembling with the aftershocks of pleasure. The same feeling from earlier fills my chest. She makes me feel so fucking invincible.

CHAPTER 7

EMMA

I've never felt anything like that before. For the longest time, it felt like something was building deep inside me, and then the sweetest release came.

I loved the sounds he made as I was pleasuring him. There's not a book on the face of this planet that could've prepared me for what I just experienced with Aiden.

He's bloody perfect. The one guy I run into, and I offer myself up not once, not twice, but three times, and he says no. But then, I have to be honest - it wasn't a no as in '*bloody hell no.*'

He made it all sweet, saying my first time has to special. Lying next to Aiden, I realize that no one has ever made me feel this good about myself.

But all good things must come to an end, and I'm sure men usually don't cuddle afterward. It's been close to ten minutes, and all he did was wrap his arms around me and hold me.

And he's still holding me.

Not that I'm complaining. Aiden's holding me, I'm not drunk, and I didn't force myself on him... this time. Pretty sure he came onto me in the kitchen.

I stare at the ceiling, trying not to squirm as the need to get dressed washes over me.

I'm naked with a guy.

Crap, I don't know what to do. I've never done something like this.

"You okay?" he asks.

He's Mr. Bloody Perfect slash Greek God and caring on top of it all.

I dare a quick glance at him, making sure my eyes stay in the region of his face. "Why are you so nice?"

"You're quiet because I'm nice?"

"No... yes. Both. You're holding me. You've been so *nice* since we met." I think I've just managed to confuse him even more.

He lifts himself onto his elbow and stares down at me. When he brushes my cheek softly with his other hand, I just about melt all over again.

"See... *nice*. Aren't men supposed to just get up and go after the... uhm... deed?"

Kill me. I'm screwing up so badly in bringing my point across.

He smiles. "No, not all men just get up and go." He starts to laugh, obviously finding me funny. "Some of us like to stay." His fingers keep trailing gently down my neck. "So you think I'm nice. Not exactly what I was aimin' for. Was going more for great, but I'll work on that."

"You're great," I say to appease him. "Just bloody great. Tell me an awful secret. Tell me you go cow tipping at night, throw eggs at houses. Anything will do right now."

He chuckles as he slips his hand into my hair and presses a kiss to the side of my temple. "Do you do those things?" His voice is a deep rumble right by my ear, making my stomach flutter wildly.

"No… it's just better than asking whether you're involved in something drug-related, murder-related, or just plain crime-related."

He pulls back a little, his eyes roaming my face, and then he presses a tender kiss to my forehead.

"I've never been on the wrong side of the law, never gone cow tippin'. When I was twelve, I threw eggs at a house. I couldn't sit for a week when my mama found out," he admits.

"Bad boy Aiden throws eggs. I feel so much better."

He chuckles, and his breath warms my skin as he lays his head down next to mine.

"So you're from Cape Town?" he asks. "What's it like there?"

I'm lying naked in bed with a stranger, and I've never felt more at peace.

"It's actually quite beautiful. It's not as hot as it is here." I don't think giving him a bit of information can do much harm. He's a student like me, after all.

"Where are you from?" I ask before he can ask more questions.

"South Carolina." He nudges at my neck with his nose, and I close my eyes. "I'm a Southern boy, ma'am," he drawls, and I become a puddle of drool next to him.

"Why did you choose Chapel Hill?" he asks.

I don't think and answer a bit too honestly, "Eagles. I read there are quite a few in this area."

He lifts his head and looks at me. Actually, it's more like he pins me down with a super intense stare.

"Why not come for a simple vacation then?"

"A student visa is longer." This is where I should start keeping quiet.

"You came here on a student visa just to see eagles?"

Once he asks the question, I realize how stupid it must sound to him.

Trying to cover my mistake, I shrug lightly. "Among other things."

His arms cage my face, and he leans in, warming my body with his muscled one.

"You'd be surprised how understandin' I can be," he whispers as his eyes lock on mine.

Oh, I think I know. What man says no three times?

"I'm just taking some time to figure out what I want from my life. Like a gap year," I explain as best I can. For some reason, I don't want to lie to him. It's as if I know that he'll know, and I just don't want to go there.

He tilts his head and stares at me, looking too deep. It's as if he's studying my soul, and then his warmth leaves me.

I glance at Aiden as he parks the car outside a mall.

"Aiden," someone shrieks as we get out of the car. I turn to see Katia coming towards us. "Emma," she squeals some more and just the sight of her makes my stomach drop. I really don't like her one bit.

I force my lips into some sort of a smile. When Aiden's arm slips over my shoulders, and he draws me into his side, the smile stretches widely.

"Hey, bud," Colton says, taking hold of Aiden around his neck, and playfully jabbing him in the shoulder.

"Hey, guys." Aiden doesn't sound too happy, or maybe it's just me.

Katia lifts a perfectly manicured hand to my face. Just like with my mother, I struggle to keep still. I try really hard for about three seconds before I give in. I just can't. My stomach lurches at the thought of this woman touching me.

I duck my face away as she reaches for me, and I end up bumping into Aiden. His hand slips from my shoulder to my neck, and he presses me into his chest. I breathe in his spicy scent.

I've been so caught up in my thoughts that the first words I hear of their conversation, is when Katia says, "Bring your girl. It will be great to get to know her." Her eyes rake over my body, and I feel a shiver of disgust rush down my spine.

"Will do," Aiden says.

I start to pull away. I don't want to go anywhere she'll be. I can't even bring myself to smile as they walk away. I'm upset that I'm letting Katia get to me.

Everything is happening too fast. It feels like my head is spinning.

"Let's go," he says, as he steers us toward the entrance.

110

Once inside, I shop fast. Well, as fast as I can with the different brands on the shelves. It's never been one of my favorite things to do. It's not fun shopping with a person who chooses everything for you.

Halfway through the shopping, Aiden steps in front of me. Standing in the middle of an aisle, he takes hold of my shoulders.

I glance up and feel confused when I see the frown on his face. "What's wrong?"

"Never in my life have I met a woman who goes through a store as fast as you do. You barely register what's on the shelves," he says.

"I just don't like shopping," I explain.

"Seriously?"

"Yeah. It's not my idea of fun." I step past him before he can ask another question.

Back at the flat, I still feel a bit tense. I try to avoid any eye contact because I'm a fast learner. Aiden is good at reading my eyes. I'm just scared he'll ask questions I'm not ready to answer.

"You're being silly, Emma. You better relax before you give him a reason to ask you questions."

I decide to check my emails, and I'm glad to see that Chloe has replied to one I sent this morning.

Sunshine,

I'm so glad you went out, even if you got drunk. Please be more careful next time. You're lucky your roommate was there.

Speaking of your roommate, he sounds hot. Don't worry too much about what he might think of you and try to become friends with him. You need a friend on that side.

Ps. I want a photo of him. Take one while he's sleeping.

I love you, around the world and back,

Chloe.

I grin at her words and press reply.

Me again,

You'll never guess what happened this morning.

Sending the email, I stare at the inbox, hoping she'll see the email and reply soon. Instead my phone buzzes. I glance at it, and seeing a voice clip from Chloe, I press play.

"What happened?"

Holding the recording button down, I say, "We got naked." I press sent and smile when she comes online immediately.

I laugh when my phone starts to ring.

"I knew that would get your attention," I tease, as I answer the call.

"Were you serious? Did you sleep with him?"

"Not really... sort of." I'm a little embarrassed to tell Chloe. "We didn't go all the way."

"Did you enjoy it, Sunshine?" she asks.

"A lot," I whisper as I close my eyes at the memory.

"That's all that matters."

"Yeah, but I think it's safe to say I officially suck at losing my V-card. I failed a third time. I must be the only girl who can't lose her virginity on two different continents. Maybe I should take a trip around the world, try another country?"

"Don't be daft. It will happen when the time is right. You're too worried about it."

"You're right," I agree with her. "Chloe, I like touching him. I love it when he touches me. I've never felt something like that before. I don't feel sick, and

113

you know that's a big deal for me. For some reason he makes me feel safe, and I know it's utterly crazy of me, seeing as I only met him yesterday."

"It's not crazy, Sunshine. You're experiencing something normal and healthy for the first time."

"I wish you were here. Everything is so overwhelming," I admit.

"I wish I was there too. My parents are constantly fighting."

"I'm so sorry. Call me anytime you need to talk about it. I hope your parents sort things out."

"Yeah, I don't think that's going to happen. Let me go, I need to get ready for a date. I'll talk to you tomorrow."

"Sure. Around the world and back," I say, feeling better after talking to her.

"I love you, Sunshine. Around the world and back."

I end the call and stare at my phone. Chloe will never know how much she means to me.

There's a knock at my door and almost fall off the bed in my hurry to open the door.

"Hi." I clear my throat so I can resemble some form of composure instead of the rampant mess I am on the inside just from seeing Aiden.

He's dressed casually in slacks and a sweater, with some sort of emblem on it. He really looks good in anything, but best in nothing. My neck and cheeks warm as my thoughts go straight to the gutter.

"I just wanted to know if you have plans for tonight? I have this thing I have to go to, and you're welcome to come along."

"Sure," I agree, then quickly ask, "What should I wear?"

"Dress comfortably," he says, and slips out, closing the door behind him.

Dress comfortably? He's wearing slacks and a sweater. Do I wear the same?

I take the safe route and change into a pair of jeans and a t-shirt. I quickly freshen my makeup and pull a brush through my hair.

"This okay?" I ask as I step into the living room.

His eyes drift slowly over me, and I feel the anxious twist in my stomach I always get when Mom inspects my appearance.

"Great, let's go." He takes my hand, and I smile widely with relief. When we walk to the door, a warm feeling settles in my stomach. My first proper night out with my roommate.

I can do this. I can be normal. It's going to be awesome.

CHAPTER 8

EMMA

We stop at a house that reminds me too much of my own back home. It's a huge mansion with a green lawn all year round.

There are already cars parked in the driveway, but Aiden stops in the street, and I'm guessing it's so he won't get blocked in.

If it's a party, we are seriously underdressed. I glance at Aiden, hoping I'm wrong. "What's happening here tonight?"

"I need you to be open-minded," he starts, and I turn in the seat to look at him. "Have you ever watched any kind of fight sport before?"

"Not really," I answer carefully, very unsure of where he's going with this. "My brother tried karate once." I'm not sure that qualifies, though. He was eleven, and it didn't last long.

Aiden rests his hand on my shoulder which only makes me worry more.

"We meet here for what we call the Ultimate Fighting Championships. We compete until there's only one guy left. The winner goes against the other guys from North Carolina who won in their individual groups. This happens once every two weeks." He stops and does that thing where he pins me with his eyes.

He's waiting for me to freak out. A part of me actually considers it for a fraction of a moment.

"So you fight?"

"Yes," he says.

I nod, not liking this one bit.

"Why?"

"Some do it for money, others for the title or the rush." His eyes drift over my head toward the house, and I can see he's deep in thought. Maybe he's worried?

118

"Why do you do it?" That's all I want to know. I don't care about other people.

"Every bird of prey looks over its shoulder before it goes in for the kill, even a hawk. Every single bird of prey knows to watch their back, except an eagle because it's fearless." I sit frozen. The fact that he knows that leaves me stunned. "I fight, so others don't have to."

When his hand slips up to my neck, my heartbeat speeds up. I'm not sure who Aiden is, but from what I've seen so far, he's just too good to be real. He might as well have stepped out of my dreams, and that's a real danger to my heart.

He draws me against his chest and hugs me. "You'll be safe in there. Just stay close to me." As he pulls away, he adds, "And don't accept drinks from anyone."

I smile sheepishly. There won't be any risk of that happening.

Just like I thought, it's clear whoever lives here has money. What I get to see of the house is glamorous.

Once we step out the back, the atmosphere shifts, it's charged with excitement. The same guys from the

119

bar are all standing around, muscles bulging and gleaming under a spotlighted area.

There's a cordoned-off circle with chairs neatly placed around it. That's probably where the fighting will take place.

And the few women that are here are dressed to impress. Tight dresses that barely cover their butts make me look duller than yesterday.

One woman approaches Aiden, and I admire her balancing skills with how high her heels are. I'd break my neck if I tried to wear something like that.

"Aiden, are you ready for tonight?" Her tone is seductively low, almost sounding like she's purring.

I try to pull my hand free from Aiden's, but instead of letting go, he tightens his grasp.

"I'm always ready. Where's Katia?"

I can't believe it. Aiden's not giving Ultimate Barbie the time of day, and she doesn't look impressed.

"She'll be out now. Why don't you go get geared up?"

Only when she turns away does he let go of my hand. I follow him as he walks toward a group of men who are standing near the ring.

My eyes widen when some of them start to strip out of their clothes, but I relax when I see they all have shorts on beneath their sweatpants.

Grabbing hold of the collar of his shirt, Aiden drags it over his head. My eyes instantly glue themselves to his well defined back. The way his muscles ripple beneath his tanned skin has me in a trance until I smack into him face first.

"Crap," I groan, embarrassed for being so obvious about drooling over him. You'd swear we weren't naked together just a few hours ago.

"You okay?" he asks in a hushed tone, making his voice sound so much sexier.

"I'm great." I want to high-five myself when I don't blush.

"Will you hold my clothes for me?"

"Sure." Taking his shirt, I watch as he steps out of his slacks. Standing in just a pair of shorts, there's so much skin that I'm starting to feel dangerously hot.

The word *Capoeira* is printed in bold white letters down the side of his shorts, and I wonder what it means.

"I want you sitting close by. We're going to warm up before the others come. Can I get you something to drink first?" Aiden asks as if everything is okay and I'm not melting into a puddle of raging hormones at his feet.

I shake my head and take the seat he points to. Folding his clothes neatly, I keep them on my lap as I resist the urge to sniff them.

Yeah, I'm in trouble. I have a massive crush on my roommate.

Warm-ups.

I don't know what I expected, but it wasn't men slamming each other to the ground.

Aiden's talking to one of the others while they watch the two in the ring fight. I'm not sure who is who, I can't remember their names, and at the moment I have them organized by the color of their shorts. Blue and Red are in the ring.

I suck in a breath when Red goes down, thinking he shouldn't get up. Hell, I wouldn't get up after being hit like that. I'd lay wheezing and counting my broken bones.

My eyes dart to Aiden, and then I hold my breath. He's separated from the group and is doing what looks like a dance move, swaying agilely back and forth. Then he moves fast, and I let out a breath as he balances his entire body on one hand, every muscle taut.

I tip my head sideways, waiting for him to tumble down, but he eases himself back to the ground without much effort.

Damn, it's just not right for one person to look so good. It could be hazardous to someone's health. Hell, I'm already struggling to breathe. Never mind the heart palpitations.

When he moves again, he twists his body into the air.

Aaanndd I'd be eating dirt if I tried something like that. Damn, the man has talent.

"Aiden, you're up," Green-shorts calls out to him.

Aiden straps on a pair of gloves before he steps into the ring. I grab hold of his clothes and press them to my chest feeling nervous on Aiden's behalf.

They tap hands, and my heart sets off at a maddening pace as they start to circle each other.

Green moves in on Aiden, kicking at him, and I shriek low in my throat for him to jump out of the way.

"The real fightin' hasn't even started yet. Relax, princess." My eyes jump to Katia as she sits down beside me. "Your man has skills."

She turns her body to face me, draping her arm on the back of my chair. She's way too close for comfort, but at least she's not leeching onto me. As long as she doesn't try to touch me, I can deal with her.

"You have a nice house," I say, not knowing what else to say. If I'm going to be around Aiden, I might as well try to get along with the people he hangs out with. Although, Katia is a different cup of tea altogether. Not sure how I'm going to get along with her.

She beams a smile at me. "Thanks." Then she leans closer to me. "Are you cold, princess? You're huggin' those clothes awfully tight."

I drop the shirt and sweats back to my lap and glance at the ring. It's empty. My eyes flit all over the place until I find Aiden. He looks intimidating, to say the least, as he stalks toward us. At first, his eyes are on Katia, and I'm just about to start feeling awkward, thinking I might have misread something between them when he reaches his hand to me.

"You don't mind if I borrow my girl, Katia?" I don't wait to hear her answer. I'm up and dropping his clothes on the chair before she can think of a response. His hand is warm when he weaves his fingers through mine.

"People are startin' to arrive, so it's going to fill up fast. I just want to get you somethin' to drink. Please don't take anythin' from anybody but me," he reminds me as we walk in the direction of the pool and bar area.

I'd rather drink pool water than alcohol. After last night I'm in no hurry to ever drink that poison again.

Aiden reaches in behind a counter and retrieves two bottles of water.

We don't head back to the ring, though. Instead, he leads me over to the steps next to the pool, where he pulls me down beside him.

"Let's just enjoy this moment before it gets crazy."

Music starts to fill the air. Even though the bass is hard, vibrating the water in the bottles, the background tune is slower, lending a trance vibe to it.

"Thank you for comin'." He places his hand right behind my butt and presses his shoulder against mine.

"It's not what I expected." Feeling worried for Aiden's safety, I ask, "Won't you get hurt?"

"Are you actually worried about me?" he teases, and as my luck would have it, I blush.

With him sitting so close, his eyes are too intense to meet. I look out over the garden, letting my hair fall between us as a smile forms around my lips. It's one thing liking him, it's another letting him know how I feel.

Some things I'd like to keep to myself for now. It's still too new to admit it out loud.

"Maybe a little," I say, surprising myself by flirting back.

I've never done anything like this. I should ask Chloe for some tips. She's good at this kind of thing.

"I can't drive you home if you get hurt. We'll end up being one with a tree on the wrong side of the road," I joke.

"I'll be fine. There's no need to worry," he reassures me.

I glance back at Aiden and seeing the letters printed on his shorts, I ask, "What does the word on your shorts mean?"

"It's the fighting style I prefer. Capoeira is a Brazilian fightin' style. It's a mixture of dance, acrobatics, and martial arts. I throw in some other things I've learned along the way. Capoeira teaches you respect and patience, which is why I love it."

Before I can say something, his hand brushes my hair away from my shoulder, slipping up my neck. There's an explosion of flutters in my stomach. He leans in, and when his mouth presses against mine, my abdomen tightens with anticipation.

I open my mouth to let him in, to experience more of him. I love the way he makes me feel wanted and safe.

The fights are brutal, to say the least. I sit shocked through the first three before life returns to my limbs.

Aiden's fight didn't even last seconds. I'm not sure what happened. The guy attacked him, tried to jab a few punches at him but missed, and somehow landed flat on his back with Aiden pinning him down.

I'm still not sure if I should be relieved or worried that Aiden incapacitated a full-grown man within seconds.

I don't know how to react to what's happening around me. Men going at each other until one is unconscious, and lying in a puddle of blood? It's not right.

Colton steps into the ring with a guy who's easily a head shorter than him.

As they start to circle each other, Katia calls out, "Kill him, baby."

I'm too tense to sit. Standing up, I walk to the side of the ring where there aren't as many people. I can see Aiden on the other side, talking to a few guys. He's not even looking at the fight.

The moment Colton pounces, my eyes flit back to the ring. I flinch as they collide with each other. The other guy throws a punch, his fist connecting with Colton's jaw. I wait for Colton to go down, but it doesn't look like he felt the blow at all. I swear these men are made of steel. He just stands and takes it with a sneer, and I get a feeling that doesn't mean anything good for his competitor.

"The fucker is going down. Colton is only playin' with him," Katia suddenly says next to me. She looks a little turned on by what's happening.

The guy gets a kick and another punch in, while Colton still hasn't started fighting back.

Katia almost gives me a damn heart attack, as she screams, "Take the fucker down!"

At her command, Colton darts forward, throwing his body against the smaller guy, who slams into the ground with a painful grunt. I stand and stare with wide eyes as Colton starts to throw punches. The other guy doesn't even have time to block any of the blows.

I cover my mouth as shock vibrates through me.

Shit! Am I the only one disturbed by what's happening?

I search for Aiden through the wire of the ring. He's watching the fight with such concentration on his face as if he's studying it. I can't believe he's okay with all this violence.

Disappointment fills my heart. I don't have time to process the emotion as Colton straddles the guy, who looks like he's passed out.

The guy's head wobbles with each blow to his face and blood splatters on the mat.

My eyes dart over all the faces around the ring, as they roar for Colton to kill him.

My heart is slamming hard against my ribs, and it feels as if I'm being suffocated by all the brutality.

This isn't right.

I dart around the ring, unable to be a simple bystander. Nothing about what's happening here tonight is right. Someone has to do something before the guy dies.

I grab hold of the wire that forms the ring and rush through the opening. When I reach them, I shove at Colton as hard as I can, but he barely moves.

Startled, Colton's head snaps up, and eyes filled with rage settle hard on me. For a moment I worry that he's going to hit me. A cold wave of fear washes over me, making dread pool in my stomach.

I don't know where the courage comes from, but I shove Colton again as I grind the words out, "Get away from him."

Colton blinks, and he actually looks stunned that I'm breaking up the fight.

Anger starts to bubble up my chest as I growl, "Move!"

When he finally gets off the guy, I kneel beside his unconscious body.

There's so much blood.

Focus on what you learned, Emma.

He needs you.

I keep chanting words of encouragement to myself as I try to assess his injuries. Leaning down I try to feel if he's still breathing. My heart thumps heavily as I wait for any sign of life.

"Oh, God." The words rush from me and panic vibrates through my body when it's clear he's not breathing.

I hope help is coming.

I grab his wrist and feel for a pulse. The seconds stretch out endlessly, while I can't feel anything. I move my fingers to make sure I have the right spot. When I still can't find a pulse, I check his neck.

No. This can't be happening.

"Okay, deep breaths, Emma. You can do this."

Not even thinking, I clean the blood around his mouth and nose with my bare hand, before wiping it off on my jeans. I start CPR, all the while chanting for him to hold on.

When Aiden kneels next to me, I hiss, "Back off." I really can't deal with him right now.

"Let me help," he says, sounding calmer than I feel.

"Back the bloody hell off!" I scream at him, losing control.

Calm down, Emma. This guy needs you.

I continue giving him CPR while my throat swells from all the emotions swamping me.

I don't know how long I do it for, until he finally sucks precious air into his lungs.

"You're going to be okay," I whisper to him even though he can't hear me.

When paramedics and police arrive, I almost start to cry with relief.

I don't know who phoned them. All that matters is he's alive.

I move to the side, and it feels as if everything is distorting around me. People all blur together, and I feel sticky from the blood on my hands. I try to wipe more of it off on my jeans as I force my legs to move.

No one even notices as I walk away from the second most disgusting thing I've ever seen, because nothing will ever compare to my mother.

When I reach the street, I start to walk in the direction of the flat.

I need to get away from that house.

From the violence.

My stomach is raw with tension as I start to notice my surroundings. It's really dark out. It's actually a good thing because then no one will see the blood smeared on my jeans.

As the adrenaline starts to leave my body, I begin to shiver.

I hate that I'm shaking like a leaf caught in a shitstorm.

I hate that I don't know exactly where I am.

I hate that I put myself in such a dangerous position.

What the hell was I thinking?

"You were looking for a flaw in Aiden. Well, now you found it."

I'm disappointed in myself for falling for someone like him. I should've seen this coming. Why do I make myself such an easy target?

I ran away from one monster only to find another.

I'm so upset that I've walked quite a distance without realizing when lights come up the street. I keep to the shadows, trying to make myself as small as possible. When the car slows, I quicken my pace.

Tears well in my throat when I hear a door slam shut. I dare a quick glance over my shoulder, and when I see that it's Aiden, it doesn't lessen any of the fear. Suddenly, Aiden doesn't look as harmless as he did before.

"Emma, please get in the car. You can't walk home," he says, still sounding calm, and it only makes me angrier.

"You're right," I snap at him. "I can't walk home because I don't know where the bloody hell I am."

Usually, I avoid any kind of confrontation, but this isn't just about me. This is about a man almost dying.

Instead of walking away, I do something I never dreamt I'd do in my entire life – I turn to face him. My body is wound tight, and I have to fight the need to cower away from him.

It's been so ingrained into me to submit, to not fight back, that I almost give in, but I can't ignore the fire that's been ignited inside of me tonight.

I saved a man's life.

I made a difference because I stood against the monsters of this world.

And it felt good.

It felt empowering.

I lift my chin a little higher as I say, "I should've listened to you last night when you warned me that you could be psycho. Not could be, you bloody are psycho!"

Turning away from him, I start to walk again.

"Will you let me explain?" He doesn't sound so calm anymore, and it sends my heart flitting into the nearest bushes.

When Aiden catches up to me and blocks my way with his body, I cringe a step back.

Even though I'm trying to put on a brave front, the fear must show on my face, because Aiden's expression quickly changes from angry to one of concern.

"I'm not gonna hurt you," he says as if he's approaching a cornered animal.

I just stare at him, waiting for his next move. There's no way I'm letting my guard down just because of a few words. Words mean nothing to me. Words are empty things, spoken by people to gain control over others.

Actions are all that matter. And right now everything Aiden has done tonight is telling me to run.

"Will you let me explain?" he asks again.

"You beat people to a bloody pulp. How do you explain that?" I ask, cynically. "You did nothing while that man almost died. What kind of person does that?" My voice falters as I cross my arms over my chest.

Taking a step back, I place some more distance between us.

"Emma," he whispers. Slowly, I glance up, and it only confuses me when I see the torn look in his eyes. "I shouldn't have brought you."

"If you didn't that guy would be dead," I say.

As my anger fizzles away, heartache takes its place. I thought Aiden was different.

He glances over my shoulder and takes a step closer to me.

"Let's just get home," he says, scanning the area around us again. "I can't talk to you out in the open like this. Once we're back at the apartment, I'll explain it all. Just get in the car."

I *do* need to get home, and that's the only reason I climb in the passenger seat. The moment Aiden parks in front of the flat, I let out a breath of relief.

When he shuts the front door behind us, I walk to the living room before I turn to face him.

He doesn't waste any time and gets right to the point. "The whole student thing is only a cover so I can get close to Katia and her gang. Girls have been going missin', and it has to do with these fightin' circles. Girls like you, who don't think, and just do." I should be upset because he just insulted me, but I'm too shocked by what he's telling me.

I'm frozen to the spot as his words sink in.

No.

It can't be.

"What are you saying?" Even as I ask the question, I start to shake my head, willing him not to answer me.

"I told you I'm not on the wrong side of the law," he says as if he wants me to figure it out for myself.

I take a few steps away from him, not wanting to face the awful truth. The edges around my vision darken as a panic attack threatens to knock me off my feet.

"You're one of them?" the words sound strangled as I force them out. "You're a policeman?"

CHAPTER 9

AIDEN

She makes it sound like I'm Satan's spawn.

"Emma – " I stop talking as she starts to breathe faster, her body shaking like a leaf in the wind.

Fuck, she's having a panic attack.

I rush forward and place my hand on her back.

"Just breathe," I say, making sure to keep my voice calm. After a few minutes, Emma seems to be calmer. "Are you feelin' better?"

She doesn't look at me as she nods. This night has been a complete fuck up. I have no idea how I'm going to fix this.

I shouldn't have taken her along.

Fuck.

I need a shower and time to clear my head before we continue this conversation. Emma also needs to get out of her bloodstained jeans.

"I think we should shower and change. Take a moment, and we'll talk when we're done," I say.

I watch her walk into her room before I go to the bathroom. I take a quick shower, and when I'm done, I wrap a towel around my waist before going to my room.

I get dressed in a fresh pair of sweats then leave the room. Seeing that the door to the bathroom is open, I knock on her door. When she doesn't answer, I push the door open and glance inside.

She's standing in the middle of the room, still dressed in the bloodstained clothes.

I hate that I've placed her in that position. It's taking a lot of strength for me to not drag her to the sink so I can wash the blood off of her hands myself.

"Emma, can we talk about tonight?" I ask. I'm not one to leave things unsaid and undone. The sooner we talk about this mess, the sooner we can move on.

"Sure," she whispers, sounding lost.

I suck in a deep breath of air, hating that I'm responsible for this mess. Walking into the room, I move around Emma so I can see her face.

She brings her eyes up to my neck before they drop back to my chest as if she doesn't have the energy to even look at my face.

"I'm still the same man as before, Emma," I say, needing to defend myself. I thought once I told her I'm with the police force, she would understand why I was at that fight tonight.

When she doesn't say anything, I continue, "I'm the same man you kissed today. The same man who held you. That gut feelin' you had about me when you let me touch you, was right. Nothin' has changed."

"Everything has changed," she whispers. "There's nothing to talk about. I came, I saw, I'm going. I was stupid to think people would be different here."

"Emma, I'm undercover. Can't you understand that?" I'm actually dumbstruck.

She looks up at me, and the pain I see there hits me square in the chest. "You're a policeman, Aiden. Policemen…" She can't finish her sentence and reverts to swallowing as she lowers her eyes to the floor. She grinds her teeth to hold back whatever else she wanted to say.

Being cautious, so I don't scare her, I take a step closer. Tilting my head, I lean down so I can catch her eyes.

"Emma," I whisper, "talk to me. Give me a chance to fix this."

She takes a step back, and I fist my hands at my sides, so I don't grab hold of her to stop her from moving away from me.

"You're supposed to be protectors." Her voice catches on the words, and it feels like a knife is being shoved through my heart. "Instead, you all use that badge to hide behind while you hurt others."

Her words hit so fucking hard, I have to take a second to breathe them away. My badge means everything to me. I would die for it.

I have to remind myself that Emma is not from here. I have no idea what things are like in South Africa.

143

Needing to know more, I ask, "Why would you say that?"

I want to reach for Emma but hold myself back. I don't think she wants me touching her right now.

"My dad never protect–" she stops, as a breath shudders through her. "I didn't put an ocean between myself and them just to move in with another policeman."

Fuck! Now I've got a million scenarios running through my head.

"Your dad's a cop?" I keep my voice gentle, trying to get more info out of her.

She nods. "He never stopped her, just like you didn't stop Colton tonight. You did nothing."

The words hurt like a bitch. Frustrated, I shove a hand into my hair which makes Emma flinch before her shoulders curl forward as if she's trying to make herself a smaller target.

What happened to this girl?

I'll find out what she's running from and help her. Right now, I just need her to know that I'm one of the good guys.

"I couldn't blow my cover, not at the expense of the women who are missin'. I have to find out where they are. I have to get them back before they're lost, or worse, killed. Those kidnapped women are my priority, Emma, not the men you saw tonight." I huff a frustrated breath. "I know we've only known each other for a short time, but do you really think I'm the same as them?" She doesn't answer me, and it only makes my frustration grow. "Last night, you turned to me to get away from Katia. Why did you do that, Emma?" I wait, my heart hammering.

"I thought you were different," she says as she finally brings her eyes up to my face.

"I am different. I made a promise to serve and protect. I'll never hurt anyone intentionally."

Her eyes search mine and I pray she can see that I mean every word.

After a moment her eyes travel back to my chest. Taking a chance, I reach for her hand and place it over the tattoo of the eagle. I cover her hand with both of mine.

"I'm sorry I took you there tonight. I shouldn't have done that. But you have to believe me when I say that I'll never hurt you."

When she nods, I don't feel any better. I can see by the wary look on her face that she didn't believe a word I said.

I'll just have to show her that I'm a man of my word.

I've been checking in on Emma since she fell asleep. I can't get what she said out of my head. The thing about her dad not protecting her has me thinking all kinds of things.

I know I shouldn't, but when I check in on Emma again, I take her phone and laptop. I need to know more about her.

I'm relieved when her phone comes on without needing any passwords.

There are more missed calls from her mother. I go into her voice messages, and as I wait for them to start playing, I open her laptop.

146

'How could you do this to me? After everything I've done for you. You won't survive out there, babes. Come home, or I'll come and fetch you.'

Shit, did Emma run away from home?

But, she's twenty-one. She's an adult. I don't get it.

The next message has my eyebrows shooting up.

'You're nothing without me! Do you hear me, babes? Nothing! I brought you into this world. I made you who you are. You need me to think for you. People can't be trusted.'

What.The.Fuck?

I sit and stare at the blank screen of Emma's laptop as the messages keep coming.

'Are you shacking up with some guy? Whoring yourself like some cheap tart? I'll never forgive you.' Then her mother's voice goes shrill almost blowing my fucking eardrum. *'You're mine, babes. I gave birth to you. I own you.'*

Emma's behavior is starting to make sense to me. Her mother is bat-shit crazy.

Are you even eating right? You better watch your weight. I won't have a fat ass for a daughter.'

147

What the hell? Who talks to their kid like that? I've met some seriously fucked-up people in my line of work, but I've never heard anything like this before.

'How can you do this to me after all I've done for you? How dare you! I'll find you, and I'll make you pay.'

I stop listening when I hear something in the apartment. Not sure what it was, I close the laptop to go check it out.

Opening my door, I hear whimpering coming from Emma's room. I rush into her room, and now that I've heard how her mother talks to her, I understand why she's having nightmares about the woman.

Emma twists and turns as if she's fighting someone, and then tumbles off the other side of the bed. I dart forward and kneel beside her as she tries to free her legs from the tangled covers. Her breathing comes in quick little puffs. When she looks up at me, her eyes are filled with so much despair, it twists at my heart.

I yank the cover away from her, and as my arm slips around her waist, Emma reaches up for me. She wraps her arms around my neck and her legs around my waist, and I have to admit that it feels good that she's trusting me right now.

Holding her tight, I climb to my feet. I carry her back to my room, and keeping her pinned to me with one arm, I pull the covers back on my bed.

"Lower your legs for me, Angel." I'll never call her babe again. It's too close to what her mom calls her.

She does as I say and I lay her down. I quickly move her phone and laptop to my desk before I get in next to her, and cover us up. Her arms wrap around me, and her wet cheek presses hard against my chest. I weave my hands into her hair and turn into her, shielding her.

"Sleep, Emma. You're safe."

I whisper the words to her again before she drifts off.

What a fucking night. First the fight, then hearing those messages from her clearly insane mother.

I lift myself slightly and look down at her sleeping face. It's not even a full two days, and she's managed to somehow crawl into my life. I've always loved being a cop, but she wakes up something else in me. A need to take care of someone else besides myself.

The thought settles warm inside of me, and I hold her tighter.

"Don't worry, Emma. I'm gonna help you."

I wake up and stretch my arm out, reaching for Emma, but the second I feel nothing in the spot beside me, my eyes fly open.

I sit up and blink the last of the sleep away, and that's when I notice the laptop and phone are missing from my desk. Darting out of bed, I race to Emma's room with a thundering heart.

If she's gone...

I stop by her door and relief washes over me, when I see her placing the laptop on her bed.

Thank fuck, she's still here.

Only then do I notice how good she looks. Damn, Emma's dressed to kill. A white silk blouse and black pants which fit her body perfectly.

I lean against the door and watch as she twists her hair up into a bun. Then she opens a box and starts putting on more make-up than I ever saw my mom and sister use combined.

"Mornin'," I say when it's clear she's not going to notice me standing here.

"Morning." She gives me a nervous smile before continuing with the make-up. I notice her hand trembling when she applies mascara and lipstick.

Emma pauses for a second, staring at herself in the mirror, and then she takes a shaky breath.

"You okay?"

"Uh-huh." She comes toward me, and taking hold of the door, she says, "I'll be out in a minute. I just need to do something first."

"Okay."

I stand back when she pushes the door closed, but as she lets go of it, it doesn't shut all the way. Moving to the right, I watch her through the crack. I should give her some privacy, but when she sits down on the bed, and I watch her whole posture change, it confirms my gut feeling that something is wrong.

I watch as Emma changes right in front of my eyes. It's like she flipped a switch. She presses something on the laptop, then folds her hands tightly together on her lap, her shoulders dropping. All emotion drains away from her face.

"Babes." I recognize her mother's voice.

Fuck, why would Emma call her mother?

"Morning, Mom," Emma says with the same whimpering voice I've heard from her nightmares, and it makes anger flood every inch of me.

"You disappointed me, babes. After everything I've done for you, everything I've sacrificed, this is how you repay me? You run away? Am I such a horrible mother that you want to hurt me like this? It would've been better for you to have ripped out my heart. Next time take a knife and dig the bloody thing out." Her mom sounds pitiful.

Fuck no! Not on my watch. I push the door open and walk into the room as Emma says, "I'm sorry, Mom. I didn't mean to hurt, Mom."

Emma doesn't even notice as I come inside.

"I have to threaten to freeze the trust account to get you to talk to me. What have I done to deserve such treatment from you? You've ignored all my calls, my messages." I hear a sharp intake of breath which makes Emma cringe. "And what do you mean by you need a break? From what, may I ask? You won't last a day without me in that godforsaken country."

"I'm so sorry, Mom. I was stupid, Mom."

As I come to stand next to Emma, I glance down at the screen. The woman doesn't look anything like Emma. Black hair and dark eyes, where Emma is soft and blond.

"Who. Is. That?" her mother hisses.

Woman, my mama would have a field day kicking your crazy ass.

"I'm Emma's roommate," I answer, crossing my arms over my chest.

Emma glances up at me as horror washes over her face. She starts to rise, then sits back down, her eyes darting between me and the screen.

"Mom," she says, her voice tight with worry. "He's just my roommate."

"Shacking up, are you? You're not even gone a full week and look what's become of you!"

I place a hand on Emma's shoulder to give her some strength.

"Mom." Emma lets out a heavy breath, and when she glances up at me, I see the fight creeping into her eyes.

My girl is torn between submitting to her mother and standing up for herself.

"You ran to him? You left me for *him!*" her mother snarls.

Emma shakes her head as she lifts her chin. "It's not like that. I needed some time on my own."

Her mother's eyes widen with surprise. I take it she's not used to Emma talking back to her.

"He's already got you back chatting me. In a fortnight he'll have you turning tri-"

I reach over and close the laptop on her mother. That's about as much as I can take because it sinks in – Emma did run away from home. She fled the fucking country to get away from that bitch.

Emma gasps and her hands fly to her mouth. She sits for a few seconds, then she leaps over the bed to grab her phone which has already started buzzing. I jump onto the bed and grab it from Emma before she can press it to her ear.

"Mrs. Bowen," I answer calmly, as I get off the bed.

Emma spins around, her eyes are wide with fear. She reaches for the phone, but I take hold of her hand, turning my body to the side, so the phone is out of her reach.

"Who the hell do you think you are?" her mother seethes over the line.

"Detective Holden. I'd be careful what you say next," I warn. "I'm not Emma, and I sure as hell am not your husband."

"You don't ever dare to talk to me like that!" she shrieks. "I want to talk to my daughter."

More demands?

She can go fuck herself. She's barking up the wrong tree.

I glance at a horrified Emma which only makes me more determined to protect her. She's so pale it's making her eyes look even bigger. Red marks are spreading up from her collarbone to her neck. I've never seen one person have so much control over another.

"I'm afraid you can't talk to Emma. She won't be comin' home either. Emma is stayin' with me."

Right there I make the decision to help Emma in any way I can.

"You can't keep her there. She's a South African citizen. She's mine," her mother fumes.

"I'll keep her away from you any way I can. I'll find a way so you won't see her again." I don't know how long I have until Emma's visa expires. I'll have to get it renewed.

"Tell her I'm cutting her off. We're freezing the trust account. You want her, you take care of her," her mother screams, and the line cuts off.

I drop the phone on the bed and pull Emma closer.

"What did she say?" she whispers. She's trembling all over.

I take hold of her chin and nudge her face up. "It's gonna be okay. I can't let you go back to her, Emma." I take a breath before I continue, "She said she's cuttin' you off." I see the flash of worry before Emma lowers her eyes from mine. I nudge her chin back up. "Hey, don't worry about it, Angel. I'll help you."

"Cut me off? She said that?" she whispers.

"You'll be fine," I reassure her. "You have me."

She nods twice before she forces a stiff smile around her lips.

"Thanks, but you don't have to worry. I'll be okay."

I watch her slam up walls. Fuck, she's blocking me out.

"Don't do that, Emma. It's okay to hurt. You can talk to me. I'm here to help you."

She nods and grimaces as if she's trying to swallow her tears down. "I don't know how... how to hurt." She rubs at her chest. "Shit, I suppose this is it." She ducks her head and then whispers, "I wasn't allowed to cry in front of her, so this is hard with you standing here."

I pull her back into my arms and hold her for the longest time, placing kisses in her hair.

"How long until your visa expires?" I need to know how long I have before I need to worry about that.

"Six months." Her breaths warm my chest.

"You've paid the apartment for six months. You're not goin' back," I spell it out for her.

"You don't understand, Aiden." She shakes her head. "If she cuts me off, I have nothing. How will I get around? What will I –"

"You said you wanted to experience new things," I interrupt her, grasping at damn straws, anything to reassure her. "Experience them here. Experience what it's like to accept help from someone. Experience what good ole' Southern hospitality is all about. Just stay and experience what it is you came to experience." I lift her face up to mine and watch her, waiting and praying she'll hear me. I've never wanted to help someone so much before.

"Stay here with me, Emma. Give me a chance to show you that there are good people in this world."

Please, Emma. Stay.

CHAPTER 10

EMMA

Mom must be having a royal fit. She saw Aiden in just his slacks. She saw his bloody tattoos.

I can't believe I talked back to her. I've never done that before. I'm scared and proud of myself all at once. It's such a foreign feeling.

I look at Aiden's ruffled hair, then drop my eyes to his chest, taking in all the ink. I try to look at him the way Mom would, but I can't. I'm nothing like her. I see his strength, and his words '*you have me*' run through my mind again.

There are so many questions I want to ask him. If I'm going to stay with him, I have to get to know him better.

"How old are you?" I finally focus on one question.

He tilts his head as surprise flashes in his eyes.

"I need to get to know the man I'll be living with, and now is as good as time as any," I explain.

"Twenty-seven," he answers.

Oh, wow! I thought he was twenty-four. What's another shock to add to my already disastrous day?

"Are you really from South Carolina?"

"Yes, I'm from Lyman. My folks and brother also live there. My whole family is in the force. My cousin Cole is a marine, but I get the feeling he'll be joinin' us as well once he's done serving."

"How long have you been a police officer?"

"I served in the army for two years. I went to college when I came back. I've been on the force for five," he says, stopping for a second, "I just made detective, but it was more luck than anythin' else."

"What is your blood type?"

He frowns.

"B positive." A smile tugs at the corner of his mouth. "Is that really important?"

"If you're bleeding to death and they ask me that, then yeah, I suppose it is." It wipes the smile from his

160

face. "I just want to know in case you get your ass kicked next time."

"I'll be in good hands then. You were pretty amazin' last night. Have you always wanted to be a nurse?"

I shake my head as I answer him honestly, "No, I studied what I was told to study. My mom wanted me to be a nurse." I can't keep the bitter laugh back. "My brother is a doctor in Pretoria. I guess she wanted me to be a nurse so I wouldn't forget I'm the lower life form compared to Byron." Saying it out loud hurts. I wish I could switch my heart off to not feel anything.

"Hey," he whispers.

I look up at him, but instead of it being a quick glance, he takes hold of my chin, lifting my face to his.

My eyes are burning from keeping back the tears. I'm not the type of person who cries over everything, but Aiden is making it hard for me to stop the tears. His other hand takes hold of mine, and he lifts it to his chest, holding it there.

"You're gonna be fine. You're gonna go to school, and have fun. Live a little." His mouth lifts at the corner

161

in the sexy grin which always makes my heart beat faster. "As soon as you're dressed in somethin' more comfortable, we're gonna go grab some breakfast because I'm starvin'." He leans in and presses a sweet kiss to my forehead.

I soak in his warmth for a minute, taking what I can get, because for some reason it's easing the pain in my chest just being close to him.

"You come to me if you need somethin'. Come to me about anythin', okay?"

I nod, swallowing back the emotion that's threatening to overwhelm me.

As Aiden leaves the room, I let a tear roll down my cheek. I can't describe how it feels that someone stood up to my mother for me.

I'll have to find a way to make it on my own now that my mother has cut me off.

But I will make it.

I have to.

I have Chloe, and now I have Aiden.

I'm not alone anymore.

I send Chloe an email explaining the latest happenings with my mother, and how Aiden stepped in. I don't tell her Aiden's a detective. I don't want to risk his life while he's undercover which reminds me to ask him more about it, so I don't slip up and ruin it all.

I change into shorts and a t-shirt then quickly wash my face and tie my hair back into a ponytail.

We step into the lounge at the same time, and I have to admit I feel insecure for new reasons; the main one being he's not just a student anymore.

Now that I know he's older and that he has a job, he comes across more masculine. He looks great in his worn jeans which hang low on his hips, and the charcoal shirt brings out the grey of his eyes.

But I try to show that I don't notice any of that or the excitement in my stomach as I leave the flat with Aiden.

He opens the car door for me, and I brush past him to get in. I catch a hint of his spicy aftershave before I slip into the car. When he walks around it, I practically devour him with my eyes. By the time he slides in behind the wheel, it feels as if I'm going to bubble over with excitement.

We grab breakfast from a drive-thru, and then he drives us out to a lake. We drive past some students settling in for a day of fun, families, couples in love, and he keeps going until the people disappear behind us and it's just us and the surrounding nature.

When he parks the car, all I can do is stare at the beauty all around me.

The glossy sheen of water is smooth beyond the trees, and I push the door open so I can take in the full sight in front of me. Most of the trees are still green, but some of the leaves have turned to gold and orange, submitting to the coming winter. The ones that have fallen are still soft, not crunchy yet.

"Are there Bald Eagles here?" I ask, my eyes already scanning the sky.

"Yeah, if we're lucky we might see one," Aiden says as he grabs a blanket from the back of the car. I take our breakfast and wait for him, my eyes going back to the sky.

I really hope we see a Bald Eagle. I've read that they came close to extinction once but with a little help and a lot of determination, they made it. That's where my hope lies. If an eagle can come back from such devastation, then maybe I can, too.

"If we don't eat soon I'm going to starve," Aiden says as he takes my hand and pulls me through the trees to an open patch of sand. It's quiet around us, and it feels as if everything is finally calming inside of me.

Right now, there's no worry or fear, just all this serene beauty.

After Aiden has spread the blanket open over the sand, we sit down and eat in silence. We don't disturb the nature around us with words. When we're done eating, he tugs me down, to lie next to him.

I can't get enough of the scenery around me. The lake stretches out wide, and not too far away I can see a dock. It's such an incredible experience. My eyes dance from the lake to the trees, then finally stopping at Aiden who's staring at me. There's a gentle smile tugging at the corners of his full mouth, which reaches all the way to his eyes.

I can't mean it enough when I say, "Thank you for bringing me here."

"You're welcome." He turns on his side, resting his head on his palm. "Tell me what you're thinkin' right now."

Seriously? I'm thinking about how I want him to kiss me. There's no way I'm telling him that.

"Grey." I blurt out. It's the color of his eyes.

"Okay, before that," he says letting out a chuckle.

Be brave, Emma. Tell him.

"That I want to kiss you," I admit.

He brings his hand to my face and caresses the line of my jaw. Leaning down, his lips follow the tingling trail left by his fingers.

"Emma," he breathes against my skin, "if you want somethin', just take it." When the tingles reach my abdomen, they feel like full-blown electric pulses, bringing every nerve in my body to life. I unclench my hands over my stomach as I close my eyes again, and the world diminishes until there's only him.

Bringing my hands up to his chest, I grip fistfuls of his shirt. I open my eyes and meeting his grey ones, I take what I want.

I pull him down and crush my mouth against his. Thank God he doesn't hold back. I open my mouth, and he slips inside, teasing me with his tongue. He takes control of the kiss until I'm breathless and sure I've got more of him than actual air in my lungs.

I want so much more. I want what we had yesterday.

I push against his chest until he's flat on his back, and I straddle him. Pressing feather-light kisses over his jaw, I move to his neck. I shift down until I feel his hardness right where I want it.

"Emma," he growls. He grabs hold of my hips, and for a moment I think he's going to keep me still. Then his hips thrust up hard.

Sensations ripple through my abdomen, and my breath explodes from my lungs. He doesn't stop. He keeps rubbing against my sensitive core until I wish we weren't wearing clothes.

I need to feel him. I need to... "Aiden," I groan when it becomes too much.

He rolls me onto my back and unbuttons my shorts. Covering me with his body, he slips his hand under my panties. When he thrusts a finger inside me, my body lifts off the ground with pleasure. I groan with desire and growing bolder than I've ever been before I shamelessly start to move my hips. My abdomen clenches, and I feel it all the way to my toes. I grab hold of his wrist and press him harder against me, as I find my release with his name on my lips. He continues placing kisses on my neck and down my collarbone, making this moment only so much more perfect.

After he pulls his hand away, and he's buttoning my shorts again, I lift my hands up to his face. I let my fingers trail over his skin, really taking him in for the first time. I don't know what's happening between us, but I like it. I press my palms flat against his jaw so I can feel more of him.

My eyes drink in every inch of him. I notice a faint cut disappearing into his hairline, and I wonder if he got it in a fight.

"I love touching you," I admit, reveling in how good it feels.

He presses another kiss to my lips before he says, "Good 'cause I love touchin' you."

A while later, I'm folding the blanket when I hear the cry far above me. My eyes jump to the sky, and I want to call Aiden, but all that comes out is a rush of air.

As the eagle soars over the lake, I'm dizzy with emotions I can't begin to describe. My chest expands and shrinks all at once. My heart stutters and I hold my breath. There's an aching pain spreading through my chest, but it's different this time. It's sweet as if something is finally being released. Something I've been holding inside me for far too long.

The eagle cries out, staking its claim on its territory and a piece of my soul. It swoops down lower on the other side, gliding gracefully, flapping once, twice, and then it's gone.

CHAPTER 11

AIDEN

I've just wasted an entire hour with Katia and Colton because I didn't get shit on when the main event will be. In a hurry to get to where Emma's waiting for me, I jog across the courtyard, watching as a guy lean into her personal space.

What the fuck? It's only day two, and already the wolves are descending.

As I come up behind Emma, the fucker says, "Come on, baby, don't be so cold. We'll have fun, and I can show you how good I am. After the fight we can go to my dorm room, and I'll show you what else I'm good at."

He tries to reach for Emma's hand, and she takes a quick step backward, right into my chest.

"Oh, sorry," she gasps, and as she glances over her shoulder, I see the panic in her eyes. But then she realizes it's me, and she visibly relaxes.

I wrap an arm around her and pull her tighter to me. I want to pound my chest when she brings one hand up, grabbing hold of my bicep, leaning her cheek into the muscle.

The fucker looks startled, and he should be for messing with my girl.

I lock eyes with him, daring him to give me a reason to beat the shit out of him.

"I didn't know she had a boyfriend," he stammers nervously. "I've seen your fights, dude. You're good. I'll be at the fight on Saturday. It will be my first one."

They're going to wipe the floor with this guy. He's half the size of most of the guys who go to these fights.

"What's your name?" I ask. I'll get Katia to set me up with him, that way I can teach him a lesson and probably save his life, so one of the other guys don't end up killing him.

"Kyle. Man, I can't believe I actually get to talk to you. This is fuckin' amazing. Do you have any tips for me?"

"Yeah," I say, "don't treat women like shit and don't get killed on Saturday."

Keeping my arm around her neck, I pull Emma away, turning my back on the poor fucker. Once we've put some distance between Kyle and us, I stop and turn Emma, so she's in front of me.

"Tha –" she starts to say, but not caring that we're in public, or how she might feel about it, I slip my hands into her hair, and pull her face to mine. I kiss her so everyone around us will fucking know Emma's mine.

So she will know she's mine.

She grabs hold of my wrists and pulls herself closer.

Fuck, it feels heavenly to fall into her.

I drop my hand to her back, drawing her body tightly against mine, and I let her sweetness fill my mouth as our tongues twist greedily.

If we were alone now, I'd forget what I said about her first time having to be special, and I'd make her mine.

I break the kiss, smiling when she inches up to follow my mouth, but I don't buckle under the temptation.

"If we don't stop, I'm going to undress you right here," I say. Emma's face flushes at my directness, and she drops her forehead to my chest. "With that said," I continue, "I don't think it's a good idea that we go home right now, 'cause I won't stop. So, a public place it has to be. Any ideas?"

She hasn't left the apartment except when she comes here for classes.

"We can go anywhere," she answers me.

"What would you normally do on a Friday?"

As she adjusts her bag, I reach for it and throw it over my shoulder. She turns half away, looking at the students passing us by.

"Really, we can do anything you want to do."

I tilt my head so I can see her face, and I try to keep mine neutral. Now that I'm starting to really fall for

Emma, it's getting harder to not lose my shit when I see the damage her mother has done to her. I better not meet that woman in person.

"Then I'll just have to think of somethin' that will sweep you off your feet," I tease.

She smiles, standing on her toes so she can reach my ear. "Give it your best shot, Detective Holden."

Heat flushes through my body and straight to my cock. I tighten my hold on Emma's neck, keeping her close to me.

"Is that a dare?" I breathe the words over her jaw which makes her grab hold of my shirt. I can't keep from smiling. I love how responsive she is and that I'm having this effect on her.

"Yes," she says, desire smoldering in her eyes.

Fuck, I can't wait to be inside this woman. I'm going to walk around with blue balls if I don't plan something special soon.

"Let's get going then. This should be fun," I say as we start to walk in the direction of the car.

My mind is racing like a wild horse during the drive home. I need to come up with something really different. Movies and boring stuff like that are out. I glance at the time, and as insane as the idea is, I decide to drive through to our family beach house. I stop at a gas station to fill up, on the way to the apartment.

I park the car, and leaning over, I place a quick kiss on Emma's lips. "Can you wait here for one sec?"

"Sure," she says, none the wiser of my plans for her.

I run up to the apartment and pack fresh clothes for tomorrow. Emma must be the easiest person to pack for. Shorts, shirt, pajamas, and underwear. I grin like a dumbass as I throw the silk bra and panty set in. Toothbrush and brush, and I almost miss the little box of contraceptive pills. I open the drawer next to her bed to make sure I'm not missing anything.

I frown when I see other bottles of pills. Reaching for them, I inspect each one. Three are still sealed, the fourth is half empty. I take out my phone and call Zac before I even think it through.

"Speak to me," he answers quickly.

"Can you check out somethin' for me? I can't right now. What is Toplep taken for?"

"Sure," he says.

"Talk to you later, bro."

I cut the call and stare at the four bottles, seriously hoping Emma isn't sick. I push it to the back of my mind for now and head down to the car with our bags.

When I steer us in the direction of Ocean Isle, I switch on the radio. I've noticed Emma loves music.

"We have a lot of time to kill, so twenty questions," I say. I can try and get to know her that way.

"Twenty questions. Wow. You're feeling brave. What if I ask you something embarrassing?" she says, her eyes lighting up with happiness. I love seeing her like this.

I glance at her. "I have nothin' to hide," I say, grinning.

"Normally the male species shies away from answering questions."

"It's in my nature to ask them," I remind her. "I like solvin' puzzles."

"You do?" she asks, an uncomfortable look crossing her face.

"Human ones," I rectify.

177

"Oh." She glances out the window and then back at me. "What's your favorite color?"

"Charcoal, yours?" I counter. She looks around the car as if she's thinking about it.

"I love any shade of blue," she says.

"Favorite thing to do?" I watch her closely. She couldn't decide on something to do for tonight, and it has me thinking about what the world is like where she comes from that she couldn't make a simple decision. With the little I know about her, I get the feeling her mother held her prisoner.

"Read, and you?" She surprises me with a quick answer, but one word is not good enough.

"What do you read? You need to explain it more."

"I read anything I can get my hands on. I love books."

A mischievous smile settles around her mouth. "What's the most daring thing you've ever done?"

I don't know if she means crazy daring or just plain daring.

"That's a tough one," I say. "It all depends. Do you mean crazy, or plain ole' darin'?"

"Both," she replies as she rests her head back against the car seat.

"Crazy first." I smile at the memory. "Laurie and I went through the academy together. We got partnered together, too. We got labeled '*The Terrible Twins*' after we drew the short straw out of all the rookies on who would prank the captain durin' our first week on the job. When he wasn't there, we turned the whole place upside down." I sigh, remembering how we took turns to keep watch. "Laurie even turned the certificates on the wall upside down. Whatever we couldn't turn upside down, we glued down. Damn, our captain was pissed at us." I laugh, and then the old pang of sadness comes, tightening its hold on my heart.

"She sounds nice. So you're twins?"

"Yeah. The most darin' thing I've ever done was four years back." I grip the wheel harder. "Goin' to Laurie's funeral took about all the courage I had."

"I'm-" My eyes snap to Emma, and she stops in the middle of saying the words. I hate it when people say they're sorry for your loss.

Emma places her hand on my thigh and smiles gently. "It couldn't have been easy."

I loosen my hold on the wheel and force a smile to my lips. We need to move on to a happier subject.

"What's the craziest thing you've done?" I ask.

I catch the smile on her face before she looks out the window. "Going to a bar and asking a guy to sleep with me."

Her cheeks flush a deep pink, telling me just how hard it is for her to admit.

"And? How's it all workin' out for you so far?"

"Better than any book I've read." The honesty shows on her face. If I weren't driving right now, I'd kiss her breathless.

Instead, I settle for second best and bring her hand to my lips, pressing a kiss to her fingers before resting our hands on my thigh.

As we reach the halfway mark of our journey, she finally starts to ask where we're going, but I don't give her any clues, wanting it to be a surprise.

THE OCEAN BETWEEN US – Michelle Heard

We keep taking turns to ask questions, and as we near Ocean's Isle, I can't wait to see her face when she realizes where I've brought her.

I've seen the view every summer when we've come down for family vacations, and I hope Emma will love it as much as I do.

Just like clockwork, the strip of blue appears, and Emma's fingers dig into my hand.

"Aiden," she breathes, a wide smile brightening her face. "It's so beautiful."

CHAPTER 12

EMMA

After driving for about three hours, Aiden stops outside a house. I don't know who it belongs to, or whether it's his.

"It's our family cottage," he says. "We come here every summer. I hope you'll like it."

Family holidays? It just reminds me of how different our lives are.

I follow him silently up the stairs, and as he opens the door, he waits for me to walk inside first. I feel uncomfortable walking into someone else's home. I don't even feel welcome in my parents' house. I've been taught to always walk behind my parents and brother and to let them first pass through doors, as a way of showing respect.

Aiden takes my hand and leads me deeper into the house. There are pictures of everyone on the wall. Children, teenagers, adults. I see one of Aiden and a woman, and I stop. Two pairs of grey eyes look back at me. She's wearing a formal dress. You can feel the love through the photo. Even though Laurie is shorter than Aiden, you can see they're twins.

I just feel so sorry for the family's loss, especially Aiden's. I can't imagine what it's like losing a twin, and by the sounds of it, they were best friends.

"She's so beautiful," I say, then I laugh when I see a photo of where they're much younger. Laurie is riding on Aiden's back, pretending he's a horse. She's even wearing a cowboy hat.

My eyes jump from the one photo to the next. The two of them doing sports. Another of them graduating.

A family portrait. I feel the pang in my heart at seeing what I've been missing out on.

"Are your parents proud of you?" I ask.

He tugs at my hand, trying to get me to face him. Eventually, he lets go and takes hold of my shoulders, turning me to him.

"Yes, very." He smiles. "We're a close family." He's watching me intently, so I force a smile to my lips.

"I'm happy for you." I'm really glad that he comes from a loving family. There's hope for the world, knowing not all families are like mine.

I follow him through a living room which is decorated in an ocean theme.

"Wow, I really like what you've done with this room." I compliment him.

"Thanks, but I can't take the credit. Mom and Laurie did all the decoratin'."

"They did an amazing job."

Stepping out onto a deck my eyes drink in the stunning view of the ocean that stretches out before us. Not only is Aiden perfect, but he comes from a perfect world.

"You want to grab somethin' to eat first, or go for a walk along the beach?" he asks.

"You can choose." I've never been allowed to make a decision in my life. I'm not sure what I'm supposed to say. We can do anything, and it will be new and exciting to me.

184

When Aiden turns to face me, he's frowning. "Emma, I'm askin' you. I want you to think about what you would like to do. Just for once stop thinkin' about pleasin' someone else, and think about what *you* want."

There's only one thing I really want to do.

"I'd really like to see your room," I say, holding my hand out to him.

I want to see more of his life.

Placing his hand in mine, we go back into the house. We pass a kitchen, and when we reach a passage, I see there are more photos lining the walls.

I stop at a picture of Aiden and Laurie, standing in full uniform next to a police car. It's weird seeing him like that. He's been going to college with me, attending classes, and pulling off the student act so well, that I keep forgetting he's undercover.

Seeing Aiden in his uniform makes it real.

"This is it," he says as he pushes a door open.

I move closer and glance inside. It's nothing like at the flat. There, he only has the bed and desk in his room. I step inside and look around. Besides the bed, there's a desk with various medals and trophies.

Plaques are up on the wall, and I'm guessing what I'm seeing is only some of it. This is their holiday home so I can just imagine what it looks like at his parent's house.

"Is there something you're not good at? Really, anything?" I know I've asked before, but this time I mean it. How is it possible that, on this whole planet, my path had to cross with the one person that's my total opposite? I'll never be able to keep up with him. He's light years ahead of me.

"I'm not good at sharin'. I recently found out I get jealous," he admits.

I look up, surprised by what he said.

"What do you get jealous of?" I ask, but his phone rings before he can answer me.

"Can you give me a sec?" he apologizes, and I nod. "Hey, Zac." He steps out of the room, but I can still hear him as I look at everything in his room.

"You did?" There's a moment's pause then he asks, "Are you sure?"

I smile when I see a worn baseball cap and brush my fingers over the top of it.

"So you're tellin' me it's for any of those four?"

I hope whatever it is isn't too bad. I hear him sigh as he ends the call.

When he walks back into the room, he looks upset.

"Is everything okay?" I ask, worried that he got bad news.

"Please sit, Emma."

I sit down on the corner of the bed and wait for him to tell me what's wrong as he pulls the chair away from the desk, and positions it opposite from me.

When he sits down and looks at me, it's with a different look in his eyes than what I've gotten used to. He's so serious, and I realize I'm getting a taste of what it's like to sit opposite Aiden the detective.

My stomach starts to twist like it does when I know I have to leave my room to go to the toilet, and I have to walk past my mother.

Crap, it feels awful.

"It's hard to figure you out," he says, which only makes confusion swirl through me. "I don't know how to word this correctly, so I'm just going to come out and ask it." My heartbeat picks up so fast, and it makes me feel lightheaded. "Are you sick, Emma?"

"Huh." Why would he ask me that? "No, I'm not sick at all."

"If you're healthy, then it leaves only two other options. You said yourself you've never been drunk, so you can't be an alcoholic."

His words shudder through me making the blood drain from my face.

"Why would you, who are healthy, be takin' such a high dosage of Toplep, a drug you need a prescription for? Can you explain that to me?"

Shit. It feels as if the ground has been ripped out from under me.

I made a mistake. I actually allowed myself to feel happy for a moment, and now the shit is hitting the fan.

I need to calm down. I take a deep breath like I do when I'm facing my mother – slow and careful.

I get up and walk to the window, unable to sit still right now.

"I used to take them so I wouldn't pick up weight," I admit part of the truth. It's all I can do. I learned at an early age not to lie. Lying only makes it worse. "My mother started me on them when she felt I was gaining too much weight."

Humiliation courses through my veins and I feel it warming my face. I rush into a quick explanation, to make it sound better than it really is.

"It's become a habit to carry them with me and to flush it down the toilet every day, so she doesn't notice that I've stopped taking them. I suppose it's stupid doing it since I'm not even at home. I can throw them all away, and she wouldn't know."

I swallow the tears back because so help me God, I won't cry, not because of her.

"Why don't you fight back?" he asks, and although his voice is gentler, the question hits hard.

I wrap my arms around myself as I laugh bitterly.

"Fight back?" A dull burning starts in my stomach, and it makes me feel nauseous. "I have. Many times."

I shake my head to stop the memories from overwhelming me. The words just burst from me when the wall I've fought so hard to keep up cracks right down the middle.

"I've tried, but to fight for hours with a person who can't hear what you're saying because they keep drinking one glass of wine after the other, only makes it worse. With time I learned to keep quiet. It's better that way."

I bite the inside of my cheek to keep the rest in and dare a glance over my shoulder, only to see Aiden leaning with his elbows on his legs, staring at the floor.

His mouth is set in a hard line, which makes a muscle jump in his jaw.

"You think I'm weak for not fighting harder, don't you?"

Instead of keeping quiet like it's been ingrained into me all my life, anger bubbles up in me, and I keep going.

"I suppose it would be easy for you to think that. Your mother loves you. I'm sure she tells you that, often, too." Turning around, I face him. "Your mother never told you that you should rather have been a boy and to be more like your brother."

I should stop, but he's just staring at me as if he doesn't care about what I'm telling him which makes a

190

wave of pain slam into me. I take a shaky breath to keep the tears back.

"Your mother never shoved a knife into your hand and held it to her throat, telling you to kill her, and by God, you wanted to with every fiber of your being. But instead, you swallow down the disgust and hold her. You hold the woman who abuses you every chance she gets. You *will* yourself not to move just so she can touch your hand, and it makes you sick to your stomach, but you do it otherwise she beats you until you're lying on the floor." I swallow hard on the lump of emotion stuck in my throat.

Now that I've started I can't stop. I've never told anyone this. In a way, it feels freeing like I've ripped the scab off and the wound can finally start to heal.

"She would beat my back raw, and then afterward I'd have to tell her how much I love her."

Aiden gets up and takes a step towards me, but I hold up my hand to stop him. I can't stand being touched now.

"I just want her to stop, Aiden, so I keep quiet. It's over sooner then." As I say the words, I realize I've said too much.

I can't walk away from the humiliation, because where would I go? I can't sink down and cry, because that would be a sign of weakness. I can't even go home. So I do the only thing I can. I run by Aiden, avoiding his hand as he reaches for me.

Feeling rejected by life, a sob builds in my throat, and as I rush out onto the deck, the first tear falls.

I grab hold of the railing as the memories tear through me. Now that I've had a glimpse of what life is really like, it hurts so much more.

I crouch down as wave after wave of anger and hurt washes through me. My fingers wrap tighter around the wooden poles as the tears I've been holding in for so long, fall to the deck.

Aiden comes up behind me, and leaning over me, he takes hold of my hands, pulling them away from the railing. Wrapping an arm around my waist, he pulls me to my feet, then turns me around and draws me into a hug.

"Hold onto me, Em," he whispers, his strong arms pinning me to his broad chest, which only makes me cry harder.

I wrap my arms around his waist and smother my sobs in his chest, letting the tears wash me clean of all the hate, the anger, the heartbreak.

I feel awful for the things I've said. Aiden's a good man. He didn't deserve any of that.

"I'm really sorry for what I said," I stammer as I try to catch my breath. "You're right, I –"

He stops me mid-sentence. "Emma." His voice is soft as his breath warms my forehead. "Don't apologize. There's absolutely nothin' for you to be sorry about. I need to know all of that so I can help you."

Taking a deep breath of his unique scent, I feel the storm dissipate inside of me, making place for the sun.

His arms tighten around me as he presses a kiss to the top of my head.

I want to stay like this forever, safe in his arms.

"I'm sorry," he murmurs against my hair. "It's easy for me to tell you to fight when I've been taught how

193

to. I... fuck. I'm sorry. I wish I could change what happened to you. I wish I had been there to stop it."

Taking hold of my hands, he pulls my arms away from where they were wrapped around his waist, bringing them up to his chest. He covers both my hands with one of his, keeping them in place as his free hand reaches for my face. With soft brushes, he wipes my tears away.

Taking hold of my chin, he tilts my face up. His eyes are soft on me. "Are you okay?" he asks, and my throat constricts.

This man.

He's the opposite of my mother.

He's my heaven where she's my hell.

"You're so different," I whisper instead of answering his question. "I can't stand anyone touching me. I wish I could explain to you how amazing it feels when you touch me." I take a deep breath, then continue, "You're the first person I've told."

"I'm glad you told me, Em." He presses a kiss to my forehead, and I close my eyes so I can savor the moment.

Grabbing hold of his shirt, I move closer until my body is pressed tightly against his. A shiver runs down my spine, settling deep in my heart.

I think I've fallen in love with him. Irrevocably with all of my heart.

I lift my eyes to his, wanting to say the words, but they get stuck in my throat. Instead, I decide to show him how much he means to me.

He tilts his head, and his mouth lifts at the corner. It makes him look wickedly handsome.

"I've seen that look before, and I'd love to know what you're thinkin'."

A smile pulls at my lips. "I'm thinking how lucky I am to have met you." I take a deep breath and gathering all my courage, I whisper, "I want you to be the one, Aiden. Tonight. You said it should be special, and it won't get more special than this for me."

"Take what you want, Em," he says as his eyes drop to my mouth. "You set the pace, and I'll follow."

Can this man get any sweeter?

I slip my one hand beneath his shirt, pressing my fingertips lightly to his abs. Feeling his muscles tighten beneath my touch, I take it as a good sign. I push his shirt up, and once I have it off, I drop it on the deck next to us.

I take in the flawless art that is his chest. Standing on my toes, I press a kiss to his neck, right where his tattoo starts.

I trail feather-soft kisses to the middle of his chest. Glancing up from under my lashes, my insides tighten with satisfaction when I see the heat in his eyes.

I want this man now. I've been ready since the dark ages.

His fingers dig into my hips as he takes hold of me, and then he lifts me up. I quickly wrap my legs around his waist. There's a sweet tightening in my abdomen when I feel how hard he is.

Nervous excitement ripples through me as he walks us back into the house. I continue to tempt him as best I can by brushing my lips along his jaw.

When I nip at the skin just beneath his ear, his arms tighten around me.

"Are you enjoyin' yourself?" he asks hoarsely.

I nod, a grin spreading over my face. "Quite a bit."

Walking into his room, he drops me on the bed, but before he can follow, I get onto my knees. Reaching for the waistband of his jeans, I slip the tips of my fingers inside and tug him forward.

His smile grows the closer he gets, until he's right in front of me, looking down. Bloody hell, he's gorgeous. I swallow to keep from drooling.

"And now?" he whispers. "Now that you have me here, what are you goin' to do with me?"

There's such an intense fluttering in my stomach that it almost feels painful between my legs.

"Get on the bed," I say, scooting back to make space for him.

Climbing on, he kneels in front of me, resting his hands on his thighs. I reach for his chest, and with a single finger, I trace the outline of his tattoo. I notice a scar just beneath the one tribal design.

My eyes dart to his. "Is this a bullet wound?"

He nods. "Yeah, but we're not talkin' about that now."

It's unsettling to know he's been shot. The idea of him being in any kind of danger makes my heart shrink.

197

I press a kiss to it and keep going, trying to ignore the new worry knotting in my stomach. I trace my fingers across the hard plane of Aiden's back until I reach his shoulders.

"One of us is overdressed," he teases as he takes hold of my shirt, dragging it over my head. With one movement, he unclasps my bra.

"I thought I'd let you take the lead," he rasps, his hands brushing up my sides, sending tingles rushing through my body, "but I think I'll take over now if you don't mind."

I nod because that sounds bloody amazing.

His head drops to my breast, and I go down with a moan.

CHAPTER 13

AIDEN

I fought hard to keep my anger in check while Emma told me about her mother. It felt like a hurricane was tearing through my chest.

I don't know how it feels not to be loved, so I can't possibly understand how Emma feels.

Fuck, if her mother were a guy, I'd beat the shit out of her.

I'm still processing half of what she told me, and as I unclasp her bra, I feel a war raging inside of me. There was a time it would've been easy to have meaningless sex, but not with Emma.

I can't just fuck her, and afterward, go on as if something significant didn't happen between us.

With my feelings all over the place, I reach for her jeans.

My mind is telling me to wait, and to think this through while my cock is telling me to go for it. I want Emma so bad it aches.

Emma wants this, and so do I.

We want this.

She's emotional. I'm an ass for not taking this slower. This is not the right time even though she told me she's ready.

I yank her jeans off and crawling back over her, I drink in her pale soft skin. Lifting my hands to her face, I slip my fingers into her hair, feeling the silkiness. Her breaths are fast against my mouth, but I take a moment to look at her. If I kiss her now, I'll want all of her.

Meeting her eyes, I see the heated desire. Before I can think about this for another second, she crushes her mouth to mine.

She kisses me with so much hunger, I'm back to teetering on the edge of heaven's bliss, and it now has a name – Emma.

She reaches for the snap of my jeans, and I hear the zip go. I should slow her down, but I can't. This is just too incredible. Her hands slip beneath the fabric, and when her fingers wrap around me, I growl against her mouth.

My body jerks against hers when she slowly slides her hand up and down the length of me.

It feels so fucking good.

Fuck, we can talk later. Right now I just want to focus on making Emma feel good.

I break the kiss and work my way down to her breasts. She moans as I softly bite her nipple.

Before I can move further down, she places her hands on my shoulders and pushes until I relent and turn onto my back.

She pulls my jeans off then steps out of her shorts and panties before crawling over me. I reach for her breasts, my thumbs brushing over her taut nipples.

What a fucking incredible sight.

She straddles me, and a cold sweat breaks out over my body as her pussy rubs against my hard as fuck cock.

It's right about then all reason and reality leave the room. When Emma begins to move, my fingers dig into her hips, and I have to grit my teeth as all my blood rushes down south. It's all I can do to not bury myself deep inside her hot pussy, and fuck her senseless.

Not being able to take much more of feeling her clit massaging my cock, I tighten my hold on her slender hips and lift her to my abs, so I can just catch my breath.

"Emma," I grind out her name between my teeth. "You're overestimatin' my self-control."

But she doesn't listen. Placing both her hands on my chest, she thrusts her body down. It happens so fucking fast, that when her pussy slams down on my cock, and I sink deep inside of her, my breath gets ripped from my lungs.

"Fuck," I growl. Unable to control my body my ass bows off the bed pushing harder into Emma.

My fingers dig too hard into her skin as I fight to gain control.

Fuck. Fuck. Fuck.

Emma gasps sharply, her arms giving way beneath her. She falls over my chest, and I feel her breaths, hot and ragged against my skin.

We're both tense for a few seconds, as I struggle not to move, not wanting to hurt her further.

I can't believe she did that.

"I'm sorry," she whispers when she finally catches her breath. "I didn't mean for that to happen," she starts to ramble. "I just wanted to move back down, and all of a sudden you were there, and…" her words trail away as a shudder ripples through her body.

"Are you okay?" I ask. That must've hurt like a mother.

She shakes her head, and I gently ease to the side, turning us over, and slowly pull out. She winces and the look of pain tightens her features.

I just took her virginity.

Fuck!

I didn't get to whisper to her how precious she is while making sure she was ready.

"Wait here," I whisper as I slip off the bed.

I rush to the bathroom and first clean myself up. The sight of Emma's blood makes me grit my teeth as anger begins to simmer in my chest.

How the fuck did this night go from good to bad so fast?

I've fucked up, and I know it.

Opening the warm water, I wet a cloth before heading back to the room. Walking in, Emma's already getting dressed.

Dropping the cloth on the desk, I grab my jeans and pull them on, then turn to Emma.

"You should have a warm bath. You'll feel better afterward." Taking her hand, I lead her to the bathroom. I open the faucets and throw in some bubble bath as well. Turning back to her, she looks so fucking vulnerable I want to slap myself upside the head for allowing this to happen. "Get in. I'll grab some fresh towels and bring your bag."

I close the door behind me and give her some time alone.

Walking out onto the deck, I shove my hands in my pockets and stare blindly at the ocean.

204

I don't even know where to begin to process this night.

CHAPTER 14

EMMA

Stripping out of my clothes, I climb in the bath, wincing when the warm water laps between my legs.

Crap that hurt a lot.

I can't believe I did that. My heart feels heavy with regret and shame.

I took advantage of Aiden. What type of person does that make me?

Even though I didn't mean for it to happen, it's still my fault. Aiden tried to take it slower, and I got caught up in how incredible it felt.

Now it's all ruined. He wouldn't even finish having sex with me.

Ugh... this sucks.

As I wash, my mind starts to run wild with everything that happened tonight.

I spilled my guts to Aiden. He knows all the sordid details of my past. I just assumed he was okay with it all and threw myself at him – *again.*

There's a knock at the door, and I pull my knees up to my chest, then say, "Come in."

Aiden only pushes half inside and drops the bag and towels on the floor. Not even looking at me, he shuts the door which just makes me feel worse.

I drop my chin to my knees, wishing I could erase tonight, and do things differently.

But I can't. It is what it is.

I've screwed up, and I don't know how to fix it. Can I even repair the damage I've done?

Climbing out of the bath, I let the water out. I dry myself, being careful between my legs. After getting dressed, I look at myself in the mirror.

I don't like the person staring back at me. Shame fills my chest until it feels like I'm suffocating. I need time alone so I can figure out where to go from here. I need to take a good look at myself and make some changes.

I can't go on like this.

Knowing that Aiden will want to talk about what happened and that he'll probably be understanding and sweet, I shove my dirty clothes in the bag and sneaking to his room, I quickly put on my shoes.

When I shut the front door behind me, I let out the breath I've been holding. Taking out my phone, I open the Uber app so I can request a ride.

The app is still loading when the front door swings open behind me, and Aiden comes out.

Oh shit, so much for slipping away quietly.

"Seriously, Emma? You're just going to leave?" he snaps, anger tightening his handsome features.

"I was going to send you a message," I say lamely. "I thought it would be best if we had some time apart."

He glances up at the sky, sucking in a deep breath. When he brings his eyes back to mine, and I see the hurt in them, my heart breaks a little knowing I'm responsible.

"I'm so s – "

Aiden cuts me off, "Don't apologize." His voice is tense. "I'll take you home. You don't need to call a cab to get away from me."

He disappears back inside and seconds later comes out, fully dressed and carrying his bag.

When he walks toward the car, my shoulders slump in defeat. I climb in and place my bag at my feet. After pulling on the seatbelt, I wrap my arms around me and stare out the window.

Aiden gets in, and not breaking the silence, he starts the car and drives away from what was supposed to be a special night for us.

Congratulations, Emma. You've just successfully ruined the best thing that ever happened to you.

CHAPTER 15

AIDEN

I'm used to communicating, but not this – whatever the fuck this is. For the past week, when I come back from my run, Emma has already left for school. We hardly see each other.

On the odd chance, I do get to see her, she's withdrawn. Starting a conversation with her is impossible.

I don't see her eat, and it worries me. When I ask if she wants something, she declines in this proper way that's starting to irritate the shit out of me. I don't know if she's eating at college. This whole thing is driving me fucking crazy.

I almost lost the fight tonight, all because I could only think of this fucked up mess between Emma and me.

It took me forever to get Joe off of me. My ribs are killing me, and I worry I won't be healed for the main event which was finally announced tonight. One week and I'll get to finally bust Katia's ass.

After taking a shower to loosen my muscles, I head into the kitchen to grab a bottle of water. Emma's been coming home later and later every day, and I don't want to think why. I try not to.

I'm about to head back to my room when the front door opens. I stop and watch as Emma tries to sneak in, softly closing the door.

She turns around, her arms full of books, and as her eyes land on me, I watch her eyes widen with shock. I'm just about to lose my temper and tell her to stop trying to evade me when she drops the books to the floor.

"Aiden, you're hurt," she cries, as she rushes forward. Nothing could prepare me for her touch. It's like lightning striking when her fingers carefully probe at my ribs.

I flinch, not because it hurts, but because it's too much. Emma can't just touch me while things are so bad between us.

"It's nothin'," I say, pulling away from her. I walk around her and pick up the books. Glancing at the books, they're all on the same subject. *The idiot's guide to English. A-Z of writing well.*

I hand her the books, and I can't miss that she looks tired.

"How's school?" I ask, unable to stay angry with her.

"It's okay," she sighs. "Turns out South African English is very different from American English. I need to learn how to spell all over again. I've been working my butt off to get all the assignments in on time. I only have one left then I'll be able to breathe again." She smiles at me, but it doesn't reach her eyes. "Well then, I better get a move on."

Fuck, I'm such an asshole. How did I not see this? She's been stressing her ass off about school, and here I thought she's still pissed at me.

"Wait a sec. You've been doing assignments all this time?"

I follow Emma to her room and watch her drop the armload of books on her bed.

"Pretty sure that's what I just said."

I follow her inside. This can be my chance to help her, to make things right.

"What do you mean, you have to learn to spell all over?"

"Some of your words are different to ours. So I'm back to learning another language," she explains.

"Like what?"

She opens the book on top and scans the page. "Color. We spell it with a 'u' where you don't."

She flops down on the bed, looking miserable. "Some words you spell with a 'z' where we use a 's'. I've been trying to study the bloody dictionary for the past two weeks. Every time I try to set my laptop to US spelling it switches back."

213

Her shoulders slump, and if it's at all possible, I feel even more like a fucking ass.

"Didn't I tell you to come to me if you need anythin'?" I say, feeling highly irritated with myself. I sit down next to her. "Where's your laptop?"

"Why?" I wish we could go back to how we were. I want her to trust me again so she'll come to me if she needs anything.

"Let me look at it so I can change your settings to US," I explain patiently.

"Oh." She reaches down to retrieve it from her bag. When she opens it on her lap, she says, "Let me just close these documents."

I glance over her shoulder in time to see the words *monthly expenses* at the top of the page before the document disappears.

She hands me the laptop, and before I click on the settings, I read the words on her background screen.

'Don't depend too much on anyone in this world because even your own shadow leaves you when you are in darkness' - Ibn Taymiyyah.

"Do you really believe that?"

"What?"

"This quote." I point to the screen.

She reads the words then says, "Trusting someone just sets you up for disappointment." Her words hit hard. I know it won't help to tell her that she can trust me. To Emma, it's all about actions, and over the past week, I haven't been a good friend to her.

I change the settings for her, before closing the laptop and placing it behind me.

I turn toward her, waiting for her to look at me.

Her eyes finally meet mine and I hate that the happy sparkle is gone from them.

"Thank you for helping with the setting. You saved me hours of studying. Now I can get going with the paper." She smiles, but it only hovers around her lips.

"My pleasure. I'm going to run out in a minute. Can I bring you somethin' to eat?" I ask.

"I'm good, but thank you for asking," she declines again.

"What have you been eatin'?" I ask as I get up.

"I..." her words trail away, and she draws her bottom lip between her teeth.

My blood runs cold as I watch her fidget. She was going to lie to me but for some reason stopped.

I really look at her, the circles under her eyes, the fidgeting, and then my gut tells me to check her nightstand.

I walk to it, and as I reach for the drawer, Emma darts forward. "No, Aiden!" Her voice is drenched with panic as I pull the drawer open. I grab the open bottle of Toplet and check how many are left.

Fuck, she's been taking them.

"If you tell me you've been flushin' them I'll believe you," I say.

But her mother's not here. There's no need for her to flush them. She should've thrown them all out. "Tell me, Emma."

She doesn't say anything.

I grab all four bottles and walking to the bathroom, I open the sealed bottles. I'll be damned if I'm going to stand around and let Emma waste away because of some lunatic on the other side of the fucking planet. Anger rolls over me in waves as I empty the first one into the toilet.

Emma grabs at my arm. "No!" She tries to get past me, but being twice her size makes it easy to just step in front of her. She slams into my back as the rest go into the toilet, and I flush.

"No," she whimpers. I hear her breath catch in her throat as she pushes away from me.

I follow her back to her room, and watch as she starts to pace, the length of the room like a caged animal.

"Why are you takin' them again?"

I have to remind myself to stay calm. It doesn't help to get all heated up when one of us is already emotional.

"Because!"

I walk toward her and taking hold of her shoulders, I make her stop.

"Why are you takin' them?" I ask again, my patience slipping. Usually, I'm a very patient man, but with matters concerning Emma, it's very hard.

"Because," she whimpers. She doesn't make eye contact. Instead, she ducks her head low, staring at her feet. "They help. They help me sleep. I don't dream

217

then. I don't have to eat. I don't have to think. They just help. They keep her away."

She looks so fucking hopeless and tired. I can't be mad even if I wanted to. She steps back from under my hands.

"I'd like to start on my paper now," she says, crossing her arms around her middle.

I nod and leave. We both need the space right now.

I need to go see Zac.

I can't fucking deal with this shit on my own.

Relief floods me when Zac opens the door, and I look into his blue eyes. Laurie always said they made her think of heaven. Well, I need some advice, so he better call on some divine intervention for this one.

"You look like shit," Zac says as he opens the door wider for me to go inside.

"Thanks," I growl. "I missed you, too." I walk to the living room and sink down on a couch.

"You gonna tell me why you look like shit?" he asks as he takes a seat on the couch opposite me.

"She's turned my damn world upside down. I don't know my head from my ass," I admit.

I tell him everything, from start to finish, and then I want to slap him upside the head because he's staring at me with a huge grin.

"Oh, you've got it bad," he says. My brother-in-law, who is always packed full of wisdom, now has nothing but a crappy comment for me.

Feeling irritated, I get up and stalk to the window.

"Seriously, Zac. I need some advice right now," I say. I don't like feeling like this. I need to be in control, and with Emma, I have no control.

"Go back to the apartment, talk things out, and afterward you can have hot make-up sex," he says.

I swing around. "Have you lost your bloody mind?" And then I laugh because I'm starting to sound like her.

"Bloody?" he laughs.

"I know, I know." I look at Zac and shake my head. "This conversation helped nothin'."

It's the weirdest one we've ever had.

"Cause you should be talkin' to her, not me," he says, grinning wider, finally giving me advice. "Just go

219

tell her how you feel. You win some, you lose some. But runnin' away won't solve shit."

He's right. He's always right.

CHAPTER 16

EMMA

Fear brings your mind to the edge of insanity, where everything is so frighteningly crystal clear you can take in every little thing that's happening around you. Your body runs purely on adrenaline, not a drop of blood pumping through your veins.

But, eventually, your body runs out of adrenaline, and then it starts to feed off your emotions, and the only one strong enough to keep you going is hate. Hate is powerful.

Sigmund Freud defined hate as an ego state that wishes to destroy the source of its unhappiness.

I stare at my laptop and the piece I've started to write on my paper. For this assignment, we had to choose an emotion, and write about it. I know all about hating someone, so I decided to write about it.

The past week has been so hard. I can't look at myself. It feels like I'm being sucked into a black hole which was created by my mother. But now I'm allowing it to grow and swallow me whole.

The missed calls and text messages from my mother haven't stopped. The threats haven't stopped.

I'm scared. I need to find a way to stay here. I need to get my visa extended, and the only way I can do that is by doing well at school.

I also need to get money somehow. I'm on my last hundred dollars. That's why I started taking the damn pills. They suppress my appetite.

I've been looking for a job, but once they hear that I'm here on a student visa, they all say no.

I've even been avoiding Chloe. I don't want her to worry about these things, but it's been too long. I bring up my email screen. I have to talk to her. It's not right hiding from her as well.

Chloe,

I'm sorry for my disappearing act. I'm a horrible friend. It's just hard at the moment. I had so many assignments to do.

I messed things up with Aiden. We started to have sex, but then things went wrong. I'm not a virgin anymore. It's what I wanted, right? I'm so upset with myself. I destroyed the best thing that ever happened to me.

I wish you were here.

Hugs,

Sunshine ;)

My phone rings a minute later. "Why are you only telling me this now?"

"I'm sorry. It's just been a really long week. My mom froze the trust account payments, as well. I need to find a job, but every place I try to apply to, tells me I need a work permit. Do you think they'd give me a visa so I can work, while I have one to study here?"

"She didn't," she says, sounding upset on my behalf.

"She did."

"She can't," she insists, "you're over twenty-one."

"She can. She's in charge of it until I turn twenty-five."

"What? That bitch."

"So yeah, she went ahead and cut me off," I say.

Yeah, my finances are a disaster. Winter is coming, and I didn't pack everything, because I thought I'd be going home for Christmas, which I'm not, so it's going to be a freezing winter wearing t-shirts and a jacket.

"I'll figure something out," she says.

"No, you won't! You've done more than enough. I'll come home if I have no other choice," I argue, not wanting to be a burden to anyone else.

I can't allow Chloe to do a single thing more. She's done so much already.

"You can't do that, Sunshine. You've not even been gone three weeks. Don't let her win so easily." She doesn't have to remind me, it's been on my mind quite a bit.

"And now Aiden really hates me because he thinks I'm a drug addict, which I'm not. Oh, wait, I didn't tell you that part." I'm starting to talk in circles, "He caught me with the bloody pills, and I'm only taking them

224

because they keep the nightmares away," I cringe, because I know admitting the next part is going to upset Chloe, "and so it will help with my appetite, but they're all gone. Now I'll have to deal with the withdrawal symptoms all over again."

"Have you finished?" she asks, her voice tight with anger.

"Yeah," I whisper.

"Why did you start taking them again? You're letting her control you from across the bloody ocean," she snaps at me. "You'd better be eating, or so help me God, I'll come and feed you myself!"

"Don't you get upset as well," I say, sitting down on the bed.

"I'm upset with that bitch, Sunshine, not you. Please eat properly. Deal with the dreams. Phone me when you have them, I'm awake anyway."

"I will," I say, then add, "I don't know how to fix things with Aiden."

"Talk to him. He's not your mother. Just have a conversation with the man. I'm sure things will be better then."

I frown when I hear the sad tone in Chloe's voice. She's always cheerful.

"What's wrong? How are things at home?"

"What home?" she snorts. "You have enough to deal with, I'm not going to bog you down with my nonsense, too."

"Chloe, come on, talk to me," I say softly, and it's like I've opened a tap. I hear her breath shuddering on the other side, and my heart clenches. Chloe is my rock, and listening to her fall apart breaks my heart.

"You know I told you I have the best parents, right?" She sounds lost, and I wish I were there to hold her.

"Yeah?"

"I love them both so much, but they're destroying each other, and there's nothing I can do to stop it. My dad shacked up with two other women. Two!" Hearing how much pain she's in, makes me think maybe it would be better if I go home. Things aren't working out this side, and Chloe needs me.

"My mom's just given up."

226

"Aww, Chloe, maybe they'll still sort it out." I should've kept quiet because it only makes Chloe cry harder.

"It's been going on forever. And when I say my Mom's given up, I mean she's sick. She doesn't want to live anymore. She's dying of heartache right in front of me, and my dad's too busy with his new flings to notice. The doctors can't find anything wrong with her. I've made an appointment with a psychologist, hoping they'll be able to help."

I sit stunned, for a second or so. "And you let me bugger off to America?" I shriek. "You needed me, and you let me fly halfway around the damn world? Why didn't you tell me this sooner? I could've at least tried to help you in some way."

"You can't change anything, and getting you away from your mother made me feel better."

"Just say the word, and I'm on the first flight back."

"I will. Right now, I want you to enjoy your freedom." How can I enjoy anything when my only friend is hurting?

"Chloe, you know you mean a lot to me, right?" I say.

"I love you too, Sunshine. I have to go. Thanks for listening to me."

"Always. You're my best friend. Call me if you need to talk."

"I will."

Cutting the call, I scroll through my contacts until I reach Gran's number.

I've been hiding from my problems for long enough. I've always been close to my gran, and not talking to her for two weeks has been unforgivable on my part.

"Emma! Emma, is that you?" she answers the phone.

"Hi, Gran. It's me. I'm so sorry I left without telling you."

She sounds breathless when she says, "Thank God. I was so worried. Where are you? Your mother is so angry."

"I'm in America, Gran. I needed some time for myself."

"You don't need to explain that to me, dear. Remember, I raised your mother. I know what she's like. Takes after her father."

"I just couldn't stay there any longer. I should've told you though. How are you?"

"The old ticker keeps ticking," she says. "Margie just came over, dear. She's doing the rounds to make sure we're all alive in the retirement village."

Smiling, I say, "I'll let you go. Have a good day, Gran."

"I love you, my child."

I press the phone to my chest and curl up on the bed.

It's time for me to get my act together. As soon as Aiden is home, I'll apologize and try to make things right.

CHAPTER 17

EMMA

I must have dozed off because I wake up with a start. It's dark in the room, except for the moonlight shining through my window.

It's already getting colder in the evenings, and as I sit up, I shiver. I rub my arms to get some warmth into them as the fuzziness of sleep lifts.

Deciding to take a shower so I can warm up, I grab my pajamas and walk to the bathroom. Closing the door, I place the clothes on the counter, then turn to open the taps.

Just as I've gotten undressed, there's a knock at the bathroom door. I wrap the towel around me then open the door a little and look up at Aiden.

"Can we talk?" he asks, looking tense as he stands with his hands in his pockets.

"Of course. I'm just going to shower quickly," I reply.

"Go ahead, but I'm gonna talk," he says, as he comes in and lifts himself to sit on the counter beside my clothes.

"Oh, okay," I say, hoping desperately that I'm coming across more confident than I feel. Aiden meets my stare, and it's obvious he's being serious about having this talk while I shower.

"This is un-bloody-believable," I mutter. This night is not getting any better. So much for me wanting to apologize.

"Emma," he says. "When we met in the bar and-"

I let the towel drop to the floor. It's not like he hasn't seen me naked. When he doesn't say anything else, I glance at him over my shoulder. His eyes are glued to my back.

Shit! I forgot about the scars. Some of my bravery flees the bathroom. I lift my chin in a last attempt to salvage the little pride I have left – naked, in front of

THE OCEAN BETWEEN US – Michelle Heard

him. It's not working. How do I manage to get myself into these situations?

"Talk, Aiden," I say, but my voice doesn't come out as strong as I would've liked. "You've seen naked women before. This should be nothing new to you, besides you've made it pretty clear you don't want me in a sexual way."

Aiden's head snaps back as if I've hit him. He jumps off the counter, and in one swift movement, he's right in front of me.

"Is that what you think?" His voice drops low. "You think I didn't want you?"

He looks up at the ceiling as if he's saying a silent prayer, and I'm starting to think maybe I should say one, too.

"Emma," he groans as he grabs hold of my hips, yanking me against him so I can feel how hard he is. "That is how hot you are. This is how much I want you. This is…" He breathes hard, and I can only stare at him in wonder, my stomach in knots. "And then you look at me like that, and I just want to fall into you until there's nothing left of me."

"You do?" I breathe, completely stunned.

"I do," he whispers, a slight smile tugging at his lips. I want him to kiss me so we can put all this behind us, but there's still a lot we have to talk about.

"I'm glad you don't hate me," I say, "but you had no right flushing the pills earlier." Even though I'm upset, I don't want to make a scene about it, but I have to let him know about the consequences I'll be facing for the next few days.

He lets go of my hips, and I reach into the shower to turn the water off, before wrapping a towel around my body again.

"I'm sorry, Em. I lost control," he explains.

Before he can continue, I cut in. "I'm sorry I lied to you, and that I didn't tell you up front that I was taking the pills. That was wrong of me, but for me to not have withdrawal symptoms, I would've had to decrease the dosage weekly, until I could finally stop. You just tossed them. Tomorrow the withdrawals will start, and I'm not done with my assignment yet."

"How bad are the withdrawals?" he asks, looking worried.

"They can be pretty bad. I was taking the maximum dosage, Aiden. I tried to stop once, and I was so sick my mother immediately caught me out. I'll be dizzy, nauseous... ugh, I hate being nauseous," I groan when I think what's waiting for me. "Honestly, we'll have to wait and see what happens. The withdrawals are different for every person."

"Fuck, I'm sorry, Em. I should've reacted better. "Wouldn't it be safer if I took you to the hospital?"

My eyes widen at his words. "No. There's no way I'm going to the hospital. I'm still on my parent's medical aid, and I'm pretty sure it doesn't cover international hospitals. I'll deal with it. I'll just have to stay up tonight and get the assignment done."

"I'll order in. I'll help you get it done."

We stare at each other for a while, then I whisper, "I'm so sorry for the past weeks hell. I didn't mean for it to get so out of hand."

"I'm sorry too, Em. Next time we don't agree on something, let's talk it out instead of being miserable for a week."

"Okay," I say, feeling hopeful that we can get past this.

"Shower quickly while I order us some pizza. We can talk some more once you're done."

I nod and watch him leave the bathroom before I open the taps again.

That didn't go as bad as I thought it would. I let out a sigh of relief as I step under the water.

We were up half the night, but at least the assignment is done and submitted. I've made us some coffee, and as we sit on the couch, I say, "I only have one lecture today."

"You sure about going?"

"Yes, I don't want to miss it, in case I'm not better by Thursday when I have this class again."

"I'll bring you to school and back home. I'm not lettin' you walk anywhere until the withdrawal is over with."

"What about your classes?" I ask, not wanting him to fall behind because of me.

"Undercover," he says, smiling down at me. "It's all for show, Em."

"I keep forgetting," I mumble as I take the last sip of my coffee.

I wait for Aiden to finish before I carry both the cups to the kitchen and wash them up. As soon as I sit back down, Aiden pulls me to his side, tucking my head in under his chin. I curl up against him, relishing the feeling of having his arms around me.

I've been feeling out of sorts since eight am. I know it's the withdrawals starting, seeing as I didn't take any last night.

"I haven't finished talkin' yet. I first wanted to make sure the assignment was done," Aiden says, drawing me out of my thoughts. "I saw somethin' earlier, and it reminded me that your mom said she's cuttin' you off, and I can really kick myself for-"

"No, Aiden. I'm not talking to you about my finances," I say, as I get up and walk to my room to get my bag so I can go to school.

"Emma, wait," he calls after me.

I close the door behind me and look at my laptop. It's showing my monthly expenses, not my paper.

"How could you, Aiden? You looked at my expenses?" I say, as humiliation courses through my veins.

"Emma, I said I'd help," he says on the other side of the door. "I told you to come to me if you needed anythin'."

I yank the door open, and my cheeks are flaming hot.

"You said it yourself, you're not my dad. I don't need another one. I'm not going to take anything from you. Oh my, God... this is wrong on so many levels." I wave my hand up and down, and my cheeks keep getting hotter. It feels like I've swallowed a whole bloody furnace. "You're not paying for a single thing. The second you pay for something, it makes me a whore. I feel bad enough. I gave you the only thing that was mine. You're not bloody paying for it."

"Emma," Aiden snaps as he steps right up to me. For a moment fear flickers through me, but then my own temper wins out, and I lift my chin, ready to fight.

237

Aiden sucks in a calming breath, then says, "You're my fuckin' girlfriend. It's normal for couples to share expenses, to help each other out. You're makin' this bigger than it needs to be."

My anger fizzles away, and I start to feel unsure about my reaction. Is Aiden right?

"But..." I chew on my bottom lip as I process what he just told me. "I don't want to be a burden, Aiden. I've fought so hard to get away from my mom. I want to be my own person and not owe anyone."

"Angel, you can never be a burden," he whispers as he pulls me to his chest. "Just because I might take care of you, doesn't mean I'll control you. That's not how it works. I'm not going to help you and expect somethin' back in return. I want to do it because I care about you."

I search his face and seeing the truth in his eyes, I say, "It will take some getting used to for me."

"I get that." He presses a kiss to my forehead, then asks, "How are you feelin'?"

I let out a burst of laughter, "Ask me again this afternoon. I better get going, or I'll be late for class."

Aiden doesn't step out of the way, but instead takes my hand and pulls me closer.

There's a serious look on his face as he says, "I really care about you, Em."

I stand on my toes and press a kiss to his lips, then say, "You mean a lot to me, Aiden."

He smiles, and as he starts to turn around, I pull him back.

"Wait." He glances back at me, and I quickly continue. "Thank you for being there for me since I got here. Thank you for letting me spill my guts, and for dealing with my mother, and for wanting to take care of me. I appreciate you, Aiden."

He brings his hands to my face, and presses a soft kiss to my mouth, then says, "You're welcome, Em."

Walking out of the flat, I'm glad we talked about everything, and that our relationship isn't ruined.

CHAPTER 18

EMMA

I didn't feel too bad during class, but as I walk down the stairs, I feel dizzy with withdrawals. I'm nauseous and tired, and just bloody groggy.

When my tongue becomes one with the roof of my mouth, I drag myself to the nearest water fountain. I gulp some down and look at the bench nearby. There's no point in sitting and waiting for it to get better. It will only get worse.

"Emma, honey, are you okay?" I hear a familiar drawl, and honestly, I don't care if she's Hitler's second in command, I'm just glad to see someone I know.

"Katia. No, actually I feel quite horrid," I admit. Getting to know her might help Aiden, too. "Have you seen Aiden?"

It feels like I'm fighting gravity to stay upright.

"Yeah, I saw him in the parkin' area. Let me walk you there." I don't trust her sudden friendliness, but right now I'm not sure I'll make it to Aiden without falling on my face.

Katia presses up against me, her arm circling my waist. "I'm so glad I ran into you. You're hard to find," she says, and I really just want to get to Aiden. "The girls are havin' a little get-together tomorrow night. Without the men, of course. You have to come. Seein' as you're with Aiden," she babbles non-bloody-stop only bringing on a headache.

I nod as I swallow the bile back. I shouldn't have had the water.

"Sure." I force the word out.

"Honey, you really do look sick," she says as if I don't know it.

Her arm tightens around me, and she takes most of my weight. *Damn, she's strong.*

I lean my head on her shoulder and try to remember never to look for trouble with her.

"Oh, there are the guys," she says. The sun is too bright, and I know if she lets go now, I'm going to fall. "So, if you're up for it, I'll see you tomorrow night?" she asks quickly.

I nod, as she starts to draw away from me.

"Katia," I say to stop her and take hold of her arm to steady myself.

"Emma?" Aiden's voice is sharp.

I squint in his direction, but the light is too bright. I close my eyes so all the spinning will stop.

"Hey, guys," her voice rattles through my head.

I press my forehead to her shoulder to ease the throbbing. She rubs my back, and I swallow to keep the bile down as her touch makes my stomach lurch.

"She's not well. I found her at the Old Well. Poor baby looks terrible." And then I feel her stroking my hair, and my body jerks involuntarily.

"I'll take her," Aiden says. Strong hands take hold of my arms, and they pull me away from Katia, who's keeping my head from splitting open, but making me feel sicker, all at once.

"Ouch." The groan slips out, and I press my palm to my eyes as arms slip under my back and knees, and then the world capsizes on me.

"I have you, Em," he whispers against my splitting head.

Even though I feel awful, his words settle deep inside me.

The ride home is a blur, and as Aiden places me on my bed, I lie still so the nausea will subside.

"Can I get you somethin'?" he asks.

"Could you close the curtains, please? The light hurts my eyes."

"You don't look good. Please let me take you to the hospital?"

"No, it will pass. I'll be fine. It's just withdrawal symptoms."

The bed moves as he sits down, and my stomach heaves.

I jump up, and it feels like my head's going to split open as I run for the toilet. I make it just in time, lurching forward as my body begins to convulse.

"Is there nothin' I can do?" he asks, as I sink back onto the floor.

I shake my head slowly, so I don't make it worse. It feels like my stomach has settled a bit, and I slide back, lying down on the cold tiles. I just need to lie down.

Aiden's phone rings. The sound echoes in my ears.

"Zac, what's up?" he says as he kneels next to me, placing a hand on my forehead. "Emma's sick. I'll call you when I have some time."

As he presses his hand to my cheek, it feels cool. "Can I take you back to bed?"

"I don't want to move," I mumble, but I reach for his hand and give it a weak squeeze. "Thank you for caring. I'll make it up to you when I'm better."

CHAPTER 19

AIDEN

Seeing Emma so pale and sick makes me hate her mom with a fucking passion. Hate is a strong emotion, one I'm getting to know really well because of that woman.

I watch Emma sleep after the long night she's had, and I open her laptop. I click on her media player and select the first song, so her personalized album will start playing. We haven't talked about simple stuff like music and movies yet.

I open the assignment we worked on and read the piece I wrote for her again.

From hate, revenge is born. From revenge, death is born. Hate creates devastation, and nothing can grow from it. Hatred consumes until there is nothing left but an empty shell of the former self. From there outrage and brutality are born.

Hate creates an act of violence whether it's against another or yourself, because somehow, somewhere, something dies.

"What are you doing?" I hear her groggy voice next to me.

"Just readin' over the paper." I set the laptop aside and lean over her. Brushing some strands from her face, I ask, "How're you feelin'?"

"Death warmed up," she groans as she presses her face into the pillow. She curls into a ball, her arms clutching her stomach.

"What's wrong?" I ask, wishing I could make her feel better.

"Muscle spasms," she whispers, her voice drenched in pain.

It takes four days before Emma starts to get better, and I swear I've fucking aged a hundred years with worry. The only good thing about this past week is that my side has healed.

THE OCEAN BETWEEN US – Michelle Heard

I'm up against Colton. I've watched him. He fights recklessly. He fights for Katia. Whoever wins will go through to the finals where the winners will face off against each other.

I haven't told Emma, but they'll be watching her. If I win, which I have to, they'll go for her. Zac just better make sure nothing happens to her, or all hell will break loose.

I just need to get behind Colton. I have training and patience. I know I can beat him.

"You look so worried," Emma whispers next to me where she's curled up under a blanket.

Things have actually been great between Emma and me. We've been watching movies all day long. She made me eat candy with my popcorn, and I have to admit, it tasted damn weird.

"Just thinkin' about the fight tomorrow."

"I can take your mind off it," she says, as she gets onto her knees giving me a seductive look.

"Em, you're sick," I say, even though she's much better today.

"I'm better. The worst is over." She trails her fingers down my chest, and I close my eyes so I can focus on her touch.

"Don't worry," she breathes against my neck. "Relax."

She climbs on top of me, and I can't help but smile as she straddles me. She's wearing one of my shirts, and it pushes up her thighs, exposing her creamy skin to me.

Fuck, I love seeing her in my clothes.

Placing my hands on her legs, I push the shirt up until I can see her panties.

"What are you doing?" I ask, feigning ignorance.

"Paying my doctor's fee," she teases as she trails a finger from my temple to the day-old stubble on my jaw.

"You look your age when you don't shave. You look really mean at the moment. All ink and broody." Her voice is silky, making my cock harden.

I don't want to think about tomorrow anymore, not with her on top of me. Slipping my hands to her ass, I yank her closer and push my cock hard against her pussy. Her breath rushes out over my collarbone as she drops her head against my chest.

"I want to be inside you, Em," I whisper, as I bring one hand back to her thigh, brushing my finger lightly up the silky stretch of skin to her pussy. "I want you naked beneath me. I want to come inside of you."

Her eyes flare with desire as the back of my fingers brush over her panties. Keeping my touch light, I love how wild it's driving her.

"I want you inside me, too," Emma admits.

That's all I need to hear. Grabbing hold of her ass, I stand up and walk to my room. As I lie her down on my bed, I have no intention of stopping.

I shove my sweats down. "Spread your legs open for me, Em," I say, as I place a knee on the mattress.

She does as I ask, and I move in between her knees. Tonight I'm going to take my time, and explore every part of her.

Sitting back, I grab her hips and yank her to me until she's pressed against my cock.

As I push the shirt up, I say, "Take it off. I want to see all of you."

She yanks the shirt off and falls back to the bed as I press a thumb to her clit. I start to massage her through her panties until the material is wet with her arousal.

I take hold of my cock and position myself at her entrance. Pushing against her panties, the ache to be inside her is almost unbearable.

I watch her face for any sign that she doesn't want this. Her cheeks flush and her lips part.

"Touch your breasts, Em," I demand, as I start to rub my cock over her clit.

She moves her hands from the covers to her toned stomach and slowly trails them upward until they cover her breasts.

"Push 'em together," I growl, and when she does what I ask, pre-cum spills from my cock at the sight of her cleavage between her fingers.

"That's so fuckin' sexy."

Needing to be inside her, I move back and yank her panties down her legs. I grab a condom from the drawer next to my bed and roll it on in record time.

Emma starts to remove her hands from her breasts. "No, keep your hands there."

I crawl over her body and lower my chest against her hands, watching her cleavage deepen.

Bringing my eyes up to her face, I lean down and press a kiss to her parted lips. She pulls her hands free from between us, and places them on my jaw, slipping her tongue inside my mouth. The second I taste Emma while feeling her naked body beneath mine, something snaps in my chest.

I thrust my tongue into her mouth and start to fall with no intention of ever getting back up. I want to stay like this forever, just Emma and me.

She moves her hands down my neck, to my shoulders and doesn't stop until she reaches my biceps. Her fingers dig into my muscle as I devour her mouth.

I'm going to explode right here. Emma bites at my bottom lip, and then lifts her hips from the bed, rubbing her pussy against my lower abs.

Breathe, Aiden. You just need some blood and air in the rest of your body, or this will be over before it can get started.

Resting my body on one arm, I push myself up as I break the kiss. I trail my fingers down Emma's warm skin, from her collarbone, over her nipple, and down her stomach.

When I reach her pussy, Emma's breaths are coming fast, her eyes never leaving mine. Taking hold of my cock, and pressing against her entrance, I glance down. I watch as I push only the head inside of her.

Resting both my arms on either side of her head, I look down at her as I start to slowly rock my hips, not going any deeper.

She wraps her arms around my waist, digging her nails into my back before dragging them up to my neck, and I almost slam into her.

"Fuck, that feels good," I growl.

"More, Aiden," she begs.

I push my right thigh under her leg and thrust a little deeper.

"I want to feel all of you," she says, breathless with lust.

I bring my mouth to hers so I can feel each breath, as I push deeper. With Emma's heat surrounding me, and her mouth on mine, it's pure heaven.

Her whole body shudders when I'm buried deep inside of her.

"Fuck, you're tight," I hiss, lost in how amazing she feels.

Moving a hand down to her hip, I dig my fingers into her skin and start to build a rhythm.

Her fingers weave into my hair, and she grabs fistfuls. It's so fucking hot, I'm struggling to not come.

"You feel incredible," she groans, and her breath races over her parted lips, mingling with my own. Then, finally, those sweet moans start to fill my ears.

"Shit, Aiden." She throws her head back and begins to meet me thrust for thrust.

"You're so beautiful, Em," I whisper, and seeing her body so fully displayed beneath me, I know I'll never forget this moment.

Letting go of her hip, I bring my hand between us and finding her clit, I start to rub circles around it.

"Aiden," she groans getting close to her release.

Picking up my pace, I drive my cock into her, deep and hard until I feel her inner walls clamp down around me.

Losing control, and needing to find my own release, I brace myself over her with one arm, then grab hold of her hip to hold her in place as I fuck her hard. The sound of our skin slapping only spurs me on.

"Fuck, Em," I growl. My hips slam forward, and every muscle in my body coils tightly when tingles shoot down my spine.

"Ah," the cry from Emma as she comes, along with her breasts bouncing with every thrust, sends me over the edge.

"Em." I grind out.

I drive my cock as deep as I can until my body tenses from the pleasure rushing through me. Unable to keep myself up any longer, I lower myself against her. Feeling her body shuddering beneath mine, I press a satisfied kiss to her mouth.

Not wanting the moment to end yet, I deepen the kiss while slipping my arms under her limp body, then roll onto my side so I can hold her tightly.

Catching her breath, she starts to draw lazy patterns on my chest.

I could fall asleep with my cock inside of her, but instead, I let go so I can get rid of the condom.

"I'll be right back," I say, pressing a last kiss to Emma's lips. "Get under the covers."

I walk to the bathroom and dispose of the condom, then make sure the front door is locked before switching off all the lights.

Climbing back in bed, Emma curls against my side and lays her head on my chest. I wrap my arms around her and pressing a kiss to her hair, I say, "Thank you for lettin' me be your first."

I'm so over my head in love with this woman, I pray I'll be her last.

"That was so much better than I imagined it would be," she whispers drowsily.

CHAPTER 20

EMMA

I think it's finally starting to sink in that someone as wonderful and attractive as Aiden really cares about me.

I feel giddy with happiness as I pour us some coffee. Placing a mug on the coffee table in front of Aiden, I sit down and ask, "What are you thinking about?"

"I'm up against Colton tonight. I'm just goin' over all his moves, tryin' to find his weak spot," he answers, as he picks up the cup and takes a sip.

"Katia's his weak spot," I say. "Let me go with you. I can help. I think she's interested in me, and maybe if I grab her and he sees, he'll be distracted enough for you to knock him out."

Aiden stares at me, looking a little shocked.

"You're willin' to get it on with a woman so I can win a fight?" he asks, flabbergasted.

"If it means you can beat the bloody hell out of Colton, but then you better get her off me before she takes it too far." I'm actually quite pleased with my idea. I can do something to help Aiden for a change.

"You're so hot right now, and that might be some guy's dream, but I don't want another person touchin' you. You're comin' with me, though, so I can keep an eye on you. I need to know you're safe."

"Good," I say. "I'd like to see you kick Colton's ass."

Since we made love last night, Aiden holds my heart in the palm of his hand. It still feels surreal that we're a couple.

Slowly, everything is starting to fall into place. I'm no longer on the medication, and I've made it through the withdrawals. Aiden and I hashed out all of our problems. My assignments are handed in, and I can honestly say, I haven't thought of my mother in a few days.

"I'm happy," I whisper over the rim of my cup.

Aiden's eyes dart to mine, and then a smile spreads over his face. "That's good to hear, Em."

"It's all because of you," I add quickly.

He shakes his head, and leaning in he presses a kiss to my mouth. "No, it's because you fought for what you wanted. I'm just taggin' along, watchin' you become stronger every day."

Tonight, I'm not wearing jeans. I'm not doing casual. Aiden's gone to see Zac, who I'll be meeting later today.

I take a bus into town hoping to find a dress for tonight at a thrift store.

I find a real vintage shop on West Franklin Street. At first, I'm a bit overwhelmed at how busy the place is, but join in the scavenger hunt and try to stay out of the other women's way.

I'm not one for browsing much, but I'm a little torn over what to get. I want to impress Aiden, but I also want to distract Katia and Colton.

It has to be something that will show off legs and cleavage, so I head over to the pile of dresses and skirts.

After searching through some scraps of material that can't be classified as clothes, a dress catches my eye.

I hold it up, and a smile stretches over my face as I look at the two-tone shift dress. I love the long bell sleeves.

Taking it to a changing room, I wiggle out of my clothes and into the dress, then turn to the mirror. I squeak when I see how incredible it looks.

I hope Aiden will love it.

It stops just above my knees, but if the wind catches it, my underwear will be on show for the entire bloody world to see.

I love the patterns which are all different shades of blue.

There's only one way to be sure about this. I take a picture and send it to Chloe, asking her opinion. True to her nature, she phones.

"You look hot!" she squeals.

THE OCEAN BETWEEN US – Michelle Heard

"Thank you, I was in two minds. You don't think it's a bit short?"

"No, it's about time you showed those legs off. They don't see the light of day enough if you ask me. Where are you going that you need a dress?"

"It's a work thing with Aiden," I answer vaguely.

"And how are things with Mr. Sizzling Hotness?"

"So good. I swear he walked right out of a romance novel."

"So he's swept you off your feet, has he?" she asks, hitting the nail on the head.

"I suppose, yeah," I admit. "How are you?" I ask quickly.

"You know me, I'm a survivor," she laughs, but she's not pulling it off. I can hear the heartache.

"Really?"

"Nothing has changed. I'll let you know if something does."

I swallow hard. I know she needs to hear it. "Chloe…"

"Yeah?"

"I love you. You're never alone."

It's quiet on the other side, and I wait. Then her voice cracks over the line. "I needed to hear that so desperately."

"I'm sorry it took so long for me to say the words."

"That's why it means the world to me."

I blink fast to keep the tears back. "You know you're the best, right?"

"No, you're the best."

We hang-up, and swallowing back the emotion, I look back at the mirror. My eyes drop to my feet, and seeing that it actually looks cute with my sneakers, I smile happily.

I've curled the ends of my hair, letting it hang down my back. I didn't put on too much make-up, keeping the eyeshadow light.

Staring at myself in the mirror, I feel proud. The dress is the first item of clothing I've bought on my own without my mother there to tell me what to wear.

When I hear the bathroom door open, I quickly peek out of my room. Seeing Aiden with just a towel around his waist makes me want to get naked with him again.

He glances my way and catches me checking him out. He tilts his head and smiles. I can't bring myself to move from my hiding spot behind the door. I hope I haven't overdone it.

"Hey, you? Why are you hidin'?"

"So... I got a dress today," I reply.

With a quizzical look in his eyes, Aiden starts toward me. He nudges the door open, and his eyes slowly sweep over me.

"Fuck, you look breathtakin' in that dress," he says as desire darken his eyes.

Aiden takes a step closer, his eyes dropping to my legs again. "Tell me," Aiden breathes. Then he moves fast, pressing me up against the wall with his body, "how do you expect me to keep my hands off of you tonight?" His voice is rough and low, and one look at his smoldering eyes has me clenching my thighs to try and ease the ache.

He eases his hands down my hips until he reaches the hem of the dress. Slipping them under the fabric, I start to squirm as he brushes them over my skin.

Aiden grabs hold of my butt, and lifts me against the wall, making a lustful breath escape my lips.

I wrap my legs around him, and it pushes the fabric up, exposing my thighs and blue, silk panties.

"You look fuckin' exquisite," he growls close to my mouth. He moves my hair away and ducks to my neck.

Biting into my flesh, his tongue flicks over the slight sting, and it sends streaks of desire straight to my core, making my panties wet. Squeezing my thighs against his hips, I try to get closer.

"I want you," I admit shamelessly as I rub my palms over his chest.

"When we get home tonight I'm going to rip this dress from your body, and fuck you so hard, you'll still feel me tomorrow."

The dirty words only make me squirm more. "I can't wait until then," I argue, wanting Aiden inside me now.

Not letting go of me, he turns us around and walks toward the bed. He sets me down on the corner of the mattress and kneeling before me, he pushes my legs wide open, and says, "Lean back."

I ease back a little, and fist the covers when his knuckles brush over my panties.

"I love seein' you wet for me, Em," he groans as he lowers his head to where I want him so desperately. My eyes widen slightly, but Aiden doesn't give me no time to wonder about what he's going to do, because seconds later, he pulls the scrap of fabric out of the way, his tongue swiping over me.

My breath catches at how good it feels.

When he sucks hard on my clit, my arms buckle as tremors rock my body.

"Shit, Aiden," I cry, grabbing hold of the back of his neck to keep myself upright so I can watch him. He keeps sucking, not letting me adjust to the new sensations. "Ah," I cry, my body frozen from the intense pleasure when he pushes a finger inside me, and his teeth bite down on the bundle of nerves.

Scraping his teeth over me, my insides spasm, yanking another cry of pleasure from me.

Aiden presses his palm hard against my clit as he starts to plunge his finger inside me. My hands fall to his biceps as he rises. He places a knee beside me on the bed, wrapping a hand around the back of my neck.

Holding me tightly as he rubs my clit feverishly, he demands, "Come on my hand, Em."

His finger curls inside me finally giving me the release I've been craving. It's so intense that I don't even care that the neighbors might hear me as a pleasure filled cry tears from me.

My body is still jerking with aftershocks when Aiden pulls his finger out and brings his hand to his mouth. I could seriously orgasm again when I watch Aiden suck my arousal from his finger.

"Now I'll have your taste on my tongue, remindin' me what my prize will be when we get home."

Shit, I'm going to be in a constant state of arousal around Aiden if he keeps talking dirty to me.

I'm touching up my make-up when Aiden's phone rings and there's a knock at the front door, all at once.

"Captain," I hear Aiden answer the phone as I walk to the front door.

I open the door to a man with dark brown hair and sky-blue eyes. His jaw is hard, and the week-old beard makes him look downright intense. He's as tall as Aiden but older.

Not wanting to assume that he's Zac, I'm just about to ask if I can help him when I hear Aiden say, "He just got here."

"Come in," I say, standing to the side so he can pass.

Knowing that he's also a policeman, makes my stomach knot nervously.

Back home we don't even stop if a policeman tries to pull us over, but drive to a public place for safety.

"You must be Emma," Zac says. "I'm Zac Hutches."

"I'm so rude," I gasp. "It's nice to finally meet you. Aiden's told me so much about you."

He reaches his hand out, and I stare at it. For a few heart-beating seconds I keep staring, but then I reach out and take it.

"Zac." I hear Aiden behind me, and I quickly pull my hand free. I make a fist, turning away so Zac can't see the look on my face. It's not his fault I can't stand touching people. "Thanks for comin'."

My eyes dart to Aiden when he takes hold of my fisted hand. I unclench it and smile when he weaves his fingers through mine. The man doesn't miss a thing.

"Sure," Zac says.

We walk over to the lounge, and as Zac sits down, I ask, "Can I make you coffee?"

I know they need to talk about work and want to give them some privacy.

"Just had some, thanks," Zac replies.

"I'll leave you guys to get down to business," I say, and start towards my room.

"Stay," Aiden stops me. "If somethin' happens to me, you need to know where to meet Zac so he can get you away from there."

I've tried really hard not to think about the possibility of Aiden getting injured, but when he puts it like that, there's no ignoring it.

There's a sharp ache in my chest just thinking of Aiden being in danger.

He must see how worried I am, because he quickly says, "It's only a precaution."

Nodding, I walk to my room to grab my phone. Coming out, I quickly type Zac's name into my contact list. "I need your number, Zac, so I can call you."

We exchange numbers, and I feel a little better knowing I can also call for backup now.

CHAPTER 21

AIDEN

I almost throw Emma over my shoulder and abandon the whole damn fight when Katia's eyes lock on her with a greedy hunger.

"You look totally fuckable, honey," Katia purrs as she takes hold of Emma's shoulders. Emma tenses visibly as Katia leans in, but she doesn't pull away, and I have to fist my hands to hold myself back, as Katia presses a kiss to Emma's lips.

"Let's go get a drink," Katia drools over my girl.

I take a step forward because there's no fucking way Emma is drinking anything this woman gives her.

"No, thanks, lovely," Emma says sweetly.

Katia scowls at her. "Later, maybe."

Wrapping my arms around Emma's waist, I pull her to me.

"I have to go warm up." She turns her face up to mine, giving me a breathtaking smile.

"I'll be cheering for you. Take him out quickly because I'm in a hurry to get home." She lowers her eyes to my mouth, and I don't know how she expects me to step away now.

Leaning down to her ear, I whisper, "I can still taste your pussy."

Her cheeks flush a soft pink as her eyes darken with desire. I've noticed she gets turned on when I talk dirty to her.

Emma wraps a hand around the back of my neck and feeling her warm breath on my ear, I struggle to keep my cock from going rock hard.

"I'm going to handcuff you to the damn bed and suck your cock until you explode down my throat."

Fuck me.

I'm glad she's blocking my cock from everyone else, cause it's trying to tear through my fucking pants right now.

I press a hard kiss to her lips and swipe my tongue inside. Emma only makes things harder when she sucks on my tongue.

Pulling back I groan, "We have to stop."

She grins up at me. "You started it."

"Yeah, I did," I admit with a smile.

I hug her to me until I have my raging hardon back under control. Pressing one last kiss to her lips, I let her go.

I strip out of my t-shirt and sweats and hand the clothes to Emma.

"I won't be long," I promise.

"Kick his ass," she says, holding my clothes to her chest.

———

The fight is about to start, but my eyes keep going back to Emma where she's sitting next to Katia.

I'm too tense. It feels like I forgot something. The harder I try to concentrate on what it is, the more it floats to the back of my mind.

I roll my shoulders and glance at Emma again. She's listening to something Katia's saying.

Dammit, she looks breathtaking tonight which doesn't help the fact that I need to focus.

"Aiden, Colton, it's time, guys," Harper calls out.

I shake my arms out as I step into the ring. Opening and closing my fists, I stretch the sparring gloves wrapped tightly around my hands.

I glance at Emma again, and the sight of my girl next to that viper only makes my stomach coil.

Colton starts to bounce lightly, and I turn my right side to him. The left is still tender.

"I've been lookin' forward to this," Colton sneers.

"Bring it," I growl.

He bounces back, and I focus my eyes on his chest. From there, I can see his feet and arms, whichever he'll move first. He keeps bouncing, slowly moving left. I wait, every muscle pulled tight.

Colton lunges forward, his right arm swinging lightning fast as he tries to take a swipe at my face.

I jump back and feel the air displace as he narrowly misses my jaw. I keep darting out of his reach, hoping all the missed swings he's taking at me will tire him out.

His leg shoots out for a kick to my knee, but I don't move fast enough to get out of the way. The sting isn't too bad, and shaking it off, I smirk at the fucker.

Colton's nostrils flare with anger, and he shoots forward. As his body crashes into mine, shock shudders through me. The second I hit the floor I look for Emma, but her chair is empty. So is Katia's.

Seconds - that was all it took them.

My body goes ice cold as my eyes dart over the patch of grass next to the ring, for any sign of Emma.

I twist under Colton as rage explodes through me. They say there's nothing as dangerous as a caged animal.

They haven't fucking met me.

Colton's legs grip tight around my waist, and he squeezes. It takes precious fucking seconds for me to twist around under him. I don't feel his fists as he starts to slam them into me. Using all my strength, I push my body from the ground, taking him with me, only to turn around and throw him back against the mat.

I hear a satisfying grunt and take advantage of the second I have, while he's winded. I slip my arm around

THE OCEAN BETWEEN US – Michelle Heard

his neck in a triangle choke and tighten my hold brutally on him.

"Wait!" he coughs, tapping at my forearm.

Tightening my hold, I cut off his air supply.

Ready to kill the fucker, I growl, "Where the fuck is she?"

"Katia," he wheezes.

"Where?" I shout.

I will snap his fucking neck.

"Insurance," he forces the word out, his face red from exertion to breathe past my hold on him.

I shove him hard into the floor and get up. My blood is boiling with rage as I glare down at him coughing at my feet.

"Fuck!" I shout as the panic sets deep in my gut.

I glare at Colton as he struggles up. "When's the fight?"

"Next Saturday." He rubs at his neck as he glares at me.

"That's a whole fuckin' week," I shout. "No fuckin' way!"

"Calm the fuck down," he shouts back at me. "She's with the other girls, dude. You know this is how it works. Just make sure you win so we can get paid."

Grabbing hold of his throat, my fingers dig in deep as I slam my fist into his face.

"If anythin' happens to Emma, I will kill you."

"Chill, man," he yells. "You'll win the fight and have her back in no time. This is how it works. I have a shitload of money ridin' on this. Just show next Saturday at the address they text you, win the fight, and everythin' will be fine."

The other guys step into the ring, and I have to let go of Colton because I'm out-numbered and I'm about to blow my cover which will only put Emma's life in danger.

Fuck, they have Emma.

They have my girl.

CHAPTER 22

AIDEN

"Calm down," Zac says again. But he's the one pacing a damn hole in the living room floor. "She's clever. She'll be fine. We'll find her." He keeps saying the same words over and over.

"Zac!" I snap. "Stop it. You're gonna drive me insane walkin' up and down like that. Sit your ass down. I can't think worth shit if you're goin' on like that."

When Zac finally takes a seat, I ask again, "How did they get by you with Emma?"

"They didn't come out the front with her. Trust me, I was watchin' that house like a hawk. No one left with a woman, not until you came out and she was already gone."

I drop my head into my hands and go over a year's worth of work again. I keep coming up with the same damn thing. I have to wait for Saturday. I have to wait and pray. They fucking outplayed us.

Six more days.

Zac stays the night, and I let him take my room. I stay in Emma's. I can smell her on the pillows, and it's driving me insane.

By the early hours of the morning, my heart is breaking.

"I'm so fuckin' sorry, Em," I whisper to the new day which doesn't bring much hope.

She's alone, and they're doing God-only-knows-what to her.

She forgot to take her phone. That's what was bothering me before the fight. I didn't make sure she took it.

She couldn't call for help.

I found the thing next to her bed with more texts and missed calls from her mother.

She never told me. Not that any of it matters now.

Day four is a killer. I'm torn to shreds with worry.

When her fucking phone starts vibrating again, rage burns through me.

Just in time, I notice the name *Chloe* flashing on the screen. Knowing that she's Emma's best friend, I bring the phone to my ear.

"Sunshine! Where the bloody hell have you been? You don't answer your emails? You don't text-"

"Chloe," I say so she'll stop talking.

"Who's this?"

"It's Aiden, Emma's roommate," I don't know what to say.

"Oh, it's nice to finally talk to you. Thank you for helping Emma." She says. "Is she there?"

I can't bring myself to say the words. I can't tell Chloe that Emma's been taken, that I failed her.

"Aiden, is Emma all right?" Her voice tense with every word.

"She will be. Can I ask you to hold on until Saturday? I know I'm askin' a lot, but everythin' will be fine on Saturday. I'll get her to phone you then," I say, not being able to tell her Emma's been taken.

I close my eyes and wait for her response. I pray it's not a hysterical one.

"I'm only agreeing because I know she trusts you. If I don't hear from her by Saturday, I'm coming to get her myself," she warns.

"Not a day later. You have my word."

"You look like crap," Zac says two days before the fight.

I just glare at him from the couch. Crap does not begin to describe all the turmoil I feel inside. My mind's turned into a goddamned nightmare. I can't stop thinking of all the previous cases I've worked. I can't stop thinking about the things they could've, and can still do, to Emma.

"You need to get up and at it. Emma needs you at your best, Aiden. Go for a run. I'll get everythin' ready for the briefin' with the team. We need to make sure everythin' is in place, so we don't screw things up for Cole and Troy."

He's right. Zac's right.

I drag on a sweater, because it's cold out, and I glance at Zac.

"Do you think they're keepin' her warm?" I ask. I just need to hear him say it.

He nods, but it's not enough. I can see the fear in his eyes, and it makes my gut twist even more.

CHAPTER 23

EMMA

I can't remember what happened. I can't remember how I ended up in this room. One minute I was still listening to Katia while watching Aiden and Colton, and the next I woke up here. I think they drugged me somehow.

It's an empty room, with a single bed pressed against a stark, white wall. At least I have a blanket and pillow.

There's something very frightening about not knowing where in a foreign country you are. I can't believe I forgot to bring my phone.

"They would've taken it anyway, Emma," I mutter to myself, wondering how I let this happen.

A shrill scream echoes through the air just as the lock on the door to my room rattles.

What's happening out there?

My eyes are glued to the door as shivers of fear race down my spine.

Pressing my back to the cold wall, I watch as Katia pushes the door open. She locks it behind her before she turns to look at me.

"I thought I'd come and visit," she says, sauntering in.

Another scream from somewhere beyond the door, makes my body start to tremble.

"Colton's testin' one of the girls," Katia says with a cruel smile around her full lips. "Don't worry. I won't let him touch you."

The way she looks at me as if I'm something edible, makes my stomach churn. I press further back into the wall and lift my chin, not wanting her to see my fear. "Where am I?

Ignoring my question, she says "I like you, honey. Don't take this personal."

"Yeah, right," I murmur, and then regret saying anything.

"Aiden's good. He'll win," she says, and I hear the warning in her voice. "He better win… for your sake."

"What happens if he doesn't?" I ask. I need to know, so he'll know what happened to the others.

I know he'll come for me.

"You go to the highest bidder. Sorry, honey. It's just business. My mama always said; 'if you could bottle sex, you'd be a millionaire.'

"Highest bidder?" I interrupt her.

"Yeah, the one who pays most for you takes you. How do you think we make our money? Bets don't come cheap." She sits down next to me, and I try to scoot away, but I bump into the wall instead. I clench my arms tighter around my legs.

When she reaches for me, I can't sit still. I flinch away from her hand. I don't want this woman touching me. I'd rather die.

"Are you cold, princess?"

"No," I snap, just wanting her to leave.

"It's goin' to be a long week," her voice drops to a purr. It raises hackles all the way from my spine to the tiny hairs on my neck. "You can either make it a nice stay or things will get ugly for you."

I glare at her as she reaches out to me again. When she tries to cup my cheek, I slap her hand away. "Don't touch me."

"Tsk… Tsk." She gets up, and just as I think she's going to leave, she spins around and darts toward me.

A startled shriek escapes my lips as she grabs hold of my shoulders and slams me back against the wall with so much force, the thud of my head hitting the plaster sounds sickening. My vision goes spotty, but I shove back against her, fighting not to be pinned down. Only when I hear the hammering of my heart in my ears, do I realize how fast it's beating.

Her fingers wrap around my neck, and she squeezes hard. "I fuckin' like it rough, kitten. Keep fightin' me, and I'll get Colton to hold you down. You'll like that, won't you? Both of us fuckin' you?"

A fear, unlike anything I've felt before, explodes through me.

"You'll have to kill me first," I scream as I fight to get her off of me.

She just smirks at me. "I've been dreamin' about this for a while now. I can't wait to taste you, princess."

Her fingers tighten around my throat, and I gasp at the pain. As she starts to cut off my air supply, I grab hold of her wrist and dig my nails into her skin.

"Oh yeah, kitten, let me feel your nails," she purrs again.

I'm gasping for air when she shoves me up against the wall and crushes her mouth to mine.

My stomach heaves, and I yank my head away, only to feel her hand grab at my breast.

"Don't touch me!" I rasp the words out. My vision is starting to blur, and I try to drag in another breath of air, but nothing is getting past her tight grip around my throat.

She leans in close to my ear. "We're goin' to have so much fun."

She shoves me hard, slamming my head against the wall again. The pain is blinding, darkening my vision.

THE OCEAN BETWEEN US – Michelle Heard

As she lets go of me, I suck in gulps of air, refusing to cry. I won't be weak. I won't let her win.

I've survived my mother. I can survive this woman.

I bite my lip until I taste blood to keep back the tears of anger. My eyes are glued to Katia as she leaves the room.

CHAPTER 24

EMMA

I've realized fear isn't a feeling. It's a living, breathing entity. Its sole purpose is to rob you of your will to live.

With every cry I hear echoing into my room, dread spins its web around me to the point where it makes it feel like my skin is stretched thin over my body. Every inch of me prickles with apprehension until it feels like death itself is scraping its skeletal fingers down my spine.

The lock on my door rattles and I scramble from the bed so Katia can't pin me down again.

Only, when the door opens, she's not alone. Colton follows her in, and before I can recover from the shock of seeing him, he charges toward me.

The force of his body slamming into mine knocks all the breath from my lungs in a pain-filled gasp. Still reeling from the blow, Colton somehow gets behind me and drags me to the floor.

Horror washes over me as his arms lock around me, and using his sturdy legs, he hooks them over mine, keeping me from closing them.

Pinned to Colton's body, I hear him chuckle in my ear. "She's all yours, babe."

My eyes dart up to Katia, and it's with a sickening feeling that I watch her undress.

Shit. No.

This can't be happening.

When she pushes her panties down her legs, I feel bile burn up my throat. She kicks the fabric to the side, and it's only then that I see the bag next to her on the floor.

"Let me go," I demand. "If you hurt me, Aiden will kill you."

Keeping one arm locked around me, Colton slaps a hand over my mouth. I scream as I try to pull myself free from him, but it only makes him use more force to keep me in place.

Katia opens the bag and takes a pair of scissors from it. "Kitten, I'm not going to leave a mark on your body. I like it too much."

She takes something else from the bag. It looks like a rubber cucumber. My mind races to catch up with what's happening, but as Katia comes closer, I stop trying to figure out what's happening and focus on trying to get free from Colton.

He tightens his grip on me until a cry tears up my throat only to be muffled against his hand. I don't stop fighting, trying to free my arms and legs.

Katia sits down between my legs and grabs hold of my dress. As the scissors cut through the fabric, the crunching sound vibrates through my mind. Adrenaline courses through my veins, making my heart slam against my ribs.

The pain from Colton's brutal hold on me doesn't register anymore, as Katia cuts the dress from my body.

Even though it's useless and my mouth is covered, I keep screaming until a copper taste fills my mouth.

With every cry, I yank against Colton only to have his cruel laughter filling my ears while Katia cuts away my underwear. My muffled cries just seem to excite them.

When Katia places the scissors on the floor, and my body is totally exposed to her, she leans forward with an evil gleam in her eyes.

As her tongue touches my skin in the middle of my stomach, my screams fade to a mixture of sobs and cries. She leaves a streak of luke-warm spit up to my throat.

"You taste so fuckin' good, kitten," she groans as she brings her face to mine. I can feel her hot breath wafting over me as she shoves her hand between my legs.

I squeeze my eyes shut as a tear escapes, rolling down until it's stopped by Colton's hand.

Katia's sharp, long nail stabs into me, tearing a battered cry from my aching throat.

"Doesn't that feel good?" Colton growls low in my ear. "Fuck, babe, that's makin' me hard."

Trying to escape this nightmare, I keep my eyes closed, not wanting to see what she's doing to me.

A hopeless anger shudders through my body. Even though I know they're both stronger than me, and that they can kill me, I fight against Colton's hold.

For a moment, my mind drifts away, only to be yanked back when something hard is shoved in between my legs. My eyes dart open from the pain tearing through me as my body lurches forward against the steel barrier that is Colton.

I wish I had kept my eyes closed, because seeing Katia insert the other end of the substitute for a cock into her, makes me feel violently ill and debased. She moves closer until her ass touches mine, then starts to ride the thing.

As my body jerks, Colton moves his arm up until it presses hard under my breasts.

With his mouth to my ear, Colton whispers, "You've got nice tits. I'm going to fuck them before you leave."

His words make a violent tremor rake through my body.

Stop. Please Stop.

I feel as he grows hard against my lower back, making a new fear spread through me like a devastating fire.

I haven't realized I've stopped screaming until silent tears spill down my cheeks.

The prodding pain becomes unbearable when she speeds up her thrusts.

"Ahh… fuck, I'm gonna come, kitten," she cries as she shoves herself right up against me, rubbing hard. "So fuckin' good," she groans.

I feel her hair on the side of my face as she presses her breasts against mine. Wet sounds of Katia and Colton kissing, and slapping skin fills my ear.

My whole body stills except for the involuntary jerks from Katia's assault.

CHAPTER 25

AIDEN

"Hey, Mama," I say as she answers the phone. I've called her more over the last few days than I have since I started this undercover job.

"How are you holdin' up?" she asks, concern lacing her words.

"Honestly, I'm about to lose my mind," I answer. "I just want Emma back. I don't care about the case any longer."

"Aiden," her voice is stern, "don't do somethin' stupid. Not only will you risk Emma's life, but also Wyatt and Cole's. My heart won't survive losin' another child."

"I'm not an idiot," I snap, but immediately feel bad. "Sorry, Mama. It's drivin' me up the wall not knowin' if Emma is okay."

"I know, darlin'. I wish I could be there."

Zac comes in from his morning run, and I quickly say, "I've got to go. Zac just walked in."

"My boys take care of each other, you hear," she warns.

"Yeah, Mama. Talk to you soon."

"Go take a shower, Aiden," Zac says as I drop the phone on the coffee table.

I close my eyes, not being able to think of something as mundane as a fucking shower.

Is Emma okay? Have they hurt her? Is she warm, or hungry?

Zac crouches in front of me, his face torn with concern. "Will you be able to focus tonight?"

Meeting his eyes, I shake my head. "Not as long as they have Emma." My voice cracks on her name and hopelessness pushes up my throat.

"I'll take the lead. You hang back until we've neutralized the scene. I'll check with Wyatt, back

THE OCEAN BETWEEN US – Michelle Heard

home, to make sure his team moves in at the same time as us, and Cole and Troy don't get blindsided. You okay with that?"

I nod, knowing I'll just fuck things up with the state of mind I'm in.

Unable to stop it, a tear slips free. "I never knew anythin' could hurt this much?"

Zac places his hand on my shoulder, and only now that I'm at risk of losing the woman I love, do I recognize the grief in his eyes.

"How do you cope with it every day?" I ask.

"I don't. You just learn to live with it. It's like a tumor, weavin' its tentacles through every part of you."

"Fuck." I hunch over and grab hold of Zac, and for the first time since Laurie was killed, I cry. Sliding from the couch, my knees hit the floor.

Feeling my brother's arms wrap around me, I cry because I know deep in my heart, I won't get the same Emma back.

CHAPTER 26

EMMA

I think it's Saturday, but there's no way for me to be sure. The days are becoming too long to bear, and the nights even longer.

The lock rattles and Katia pushes the door open.

Keeping the blanket wrapped around me, I dart from the bed, ready to fight. I can't help but try. I can't just lie still and let Katia have her way with me.

"I brought you a present. You can change into this." She throws a sheer piece of fabric at me. I wait for the door to close behind her before I look at it again. It's a filmy piece of scrap material.

I stare at the door, then back to the single item of clothing.

Does this mean the fight is tonight? Will I see Aiden?

I've been trying to be strong, but just the thought that I might see him in a matter of hours makes this all unbearable.

Every day I had to fight Katia.

Her touching me. Her kissing me. Her biting.

It was so bad yesterday, her teeth tore through my skin. I look down at the bloody bite mark on my breast, and it all becomes too much.

Sagging down on the concrete floor, I pray, "God, please let it end today." It's nothing more than a rasp, my voice gone from all the screaming.

Knowing I don't have a choice, I drag the dress over my head and still feel naked with it on. It's see-through with only two leather strips to cover my private parts. Not that it helps. It's so tight that the swells of my breasts are clearly visible.

The door slams open making me cower back with trepidation.

Colton. My heart launches into my throat at the sight of him.

"Your boyfriend's late," he growls at me. The room feels too small with him blocking the only exit.

When he comes in with Katia behind him, I move back until I feel the wall behind me.

Oh God, please. Not again. I won't survive it.

Colton tilts his head to the side as his eyes take me in from head to toe.

"You were right, babe. The dress looks good on her," he says in a low voice. The look in his eyes is dangerous and ravenous.

"Maybe we're lucky, and Aiden doesn't show. I'd like to keep this one," Katia says.

"Aiden will come for me," I whisper, hating that I can't talk louder. My throat is still achingly raw.

Colton's eyes snap to mine, and I see it, the fear. He's scared of Aiden.

I lift my chin and pray I'm right, I hiss, "He's going to rip you apart, and I'm going to enjoy watching."

"Nah," Colton steps closer to me, "I think he's bailed on your ass."

Meeting his eyes with a disgusted glare, I say. "Aiden loves me. You're as good as dead for what you've done to me."

Colton stalks right to me, and I flinch back, with a shriek. The punch to my cheek takes me down, and all I see is black.

Through dizziness, I hear Katia say, "Don't mark her face, idiot!"

Colton's on top of me before I can regain my sight and his hand wraps around my neck.

"You're a fuckin' nobody, a piece of trash. I'm not scared of Aiden. Don't fuck with me, whore. I won't be as gentle as Katia." He shoves me back down, and I scramble to cover myself, terror coursing like lava through my veins. "Get your worthless ass up. It's time to go."

Relief claws its way up my spine and climbing to my feet, I cover my bruised jaw with a trembling hand.

They lead me down a passage and up a set of stairs. When I see the other girls, my heart shatters.

The smallest of us, a girl in a purple dress, looks terrified, to the point that she might faint. She's

THE OCEAN BETWEEN US – Michelle Heard

positioned at the far end as they start to line us up against a wall.

I wonder if I look like that? Like I might pass out from fear.

Colton shoves me hard against the wall, making my shoulder blades dig into the plaster, but I bite back the whimper of pain. I won't give him the satisfaction of seeing that he's hurting me.

"Stand still, whore. Move, and you'll regret it," he hisses, slapping my aching cheek.

They say everything happens for a reason. Maybe I was abused by my mother to prepare me for this past week so they wouldn't be able to break me.

We're at a different location from the house where they kidnapped me. There's an empty pool to my right with sand and patches of dead grass covering the area around it.

A guy comes running toward us, and I hear a strangled cry as a girl wearing blue grabs hold of him, weeping in his arms.

I keep standing, watching as the fighters arrive, each of them rushing to a girl.

All the girls are crying, but I can't manage anything past the lump in my throat. It's lodged so hard it's starting to cramp when I breathe.

Closing my eyes, I picture Aiden. Trying to visualize an eagle soaring throughout my ordeal doesn't help anymore. Only the image of Aiden can keep me calm now.

CHAPTER 27

EMMA

Aiden, where are you?

My eyes feel heavy as I lift them to scan all the fighters, but then I see men dressed in dark blue with black vests running across the yard and for a moment I'm confused. Their appearance is in total contrast to the fighters gathering around the other girls.

I take in the rifles and guns, and then chaos erupts around us as people start to run and shout, but none of it makes sense to my dazed mind.

Fingers dig hard into my arm, and my body moves automatically forward as Colton yanks at me.

My vision becomes tunneled as I see fighters, the ones who came to get their women, being thrown down into the dirt by the men in blue. Their hands are being tied behind their backs with something that looks like cable ties, not even handcuffs.

Caught in a trance of shock, I turn my head and follow the hand gripping my arm up to Colton's distressed face.

Suddenly Colton stops dragging me, and as he lets go of my arm, I stumble forward. My knees slam hard into the ground causing stones and sand to scrape my palms and legs raw.

I slump down to the side and onto my butt while the sound of crying women and men shouting continues to fill the air.

"Don't shoot," Colton shouts next to me, and I flinch at the volume of his voice.

"Let me see your hands. Let me see your hands," someone else yells.

In a daze, I look up at Colton and watch as he raises his hands above his head.

"On your knees!" the same person as before shouts.

Colton hits the ground right next to me. He grunts as a man presses a knee into his back, restraining his hands with cable ties.

"Emma?" My eyes dart up, and I recognize Zac as he keeps Colton shoved down into the dirt with his knee and one hand. In his other hand is a gun.

He's dressed in caramel-colored chinos with a black t-shirt and a black armored vest wrapped tightly around his broad chest.

Unable to move or speak, I watch as Zac keeps his gun trained on Colton while yanking him up to his feet. He shoves Colton towards another officer.

I don't understand how I can take all of this in but not move.

"You have nothin' on me," Katia screams.

Raising my eyes, I see how an officer has to forcefully shove her into the back of a black armored vehicle.

Colton and Katia have been arrested.

Exhaustion creeps through me, and my mind shuts down, now that I know they won't be able to hurt me any longer.

Tiny prickles start over my scalp, then spread out over my eyes and cheeks. Chills numb all my senses, and I struggle to slowly turn my face away from Katia and Colton as a familiar voice drifts to me from the chaos.

I watch as someone who's dressed the same as Zac runs toward me while holstering his gun.

It takes me a few seconds to register that the person is Aiden. The only thing familiar about him is his face. He stops a few feet from me, and reaches a hand out to me, palm up, as if he's approaching a beaten dog.

Transfixed, I watch as his hand slowly comes closer, but it disappears as someone moves between us.

I'm losing my mind.

"Aiden," I croak painfully. "Aiden."

Panic hits hard, gripping my chest until it feels like my heart's going to stop. I close my eyes, wishing all this madness would end.

"Emma," Aiden breathes my name.

My eyes snap open, and I lift my head. I choke on a sob as he crouches down in front of me. He doesn't touch me, though. His hands hover near my face as if he's too scared to touch me.

"I should've brought a jacket," he whispers.

He moves away and grabs hold of one of the men in blue. He says something to him, and the man takes off running.

Aiden sits down right in front of me, and I see the hesitation on his face as he lifts an arm, but then drops it again.

What if he doesn't want me any longer?

I close my eyes against the devastating thought, but then something falls over my shoulders, and I cringe to the side to get away from it.

"Fuck. I'm so sorry, Em. It's just a blanket," Aiden says, his voice sounding impossibly tense.

Then he brushes a finger lightly over my bruised cheek. Tears flood my eyes, but I blink them back, not wanting anything obscuring my vision, too scared Aiden will disappear if I blink.

His arms slip under me, and he lifts me to his chest as he rises to his full height.

"Let's get you out of here," he whispers against my hair.

I have to answer questions before Aiden can take me home. Zac and another man ask them because

Aiden's not allowed to. In a daze, I answer them, just so I can go home.

"No, they didn't hurt me."

"No, I was alone."

"I didn't see any of the other women."

"No, they never talked business near me."

"I'm sure I'm fine."

"No, no hospital."

"I'm not hurt."

"I'm fine."

"I'm okay."

"I'm fine." I lie, not able to force the words of my shameful assault over my lips.

CHAPTER 28

EMMA

I head straight for my bedroom when we get home. I grab my pajamas and walk back to the bathroom so I can shower.

I only open the hot water tap, then drop the blanket the police gave me to the floor. My body aches as I gingerly drag the dress over my head, then throw it away from me. I never want to see it again.

I step into the shower and lifting my face, I let the water wash over me before I reach for the soap. Even though the scrapes and bite marks burn, I scrub, needing to rid myself of the awful memories.

When I'm done washing every part of me, I sink down in the corner, wishing I could cry. But I can't, and it makes the ache in my chest grow.

Closing my eyes, I pretend the drops of water pelting me are tears.

Suddenly the water stops, and my eyes snap open. I scramble to my feet and plastering my back against the tiles, my breath explodes over my lips.

Then my eyes focus on Aiden where he's standing with a towel in his hands, a distraught look on his face. He sucks in a sharp breath as his eyes sweep over my body, stopping on every mark left by the ordeal.

"I'm takin' you to the hospital," Aiden breaks the silence between us as he steps forward ready to wrap the towel around me.

I grab the towel from him and start to dry myself.

"I'm not going," I refuse, my throat burning from the strain I'm putting on it.

My mom will see that something happened to me. I don't have the strength to face her on top of everything else.

"You need to get a tetanus shot, Em. At the very least," Aiden keeps insisting.

"I've had one," I lie.

I don't care about the scapes and bruises. None of that matters. I can't deal with what's been done to me, and at the hospital, they'll ask questions, ones I can't answer. I just need time to work through the devastation that's been left inside of me.

"Emma–"

"Stop, Aiden!" The words are harsh even though my voice is scratchy. "I can't…" I shake my head as I put on my pajamas. "Too much," I whisper as I push past him to get to the sink. I brush my teeth, then leave him standing in the bathroom.

I understand that he's concerned and that he doesn't know what Katia and Colton did to me, but I'm struggling to hang onto what's left of my sanity.

I crawl onto my bed and hug my pillow to my chest, and just as I try to switch my torturous mind off, Aiden comes in.

"You need to phone Chloe. Just let her know you're okay," he says softly.

I'm drained. I want to sleep, but I know Chloe will worry.

I sit up and taking the phone from Aiden, I search for Chloe's number and press dial.

She sounds tearful when she answers.

"Emma?"

"Hey, Chloe."

"Are you alright? What's wrong with your voice?"

"I have the flu."

I can't tell her what really happened. It will crush her. She has enough to worry about. I can't allow myself to dwell on this horrible week. If I do, I won't survive. I'll have to find a way to just put it behind me.

"How are you?" I ask to divert the subject away from me.

"Oh, Emma!" She bursts out crying, and it's only then I realize she's been calling me by my name.

"Chloe, what's wrong?"

Aiden sits down next to me, his face tight with worry.

"It's my Mom," she sobs. "She's gone."

I don't know if it's from the trauma I suffered, but I don't understand what she's saying.

"Gone where?"

"She gave up. She's dead." She takes a shaky breath. "I hate to ask this, but I need you. Come home, Emma. I'll book you a ticket. You can stay with me."

"Of course. Email me the details."

"You know you're the best, right?" she says my line back to me.

"No, you're the best." It's all I can say as I sit frozen, trying to absorb the new blow life has dealt me.

I sit with the phone to my ear long after Chloe has cut the call.

I have to go back.

Chloe needs me.

Slowly, my hand slips down to the bed.

How am I going to tell Aiden?

Before I can say anything, his phone rings.

"Hey, Zac."

There's a moment's silence before Aiden shoots up off the bed, rushing out of the room. "What the fuck?"

From the bed, I watch as he stalks up and down in the living room.

"What do you mean it went south? Are Wyatt and Cole okay?" I can hear the panic in his voice, and my heart clenches.

He shoves a hand into his hair, gripping a fistful. Every muscle in his body is tense.

My heart starts to pound as he turns his back to me so I can't see his face.

"Troy's dead?" he whispers. "How did it go so bad?"

I cover my mouth with trembling hands as I watch Aiden's shoulders drop.

"But we had to go in. Wyatt knew we were goin' in. Why weren't they prepared on that side? I need to phone my mom. I need to know how Cole's surgery is goin'. I'll talk to you later."

I gasp as it hits. People were hurt... people were killed because Aiden came for me.

"Mama," Aiden can barely get the word out. He clears his throat. "Is Cole okay? How bad is it?"

I can only sit and listen as guilt consumes me. This is on me - because I came here. Because I let myself be taken.

I force myself to listen.

"They had Troy's sister? Did they-" I watch him flinch, and he brings his hand to his hair again, gripping a fistful. "The girl's in shock, Mama. They assaulted her and killed her brother. Give her time. Let me know how Cole's surgery goes. I'm just gonna wrap things up here, and then I'm comin' home."

I can't look him in the eyes when he comes back into the room, knowing I'm the cause of so much heartache. It's best I go home to Chloe. I need to face my own demons now.

"We have to talk," I murmur as he sits down on the bed.

Our lives are at crossroads now.

"We do," he agrees. "I'm sorry you got dragged into this mess." I can hear the regret and hurt in his voice. "Do you want to talk about it?"

I shake my head. "Nothing happened."

"I've never felt so helpless in my life. I kept wonderin' if they were feedin' you, where you were sleepin'. It drove me insane not knowin' whether you were okay."

"I'm here now. It's all that matters." Needing to move on, I ask, "What happens now that you're no longer undercover." I keep my voice soft, so I don't hurt my throat more.

"We have to wrap things up on Monday with the office here before we report back in Lyman, to our own department. We were only helpin' here because they couldn't use their own guys, with them bein' recognizable and all, and it bein' part of our case. We work the Lyman and Duncan area with Wyatt." He takes a breath, and I steel myself for what he's going to say next. "We'll be headin' back on Tuesday. There will be a lot of paperwork to get ready for the court case against Colton and Katia."

Just hearing their names makes shivers of shame and disgust rush over me. I'm glad they'll be dealt with, but right now, I don't want to know about it.

"How far is Lyman from here?" I ask, staring down at my scraped hands, feeling exhausted to my very core.

"About two hundred and twenty miles," he says, as he reaches for one of my hands. I almost pull away, but then his fingers brush against mine, and I let him hold it.

"How many hours is that?"

"It's just shy of a four-hour drive," he explains.

"Oh."

"I was thinkin' we could drive through to Lyman tomorrow. I'd like to go see how Cole's doin' and you can see where I'm from."

Silence follows his suggestion. I should tell him I'm going home, but instead, I agree, "Okay."

I'll get to spend time with Aiden before I leave.

I'll pretend I'm fine for three days.

It's better than facing my reality.

CHAPTER 29

AIDEN

Last night, when I saw the bite mark on Emma's breast, and all the bruising around her neck, over her ribs and on her legs, my mind started going down a dark path.

She keeps saying she's fine, but I know she's hiding something from me. Fuck, I can *see* something happened to her. *Something really fucking bad.* It's ripping a hole through my gut, not knowing what they did to her.

If Emma confides in me, it might just fucking kill me, but I'll have to remain strong for her. Right now it doesn't look like she's going to talk about her experience.

She's been quiet during the drive to Lyman. We're minutes away from reaching my place. I thought it would be good if we stopped here first before we drive to the hospital.

We haven't talked about my having to return home, which is an added worry on top of my concern for Emma's emotional and mental state.

"Things won't change, Emma." I break the silence that's suffocating me. "I'll visit every weekend. I don't like the idea of you being alone durin' the week, but, for now, we have to make do."

She only nods, not taking her eyes away from where she's staring out the window at the passing landscape.

Pulling into the driveway, Emma's eyes dart to me, and I see the worry.

"It's my place. We're stoppin' here first before headin' to the hospital." I try to set her at ease.

"Yours?" she whispers as her eyes go back to the house.

I get out and walk around the car to open her door. When I do, she gets out slowly and steps away from me.

I hate that she's distant. I wish she would talk to me so I can understand what she's been through. I'll be able to better help her then.

I want to reach for her, but she takes another step away, keeping her eyes on the house. It's a two-story I've been fixing up whenever I have some time off from work.

When I open the front door, Emma forces a smile to her lips, but I can see it doesn't reach her eyes.

It feels like I've lost her, and my heart clenches painfully.

Emma steps inside, her body tense as she glances around the foyer, and up at the stairs.

I hate that she's uncomfortable in my home.

Having little to no strength left after the nightmare of a week, it feels like I'm about to break.

"Emma." I close the door and take a step closer to her. "Tell me what happened. What you're feelin' and thinkin'? Let me help you."

My eyes get stuck on the purple discoloration around her neck.

I know from experience what causes marks like that. Emma was choked. It explains why her voice is practically gone.

Rage makes me bite the words out, "What happened to your neck?"

When she presses her lips firmly together, refusing to talk, I take a step closer to her. Her body instantly goes tense, and she clenches her hands.

Fuck, not that.

"Emma, what did they do to you?" My voice is low with fear.

"Nothing," she whispers.

I can't stand the distance between us and I take the few steps separating us. I take hold of Emma's clenched hands and pin them to my chest. She won't open them or look at me.

"Please, Em. Let me share the pain. Let me help you through this." She shakes her head, her breath catching in her throat. I brush my fingers over her cheek and lean closer. "Who hit you?"

She opens her mouth, and at first, only a rasp of air comes out.

It hurts like hell to see her like this.

Then she presses her forehead against my chest and finally whispers, "Colton."

Fucking bastard. I wish I'd killed him when I had the chance.

I wrap my arms around her, wishing I could give her all of the strength I have left. I'm used to being in control, to being able to handle everything, but all my power has been stripped away from me.

Pressing a kiss to her temple, I softly say, "Tell me what they did so I can make them pay."

She pushes against my chest, and I take a step back.

Her face is tight with anger. "You think you can actually do something about it?"

I frame her face and make her look at me. "Emma, I can. I'm not your dad. I'll prosecute them with everything I have."

"This is not about my fucking dad," she screams, her voice breaking over the words. "You can't do anything about it, Aiden. It fucking happened. It's done. Nothing you do will change that."

Her arms wrap around her waist, and hunching over, a broken cry tears from her. My heart shatters at the sight of her crumbling right before my eyes.

I move forward, but she sags to the floor, whimpering, "Don't touch me."

Feeling helpless as fuck, I watch the woman I love with every single beat of my heart, fall apart.

I sit down beside her, needing to let her know I'm not going anywhere.

Emma's been sitting in a curled ball, tightly hugging her knees to her chest, for the longest time.

With my elbows resting on my knees, and my head leaning back against the wall, I close my eyes.

"I fought so hard."

Hearing the soft whisper my eyes snap open.

I'm just starting to think I imagined it, when Emma continues, "They were so much stronger than me."

A new wave of rage rips through my chest. Emma is finally talking, and I don't want her to stop. I want her to purge herself.

"I couldn't stop them."

322

I hate the silence that follows her words. I steel myself for what's to come.

"Stop what?" My voice sounds strained to the point of breaking. "What did they do?"

"He restrained me."

I know how strong Colton is. There's no way Emma could've fought him off.

"The marks on your neck, was that Colton?"

She only nods. "I couldn't stop them."

My gut feels like it's been shredded. My girl's been hurt in ways I can't begin to process.

"Can I hold you?" I almost beg, needing to touch her.

Slowly, she lifts her head. Seeing her tears, I'm unable to hold myself back. I turn to her and wrapping my arms around her trembling body, I pull her onto my lap. I tuck her head into my chest and press kisses to her hair, as my own tears begin to fall.

"I'm so fucking sorry." It's all I can say even though it sounds hollow in my ears.

After a while, Emma pulls back and her eyes finally meet mine. "I need to tell you something."

323

"You know you can tell me anythin'," I encourage her.

She stands up, and I quickly climb to my feet.

"You've been amazing." A breath shudders through her as she takes a step away from me. "I'll never be able to tell you how much the past few weeks with you meant to me."

Fear ripples through me as I realize what she's saying. I move forward and framing her face, I lift it, so she has to look at me.

"Don't say it." My voice is hoarse as my heart breaks all over again.

"Chloe's mom died. I have to go to her."

Pressing my forehead to hers, my gut twists in anguish.

I have to get her to stay. I can't let her go back.

"You can't go back, not to your mother." I'm a second away from begging her. I can't protect her if there's an ocean between us.

"I'll be staying with Chloe," she whispers. "We weren't meant to last, Aiden. You're way ahead of me, and the gap between us is too big. Your life is here.

324

You have a house, a career, a family. Chloe is my family. I have to start working as well. I can't keep studying and hiding from life."

"We'll find a way to bridge the gap."

It's starting to sink in. She's really doing this.

Emma's leaving me.

"How do we bridge this gap? My visa should've been revoked the second my Mom cut me off. One of the requirements for a visa is finances, another is me actually studying. I've missed two weeks of school. I won't be able to catch up before exams start." Her voice starts to tremble, and I move in as close as I can. I feel her breaths rush over my lips.

"I can't lose you," I whisper. "It's all things I can take care of if you'd just let me."

"And Chloe? I can't turn my back on her."

In my desperation, I haven't thought about that. Knowing I can't be selfish, I say, "You need to be there for Chloe. I get that. But come back afterward."

For a moment she just looks at me with eyes swimming in sorrow, but then she nods.

It doesn't make me any feel better because her eyes are still telling me goodbye.

I watch her every move as we walk through the house. She stops in the den and glances up at the high ceiling. It's my favorite room. I hardly use the rest of the house.

Emma walks over to the fireplace and brushes her fingers over a photo of me that was taken while I was serving as a marine.

She turns around, and her eyes fall on the stairs.

"What's up there?" It's the first question she's asked about my home.

"My office."

I watch her walk up the stairs, and reaching the top she must've seen the shelves at the back of the room because she glances back at me. "You have books. I didn't know you liked to read."

"Most of them belonged to Laurie," I say, as I climb the stairs. "Zac isn't much of a book lover, so I took them. She loved books. You would've liked her."

Emma trails her hand over the spines, then whispers, "Words have no power to impress the mind without the exquisite horror of their reality. I love Edgar Allan Poe." She pulls a book out and pages through it. "Laurie had great taste."

She puts the book back, then turns to me.

"Laurie and Zac were married right?"

"Yes, for four years. They met at the station. Laurie was going up the stairs, and he was coming down when he stopped her. It was the first time he ever saw her, and right there he told her he was going to marry her." I watch Emma's eyes as she starts to blink faster. "They got married three weeks later."

"It's so sad," she says.

"No, if they hadn't eloped, they wouldn't have had their four years together, and Zac wouldn't have his memories now. Laurie wouldn't have died happy. They taught me how precious time is, and how quickly it can be gone."

I take a deep breath as I slowly walk toward her.

"I almost lost you once, Emma. Please don't make me lose you again. Give me a chance."

"We still have a couple of days together. One way or another, I have to go back. Even if I can find work here, I still need to go back for Chloe."

"I'm scared," I admit, and it takes a lot for me to utter the words. I hold her eyes with my own, willing her to see all my fear. "I'm so scared you'll go back and that you'll learn to survive on your own, without me, because I've fallen, and I don't know how to get up without you."

"No," she whimpers as she rushes forward, wrapping her arms tightly around my waist.

"For the longest time, half of me was missin'. Then you-" I push Emma back so I can see her face, "you walked into my life with your beautiful smile and unbreakable will, and the hole was gone. I need to take care of you. I need to touch you. I need to see you. You have to give us a chance," I beg. "You're my heaven, Emma."

I don't know what else to do. I've said everything there is left to be said.

CHAPTER 30

EMMA

Aiden broke my heart yesterday. I wanted nothing more than to tell him that I'd stay, but I have to go back for Chloe.

We left his house soon after and stopped at the hospital, but Cole was asleep so we couldn't see him. The nurses said he will heal quickly, that the bullet didn't do a lot of damage. It was a big relief to hear.

Getting back to the flat, I didn't sleep last night, even though I'm miserably tired. I just laid in Aiden's arms wondering how I was going to go on living without him.

Taking a sip of coffee, I almost choke as Aiden comes out of his room all dressed for work. By dressed, I mean holster, gun, and badge, too.

Damn, he's never looked so hot before. He looks intimidating and drop-dead handsome all at once. I'm so shocked by the fluttering feeling in my stomach that I can only stare as he pulls a jacket on and comes over to me, pressing a kiss to my forehead.

Shit, this is it.

Aiden is going to walk out the door and go to work.

"I'm meetin' Zac at the office," he says, his eyes searching my face for answers I can't give him. "We need to complete the paperwork here in North Carolina before headin' home to Lyman."

Home.

There's nowhere on this earth I can call home.

Except for Aiden.

I put the cup down, and standing on my toes, I press my mouth to his. I close my eyes as he wraps his arms around me. The kiss is filled with our heartache, our broken dreams and scattered wishes.

Pulling back, I force a smile to my lips. "Have a good day at the office."

It looks like he wants to say something, his eyes locked on mine, but then he lets me go and leaves.

While Aiden's at the office, I go to the university to explain what happened. They understand, but yes, I've missed too much. I should start fresh the next semester, but there won't be a next semester for me.

When I get back to the flat, I call Chloe to see how she's doing.

"Hello," Chloe rasps. Her voice must be raw from all the crying.

"Hey, how are you holding up?"

"I'm not," she answers honestly. We made a promise not to lie to each other. I broke mine when I didn't tell her about the kidnapping.

Chloe continues, "I managed to get a flight for Wednesday. I'll fetch you from the airport."

"Thanks. When's the funeral?" I ask.

"This afternoon." She starts to cry, and all I can do is listen.

"I wish I could hug you right now." My words only make her cry harder. "I'll see you soon, okay."

"Okay," she whispers.

After the call, I try to sleep a little, but only manage to doze off for a few minutes before jerking awake.

I hear the front door open, and get up from the bed. Straightening my shirt, I walk out into the living room.

Aiden starts to remove his holster, gun, and badge while walking to his room. Glancing up he sees me and stops. "How was your day?" he asks.

"Okay," I answer and walk closer when he quickly darts into his room to lock his gun in a small safe.

"I went to the university," I continue when he turns back to me. "They agreed with me. I've missed too much. They were very nice about it, but they recommend that I start over next semester." I try to keep my tone light.

"That's good, isn't it?" he says as he closes the distance between us. I lift my face to him as he leans down to press a quick kiss to my lips. "Then you just need an extension," he says, looking somewhat relieved.

"Yeah," I smile. "How was your day?"

Aiden doesn't answer and stares at me until I lower my eyes to his neck, not being able to meet his searching eyes any longer. I know what he wants me to say, but it's the one thing I can't give him. I have to go home.

Eventually, he says, "I missed you today. I just want to hold you for however long we have left together."

I nod, knowing that if I tried to talk, I'd cry.

Aiden's lips graze my bruised cheek, and moving up to my forehead, he presses a firmer kiss there.

I've created this little box of memories deep inside me, and I'm stuffing it full of Aiden.

There is one more memory I'd like before we go our separate ways.

Just one.

After I've showered, I find Aiden standing in the dark lounge, staring out the window.

"Hey," I whisper. I don't want to disturb the night.

"Hey," he whispers back, turning to face me.

"What time will you be leaving?" I ask, needing to know just how long we have left together.

"At five am," he answers.

Oh, that's really early.

He reaches forward, and taking hold of my hand, he tugs me toward him.

"When are you leavin'?" he asks as he wraps his arms around me.

"Wednesday," I answer, then quickly add, "I don't know when I'll be back."

"I'm not stupid, Emma. I feel the goodbye when it's hittin' me right in the gut. You're not plannin' on comin' back, are you?"

I drop my head to his chest, and I can't keep the tears from falling because this is killing me. He holds me, but he offers no words of comfort. There are none for how much it hurts to say goodbye to him.

When the last broken sigh shudders through me, he frames my blotched face, and I almost start up again.

"Please Emma, will you let me make love to you?" his voice cracks and I watch as a tear rolls down his cheek.

I nod because I want my last memory of my time here to be of Aiden and not everything else.

He lifts me to him, and walk us to his room. Placing me gently on my back, he lies down on top of me and kisses me with an unwavering passion.

Needing him to remove Katia's touch from my skin, I break the kiss and pull my shirt over my head, before shoving my slacks off. My eyes never leave Aiden as he strips out of his own clothes.

When he rolls a condom on, it's a reminder that I'll have to go for tests once I'm home. Just to be safe.

Shoving the awful thought to the back of my mind, I reach for Aiden. I wrap an arm around his neck as he takes hold of my hips, and pushes me back down.

My heart races to my throat, and I feel a twinge of anxiety as Aiden settles between my legs.

But then our eyes meet, and all my fears and doubts fade away as he says, "You're mine, Emma. No matter how far apart we are, you'll always be mine."

I said I wouldn't, but I can't hold back the words. "I love you, Aiden," I whisper, barely audible to myself.

His whole body tenses over mine.

"What did you say?" His eyes darken with desperation. "Say it again."

"I love you," I whisper breathlessly, my heart pounding in my ears.

He crushes his mouth to mine, our tongues twisting feverishly. He breaks away and moves down my body, trailing kisses over my breasts, paying particular attention to the bruised parts.

He slides one hand down and cups me, and I want to cry at how good it feels, how safe and right.

"I need you inside me," I beg near tears. "Please."

This isn't about getting to orgasm, but instead, just knowing Aiden still wants me – to feel him consume every broken part of me.

Taking hold of my knee, he lifts it to his hip.

"Emma," he whispers as his cock presses to my opening, "I love you." His hips move forward, and he fills me slowly. "I won't let the ocean between us keep you from me."

CHAPTER 31

AIDEN

After she fell asleep, I ended up crying against her hair like a fucking baby. I can't even begin to try and work through the pain that's eating me alive.

Slipping quietly out of bed so I won't wake Emma, knowing she hasn't been sleeping well, I leave the room to call Zac.

"Mornin'," he answers on the second ring. "How're you holdin' up?"

"Still standin'," I reply. "I need to ask a favor."

"Anythin'."

"Emma's leavin' tomorrow. Can you cover for me? I won't be worth shit at work. I need to be with her."

"Of course, you don't even have to explain."

"I'll see you Thursday."

"Good luck. Call me if you need anythin'."

I drop the phone on the counter and stare at the apartment where my life changed irrevocably.

We stayed in bed yesterday, just holding and loving each other.

Today, I have to say goodbye to the woman I love.

When she puts her bags at the door, my gut twists. I can't even look at the damn thing. I've been sitting in the living room while she packed. I can't beg, and I can't think of any more ways to keep her here.

"Aiden." I nod and get up. My gut is raw as if someone has taken a grater to it. "I'll take the bus."

"I'm takin' you," I growl, unable to control the hurt crashing through me.

"I don't want to put you through that."

I take a deep breath to calm down. I don't want our last words to be in anger.

"I'm takin' you, Em," I say much gentler than before.

"Thank you," she says, and she smiles, trying to be strong.

I load her bags into the car and turn to her, my movements jerky.

"I've put my numbers on your phone, my email address, Skype address, everythin'," I say. I know long distance doesn't work. I've seen relationships go to shit in the army over and over.

"Thank you," she says again, but her smile falters. "Will you email me a photo of you?"

My eyes start to burn as a tear rolls down her cheek.

"Send me one, too." My voice is hoarse as I have to swallow my own tears back.

I open the car door. There's no delaying the inevitable anymore.

As we both get in the car, I realize we don't have a photo of the two of us together. I quickly mount my phone to the holder on the dash. Opening the camera function, I press record.

I turn to Emma, and framing her face, I kiss her with all of my love, all of my sorrow, and all of my fucking determination to get her back.

339

"This is not goodbye, Em. You're comin' back to me."

She stares deep into my eyes, then says, "I love you so much, Aiden."

I soak in her words, needing to believe that she loves me enough to fight for us.

After stopping the recording, I forward it to Emma and then start the car.

We drive in a heavy silence, and as if we're not in enough pain, the worst song possible comes on the radio. I reach to turn it off, but Emma lunges forward, and, taking hold of my hand, she holds it in both of hers on her lap.

She cries silently as *Almost Lover,* by *A Fine Frenzy* rips me to shreds.

At the airport, I'm completely dazed with pain. I go in with her and walk her to the gates. I pull her to me and hold her too tight. I kiss her too hard.

And my heart shatters, my soul disappears back into the hole it's been in for the past four years.

"I'm going to miss you so much," she whispers into my chest.

"I love you so fuckin' much it hurts." It hurts to breathe.

She pulls back, and my arms fall to my sides.

"When I'm standing on the beach, and I look at the ocean." Her voices cracks as a tear slips down her cheek. "I know you'll be on the other side along with my whole heart."

The gaping hole in my chest widens as she turns and walks away from me.

CHAPTER 32

AIDEN

I thought coming home to Lyman would make me feel better, but it doesn't. It's been the longest day of my life, not being able to talk to Emma.

Her flight left at six yesterday evening which means she should be landing any time now.

I'm just glad the fucking day is over, and I can leave work. By the time I walk into the house and head up to my personal office, another hour has gone by. I sit down and open my laptop.

I start an email to Emma, and first add photos of myself. I sure as hell don't want her to forget me.

Em,

I keep hoping I'll wake up and it will all be a nightmare.

They say people come into your life so you can learn from them and they from you. There's still so much I want to learn from you.

I hate the time difference. It sucks.

I miss you so damn much.

Loving you, Angel.

Aiden.

I press send before I rattle on about the damn weather that's starting to turn cold.

I open the case file so I can get lost in work, and just after ten my phone rings. Feeling miserable I almost don't answer. Glancing at where it's vibrating on the desk, I dart forward to grab it when I see Emma's name.

"Emma?" Her name rushes over my lips.

"Hey, am I bothering you?" she asks. She still has to ask? Doesn't she know my world revolves around her?

"Of course not," I assure her, taking the stairs down to the den. "Isn't it four A.M. there by you?" I ask.

"Yeah, I'm going to bed now. I wanted to phone you first." She sounds exhausted, and I stop in the middle of the room.

"Why are you going to bed so late?" I ask.

"I had to get a connecting flight from Johannesburg to Cape Town. I've also been sitting with Chloe just catching up."

"How was your day?" she asks, trying to change the subject. "Have you been assigned to a new case yet?"

"I want to talk about you," I say, ignoring her question. "Not about work. Are you in bed yet?" I ask.

"Yeah, Chloe's cat is giving me the evil eye because I've taken his spot."

I smile. "Do you like cats?"

"I do," she admits. "Do you like cats or dogs?"

"Dogs. I don't understand how cats work. They're like women."

Emma's laughter fills my ear, and I close my eyes so I can absorb it.

"Such a guy thing to say," she teases.

"Last time I checked I was a guy," I can't help but tease her back.

"Oh, definitely. I can vouch for that."

I let out a burst of laughter. "If you were here, I'd remind you."

This is the hard part. Hearing Emma's voice but not being able to touch her.

"You owe me an email," I add quickly before the conversation can get all heated.

"You sent me one?" I hear her move.

"Yeah, you can read it when you wake up. Get some sleep, Em."

"I miss you already," she whispers.

"I'll talk to you tomorrow." I swallow the emptiness down that's already threatening to overwhelm me, and we haven't ended the call yet.

"Okay. I hope you have a good night's sleep."

I close my eyes. "Night, Em."

I don't know how to give up, so I sit down, open my laptop, and I start to research visas, marriage licenses and how the hell to get her back.

CHAPTER 33

EMMA

I make Chloe some breakfast, hoping she will eat. I have to admit, the two of us make a pretty pathetic pity party.

I place the bowl with muesli and yogurt in front of her. "You have to eat."

"I know. I just don't have an appetite," Chloe says, but takes a bite to please me. Once she's swallowed it down, she asks, "What are your plans for today?"

"I'm just going to visit my gran, then I'll be back. Is there something you want to do?"

"I need to clear out Mom's closet so you'll have space for your stuff." Her eyes tear up, and she sags back against the couch.

Chloe's so lost without her mom, and I don't know how to help her. Her brown hair hangs listlessly around her face, and the usual spark has gone from her eyes.

"You don't have to do that. I don't need a lot of space."

"It needs to be done," she whispers.

"I'll help as soon as I'm back from my gran. Why don't you take a relaxing bubble bath while I'm gone?"

"Is that your way of telling me I smell?" Her lips twitch at the corner as if she were going to smile but doesn't have the energy to.

"Yeah. Even Kit is avoiding you," I tease.

"Where is Kit?" she says, glancing around the flat.

"Claiming the bed. He's not happy sharing with me."

"Poor cat. Kit misses my mom too. He was more her cat than mine."

I close the distance between us and sit down next to her. Placing my arm around her shoulders, I give her a hug.

She rests her head against my chest, then says, "You've changed. I couldn't come near you before you left, now you're hugging me."

I don't comment on her observation, but after a moment's silence she whispers, "Do you miss him?"

My shoulders slump as the tears push up. Being so far away from Aiden is unbearable.

Chloe lifts her head, and when she sees my face, she immediately pulls me back into a hug.

"I'm sorry I asked you to come," she apologizes.

"Don't be. Aiden and I couldn't last forever," I say as I wipe my eyes.

"Why not?"

I get up and looking out the window to where the ocean lies, I whisper, "Because there's an ocean between us."

I walk to the village where Gran lives. I need to see the only person I consider family. I've missed her terribly.

She has a neat little one-bedroom flat in a retirement village not too far from Chloe's. My grandmother is a stubborn, independent, God-fearing woman, and I hope I can become half the woman she is. I feel guilty for not seeing her as much as I would've liked to.

I get buzzed in, and she beams when she sees me.

"Emma-dear," her smile is so wide. I really should've come sooner. "What a nice surprise."

"Hey, Gran." I hold her tightly as I soak in her love. I feel guilty for forgetting about her. Aiden doesn't even know about her.

"Come in. Let's have a cup of tea."

I follow her into her flat and take in all her mementos. She has a picture of me above her TV. I frown. "Where did you get the photo of me, Gran?"

"I made your mother give it to me," she says, chuckling. "The bloody wench has so many, she can spare me one of my own granddaughter. I wanted something. I wanted to see your beautiful face after you just up and left me."

"I'm sorry." That's all I can say.

She taps on the seat next to her. "You went and had yourself an adventure, now, did you?" she asks. Then she folds her hands together and settles in, waiting for me to tell her.

Sitting down, I smile blushingly. "I did." I fish my phone out of my pocket and bring Aiden's photo up. "I met a guy." I turn the screen so she can see him. I watch how she fumbles for her glasses and nudges them onto her nose, then she stares long and hard at him.

"Oh… he looks like a charming young fellow." She slips her glasses off, and I glance down at his photo. It's one where it looks like someone caught him sitting at his desk and called to him. He's leaning back in his seat, glancing at the photographer. The reason I like it is that I can see his eyes and the color of them, really well.

"He is," I say, deep in thought.

"And now, love?" she asks.

I let out a deep sigh. "And now I'm here, and he's there, and there's not much to do about it." I smile at her. "How are you? I feel horrible for leaving you."

"You're young. I expect you to go and have fun," Gran scolds me. "I have a new neighbor. A bloody old nagging man. He wakes up nagging and goes to sleep nagging," she huffs, and I can't keep back the burst of laughter. She's adorable when she starts in on her neighbors.

"Every second day he's found a new religion, and he drives me up the bloody wall with it. Today, he's a Jehovah's Witness. Crazy old fart."

I sit smiling as she brings me up to speed on the happenings of her little village.

And then, as if I haven't been feeling bad enough, she says, "And the other day I was cooking. The bloody pot fell on my foot. It wasn't that bad, though, only a bruise," she says.

"What? Let me see." I drop to my knees at Gran's feet and start tugging her slippers off.

"It's looking so much better already," she says. "Just a little purple still."

I caress her foot gently. It doesn't look too bad.

Seeing how dry her skin is, I ask, "Do you have some lotion, Gran?"

I get up to go and look in her bathroom.

"On the side of the bath, dear," she calls from the small lounge.

After I fetch it, I sit back down in front of her. I place a pillow on my lap and gently lift her feet onto it. Then I squirt some into my hand and warm it a little.

"He's a detective," I say, as I start to massage the lotion into her frail skin. "He's so handsome and caring, you'd really approve of him. I wish you could meet him."

"Your granddad was a handsome fellow. Oh, he had the girls running after him," she says, a sweet smile playing around her lips. She always gets that smile when she tells me stories of her past. "But I made him work hard. I sure did." She closes her eyes, and I concentrate on a particular spot by her ankle. "Oooh… that's nice."

Yeah, look at me who hates touching people rubbing my gran's feet.

"I have to go look for work. I don't know what, though. I'm not sure I want to be a nurse." I tell her what's been weighing heavy on my shoulders.

"Why don't you pop in at the office here? They need someone to help. At least it's a start until you figure out what you'd like to do. I'd get to see you every day then," she says.

"I'll pop in when I've finished here, Gran. From now on, I'm going to spend more time with you. We see each other far too little," I say.

It's just like Aiden said: time is precious, and Gran isn't getting any younger. I don't know how much time I have left with her.

When I leave her, I go to the office to see about the nursing position. They ask me to bring in proof of my qualifications. I doubt I'll get it without any experience, though. On the way to the gate, I stop to help an elderly man move his chair into the sun.

I'd like to work with the elderly. They're often rejected by family and forgotten by life.

I'll fit in here.

***

Walking home, I wonder what Aiden's doing, and whether he'd mind if I phoned him now. It's just past twelve here. That would make it around six A.M. by him. He shouldn't be at work yet.

I press dial, waiting while it rings. Nerves start to nibble at my insides. With every ring, my stomach clenches more, and I fumble to cut the call. I take a deep, shaky breath. I can't just call him anymore. He's not mine to phone whenever I feel like it. I need to learn how to let him go.

When my phone starts to ring, I jump, staring at his name flashing on my screen.

"Hey," I answer, feeling anxious.

"Hey, you," he greets back. "I'm just pluggin' you in so I can drive, give me a sec'." I listen to him moving, and a smile spreads across my face. I can picture him getting into the car. "There we go, we're all set. So, what have you been up to?" he asks. I hear the car roar to life.

"I went to visit my gran," I tell him, my smile growing wider. "She thinks you're charming."

"She does? You told your gran about me?"

He sounds pleased, happy even.

"I did, and I'm applying for a position at her village. There's a nursing position open she told me about. We'll have to see how that turns out."

"You are?" his voice drops a bit, or it could be my imagination.

"I love elderly people. I think I'll like it there," I admit.

"Where are you? I hear cars," he asks, changing the subject of my career.

"I'm walking home, talking to you," I say, looking at the houses around me.

"I'll keep you company then," he says.

"I wanted to hear your voice," I admit, not knowing if that is wrong. I don't want to cause Aiden any more pain.

"I miss you, Emma," he says. I hear him open the car door.

And then I hear a woman in the background, "Aiden, this is a surprise. Come in, darlin'."

"Give me a sec'," he calls back to her.

"You have to go, I understand." The words tear from my throat because it still hurts so much to say goodbye.

"Love you, Em."

"Love you more," I say, and hanging up I run up the road, just wanting to get back to the flat.

CHAPTER 34

AIDEN

I cannot believe how much red tape there is. It's like the world is conspiring to keep us apart, but I won't let that stop me. I meet with the consulate twice to make sure I have all the facts straight. There will be a lot of interviews once we're back. People marrying just to get into the country are making my life hell.

What's worse is Zac and Wyatt not taking no for an answer. They've decided we're going out for breakfast.

I'm not in the mood for anything that doesn't involve Emma.

I grab my car keys and phone as I stalk off to go endure a morning of torture with my brothers.

I pick up Zac and drive to Wyatt's apartment.

"Have you decided when you'll go?" Zac asks.

"Next week, I hope. Don't tell Wyatt, he'll tell Mom, and she'll ask questions, and I don't want to talk about it right now. I want to get it all sorted out first," I say, glaring at him for extra effect.

"I won't tell. Where are we havin' breakfast?" Zac asks as I pull up to Wyatt's.

"I don't care where. Y'all can decide. Will you take over drivin'? I want to call Emma."

"Sure," Zac says.

Thankfully he's been very understanding the past week.

I get out and walk around the car, taking out my phone. Climbing in the passenger side, I call Emma.

"And now?" Wyatt asks, getting into the car.

"Aiden's phonin' Emma, so be quiet," Zac answers for me.

"Seriously, Aiden. Just for one day give the girl a break," Wyatt says from the back. I'm about to snap at him when the phone starts to ring, saving his butt.

"Hi," Emma's voice suddenly comes over the line.

"Hey, Em. How's your day?" I ask.

359

"I made a mess of Chloe's hair," she says, and I can hear she's trying not to laugh.

"This is not a mess," I hear Chloe shout from somewhere in the apartment. "It's a bloody natural disaster! I'm heading to the hairdresser. See ya."

Emma's laughter fills my ear, and I smile as it warms my body.

"How's your morning so far?" Emma asks when it's finally quiet on her side.

"I'm on my way to have breakfast with Zac and Wyatt," I reply.

"Hey, Emma," Zac calls out.

I hear her chuckle. "Tell Zac I say hello."

Before I can say something else, Emma says, "There's someone at the door. Give me a second."

"Sure."

I hear as she opens the door, and then the phone drops to the floor.

"No!" Emma says sharply. "Leave. You're not welcome here."

"Is that the way you greet your parents." I hear her mother's cold voice.

"Fuck, no," I whisper as dread fills my veins.

"What?" Zac asks. I hold my hand up so I can hear what's happening.

"Get out!" Emma screams, and I can hear scuffling.

I swear I can hear breathing come over the line, then, "I told you she's mine," her mother sneers.

"If you hurt her –"

"You're going to what?" She chuckles, and the sound alone sends chills racing down my spine then the line goes dead.

"Pull over," I hiss through clenched teeth.

The car has barely stopped before I'm out and running. I have to let it out somehow. I've let her down just like her dad.

I didn't protect her.

Zac catches up to me, and taking me down to the ground, he wraps his arms around me from behind.

My shout echoes over the field as I try to ease some of my raging emotions.

CHAPTER 35

EMMA

"Here I was worried about you, and you were shacking up with this..." Mom walks into the bathroom and throws my phone in the toilet. "*Commoner*," she says as she turns back to me.

"You need to leave. You're not welcome here," I say again, knowing she won't listen to me.

Dad's right outside having a cigarette. Keeping that in mind, I slowly inch closer to the kitchen. I just need a weapon.

"Class and culture are important," she continues, ignoring my request for her to leave. She starts to look around Chloe's place, picking at things as if they're dirty. "You don't know what the children will be like."

Her mouth pulls down with disapproval as she wipes her fingers over the coffee table.

"Mom," I whisper, my voice hoarse, "He's not like that. He's gentle. He's caring." I finally make it to the block of knives next to the microwave and grab the biggest one.

"Aiden is everything you're not," I say, holding the knife in front of me.

"Next you'll be telling me you're off to marry him," she sneers, and as she turns around, her eyes lock on the knife. "Are you going to use that on your own mother?"

As she takes a step forward, I square my shoulders and give her a look of warning.

"I'm not the same person you used to abuse," I growl. "I've met the devil face to face, and you're nothing compared to her. I'm not afraid of you. You have no control over me anymore."

Her mouth sets in a grim line. "Is this *him* speaking? Did *he* brainwash you?"

"This is me sick and fucking tired of your shit. Get out, or I will use this. I swear I will."

"Did you stop taking your pills?" she asks, looking for a reason because she can't believe that I could possibly stand up for myself.

"Leave. Now," I grind the words out.

Suddenly Dad opens the door, popping his head in. "Lovey, Chloe's car just pulled up. Time to go."

I can't believe he was keeping watch for her.

"This is not over," Mom sneers.

I let out a breath of relief as I watch them go.

Chloe comes rushing through the door, her eyes wide with fear. "Emma! I couldn't get an appointment. Just as well. Was that your crazy mother I saw leaving?"

"Yes," I say, still holding the knife.

Chloe spots the weapon and her eyebrows dart into her hairline.

"Sorry," I whisper, dropping the knife onto the counter. I walk to the bathroom and fish my poor phone out of the toilet. I try to switch it on, but it's dead.

"She killed my phone," I say as I walk back to where Chloe is still standing looking a little shocked.

"Sunshine," she says, sounding emotional.

My eyes dart to her face and when I see the proud look in her eyes a smile pulls at my mouth.

"You totally stood up for yourself."

"I did." The impact of what I did, finally hits. "It felt so good."

Chloe rushes to me, and we hug each other as some peace returns to my battle-weary soul.

I beat one of my demons.

CHAPTER 36

AIDEN

The last day has been a total blur. Right after the call I packed and got my ass to the airport to catch a flight to South Africa.

I didn't even last two weeks without Emma.

I've tried calling her, but it keeps going to voicemail. I can kick my own ass for not taking Chloe's number.

A million thoughts torment me. I have no idea whether Emma is okay or not.

Now that I'm sitting in the back of a cab, in a foreign country, I don't take in any of my surroundings. I just want to get to Emma. I need to see that she's okay. I'm going out of my fucking mind with worry.

The cab driver drops me off in front of some luxury apartments. I run up the stairs, and almost bust the door down.

"Hold your damn horses," I hear Chloe's familiar voice yell from the other side. She yanks the door open, and when she sees me, her scowl falls from her face. "Aiden?"

"Hi, Chloe," I say, then get straight to the point. "Where's Emma? Is she okay?"

"She's fine," she says, still in shock from seeing me. "What are you doing here? Emma didn't say you were coming."

"She doesn't know I'm here."

"Come in," she gasps once she realizes that I'm still standing outside.

"We were on a call when her mother showed up here. Is Emma okay?" I ask again.

My eyes search through the living room for any sign of Emma.

"She's really okay. She chased her mother away." Chloe walks to a huge set of floor to ceiling windows. "Come here."

I walk to her, and she points at something. "There she is. On the rocks."

I see her blonde hair waving in the wind, and for the first time, I can breathe easily again.

"How do I get to her from here?"

"Take the stairs down, then turn right. There are two more flights of stairs. Cross the main road, and you'll come out by those robots."

"Robots?" I ask.

"The set of traffic lights."

"Oh, right," I say, then remember my manners. "It's nice to meet you in person. I just need to get to Emma."

"Go," she laughs. "Go get your girl."

I jog out of the apartment and try not to break my neck as I rush down the stairs. I have to wait for cars to pass before I can cross the road.

I only slow down when I reach the beach. Walking to the cluster of rocks, I hear Emma shout over the waves, "I love you, Aiden."

"I love you, Emma," I say when I finally reach her.

She spins around so fast, she almost loses her balance. I dart forward and grab hold of her.

THE OCEAN BETWEEN US – Michelle Heard

She grabs hold of my shirt, then spreads her hands over my chest.

"Aiden," she whispers. "You're here."

"I told you I'd come. I'm not leavin' without you."

Her eyes start to shine with unshed tears, and the smile I have missed so much spreads over her face.

She shrieks as she throws her arms around my neck. "I can't believe you're here. You crossed an ocean for me."

"Dammit, I missed you," I whisper into her silky hair as I practically squash her body to mine.

I take a deep breath, filling my lungs with her scent.

"Oh, God, please be real," she murmurs as she starts to press kisses to my neck and up my jaw. I turn my face to her and grin when she crushes her mouth to mine.

The grin quickly fades as her tongue swipes over my bottom lip. I kiss her with all the longing I've felt since she's left.

I pull her face away and look down at the happy tears. Cupping her cheeks, I wipe them away with my thumbs, then press a soft kiss to her swollen lips.

"Hi, Emma." I just want to hold her, and I do. This is what I flew thousands of miles for – to feel her arms around me.

"You're here, you're really here," she whispers as she clings to me.

She lets go, and I drink in her beautiful face like a man dying of thirst.

"Why haven't you answered your phone?"

"My mom drowned it," she says. "I tried to call your work from Chloe's phone, but they said you weren't in. But you're here now, so that doesn't matter."

"Yeah, I'm here now."

Keeping my arms around her, I just hold her not wanting to let go.

CHAPTER 37

AIDEN

"Night, Chloe," Emma says as she closes the door.

She turns and again smiles when she sees me lying on her bed.

"Come here," I growl, wanting her something fierce.

She sprints forward and jumps on the bed with laughter bubbling over her lips. Grabbing hold of her, I tuck her under me and smother her laugh with a kiss.

The urgency to be inside her grows until I almost rip her clothes off in my hurry to get her naked.

Our breaths mingle as I help her get my sweats off.

When we're finally naked I kiss my way down her body and pushing open her legs, I bury my face in her pussy, sucking her clit hard.

Glancing up, I suppress a grin as she grabs a pillow and presses it over her face to muffle her groans.

I nip and suck at her until her hips are pushing down on me, then roll on a condom at the speed of light. Not being able to hold off any longer, I crawl back over her, sinking my cock deep inside her body.

I shudder from how amazing it feels. Ripping the pillow from Emma's grip, I throw it to the other side of the bed.

"Finally. Fuckin'. Home," I growl with each hard thrust.

I crush my mouth to hers, swallowing all of her groans as I keep driving my cock into her until her body starts to shudder beneath mine as pleasure takes her.

Not breaking the kiss, I move both my hands down to her ass. As my fingers dig into her flesh, with my chest pressing against her breasts, I thrust as hard and deep as I can, wanting to become one with her. When tingles sizzle down my spine as I empty myself inside of Emma, the pleasure is so intense, it robs me of my breath.

Waking up with Emma in my arms is something I'll never take for granted again.

Not thinking, I only pull on my sweatpants before I open the door to go grab some coffee.

Emma and Chloe stop stalking, and they both stare at me from where they're sitting on the couch.

"What?" I ask.

"Shirt," Emma says as she starts to laugh at Chloe's comical facial expression.

"Don't wear one on my account. I like the view," Chloe teases, then she has to duck as Emma grabs one of the throw pillows and tosses it at her.

I shake my head as I walk back to my bag to grab a shirt.

"Mornin'," I grumble, trying to suppress my smile as I drag the shirt over my head.

"Do you guys have any plans for today?" Chloe asks.

"Do we?" Emma asks as she joins me in the open plan kitchen which has a view of the living room.

She pours me some coffee as I answer, "We do."

THE OCEAN BETWEEN US – Michelle Heard

"I have a date with Netflix," Chloe says, making herself comfortable on the couch.

"What plans do we have?" Emma asks, looking curious.

I glance at Chloe, but she's already lost in a show on Netflix.

"Do you have a car?" I ask.

"No, but I can borrow Chloe's. Why, where do you want to go?"

"Your parents."

Emma's mouth opens, but nothing comes out, then she frowns. "Why?"

"I want to meet her. This fuckin' hold she thinks she has on you, ends today," I say with finality.

She takes a deep breath, then nods. "Okay. You're right. It's time I close this chapter in my life."

"I still have keys to get in," Emma says as we stand outside a large mansion. "I'm not sure if I should use them, or knock."

I can hear how uncomfortable she sounds, and give her hands a squeeze for encouragement.

"Unlock the door, Em," I say, not wanting to even bother with knocking first.

My heart starts to beat adrenaline through my body as she pushes the key into the lock.

I've been ready for this moment since I heard those messages from Emma's mother. Today I'm putting a stop to that crazy bitch.

I push open the door, letting myself inside the mansion - the place that's supposed to be Emma's family home.

Inside it's gloomy and dark, even though it's hardly noon. The house is spotless giving it a cold and clinical feel. You could eat off the floor.

Large pictures are hanging on the walls, and as we walk close by one, I notice they are actually puzzles that have been built and then framed.

She leads me down a passage, and her body starts to grow tense, as her fingers tighten around mine.

When I see the photos on the wall, I clench my jaw to hold back all the rage I feel inside. Graduation photos of a guy, who I assume is her brother. Wedding photos of her parents. Pictures of a happy boy. There are others - they must be of the rest of the family.

I stop and pull Emma close to me as my heart aches for her. There's one of four boys standing around a birthday cake. A little white-haired girl's cherub face peeks out from behind the one boy. She's the most adorable fucking thing I've ever seen.

It's the only photo of Emma on the entire wall.

"You matter to me," I say the words slowly, so she can hear every syllable and know I mean them.

She tries to smile, but gives up, and instead, she leans up to kiss me. I savor it, drinking it in.

The atmosphere is cold as we near an archway to the left of us. Emma moves in front of me as if to protect me, as we step into the kitchen.

"Mom," Emma's tone is cautious. "We need to talk."

"Well, well, look what the cat dragged in," her mother sneers.

Emma glances at me, looking on edge. "Aiden, this is my mother."

I pick up on the fact that Emma doesn't say her mother's first name.

"Mom, this is Aiden Holden."

I'm not here to meet the fucking woman. Taking Emma's hand, I pull her behind me as I take a threatening step forward.

The woman is seated at a large, dark oak table in the middle of the kitchen, with a glass of fucking wine in front of her.

Her mom doesn't move to get up. She glares up at me, her dark eyes filled with hatred.

"Finally we meet... Aiden." She practically spits my name out.

"I'm not here to play your fuckin' games. Where's your husband?" My entire body starts to vibrate with anger.

She arches an eyebrow at me. "Why may I ask?"

"I don't make a habit of repeatin' myself. It's best he's here when I say my piece to y'all."

"Emma, go fetch your dad," the woman orders.

"No," Emma says and she tightens her grip on my hand. "I'm not leaving Aiden's side."

377

"Is that so?" her mom sneers. "Seems you've forgotten your manners while shacking up with *this* man."

I shake my head, and I let out an aggravated chuckle. This woman has some nerve, doing this in front of me.

"You don't want to go there with me," I warn her. "I don't care if you're a woman. I swear, if you disrespect or threaten Emma one more time, I'm gonna lose my shit, and my mama taught me better than that. Now, get your fuckin' husband."

Lucky for her the fucker comes around the corner. My first impression of Emma's father is that he looks like a weak rat. His entire posture is hunched in. This man doesn't have a backbone to speak of.

"I don't really care what y'all's names are," I start. I take a deep, calming breath as I glare at Emma's mother. "If you were a man, I'd beat the shit out of you. You can be so fuckin' glad you didn't abuse Emma in my backyard. You'd be rottin' behind bars."

I take a step towards her dad, and he cowers backward.

"You're a fuckin' coward that's a disgrace to your force. I'm reportin' you first thing I can because you shouldn't be trusted with people's lives. You can't even protect your own daughter against your insane as fuck wife."

Emma's mother lets out a disgruntled snort while the father appears to have enough self-preservation to at least look scared.

"Don't come after Emma. Don't phone her. Don't fuckin' contact her in any way. If you so much as step foot on U.S. soil, I will fuckin' end you." I lock eyes with Emma's mother. "You don't want to see what I'll do to y'all in my country."

"Don't you threaten me in my own house," her mother hisses as she stands up.

"Lady, that wasn't a threat. It's a fuckin' promise," I growl, matching her step for step as she comes toward me.

When we're in touching distance from each other, she looks up at me with contempt.

"I should give you the beating your mother obviously never did," she snarls, and it makes fumes of her wine-drenched breath waft in my face.

Clenching my jaw, I take another step closer, putting my chest right in her face. Fuck, I've never wanted to hurt someone as badly as I do this woman.

"Try," I growl. "I fuckin' dare you."

"Lovey," Emma's dad almost whimpers, his voice trembling with fear as he leans forward, and taking hold of his wife's elbow he tries to pull her away from me. He looks like he's about to piss his pants while his eyes stay glued to me.

She yanks her arm free from him, her hate-filled eyes never leaving mine.

Taking a step forward, Emma takes hold of my hand, and says, "I have something to say." It's the first time I've heard her voice so tense with anger.

Emma's mother glares at her, her eyes take on a beady look.

Emma's dad quickly moves forward. "Calm down, lovey," he whispers to his wife.

"Don't tell me what to do! This is *my* house, and here *my* word is law. Emma is *my* daughter, and he's not going to poison her against me," she shrieks at him.

Pointing a shaking finger at Emma, she sneers, "Are you going to let him talk that way to me?"

Instead of answering the question, Emma asks, "Why? Just tell me why you abused me. What did I do to make you hate me so much?"

Her mother lets out a bitter bark of laughter. "I never abused you. Don't be so dramatic."

I fist my hands so I won't do something I'll regret.

"You've always been so temperamental. You wouldn't even let me breastfeed you as a baby."

My mouth drops open at the pathetic reason she gives Emma for all the hell she caused her.

"And that justified you hurting me?" Emma asks, sounding as dumbfounded as I feel.

"You look like your good-for-nothing father. From the moment you were born, I no longer existed. He only had time for his precious little girl. I thank God every day that Byron takes after me, but you're a constant reminder of how I had to compete with my own daughter for the love of my husband. "

Confused I glance between Emma and her mother, because she looks nothing like her pathetic father.

"I was a baby!" Emma cries. "I can't even remember him."

Fuck, now I'm really not following who they're talking about.

Emma continues, "Where's my father now?"

"Oh, he died not long after I took you and left. He drove off Van Reenen's pass during a breakfast run with his motorbike club."

"This man isn't even your father?" I ask as I point to the sack of shit hiding behind Emma's mother. Now it all makes sense.

"No, he's my stepfather," Emma says, looking exhausted from the confrontation.

There's nothing more I have to say to these people. I tug at Emma's hand to get her attention. "Let's go, Em. You can't reason with insanity."

"Wait," she whispers. There's no emotion on her face as she looks at her mother. "I don't want to hate you, because it means I will have to think of you, and I never want to think of you again. I'm going to forget you. You're an unhappy, old woman and that's really just sad. Wallow in your bitterness, and when you think of me just remember that I am *nothing* like you."

"We're done here," I say as her mother sucks in an offended breath.

As I pull Emma toward the hallway so we can get out of this hellish house, her mother grabs hold of her arm.

Emma twists around, yanking free from her mother's hold, and with a heaving chest, she practically growls, "Don't touch me."

"I'm your mother! I own you," the woman shrieks, her voice shrill with anger.

"You're not my mother. You've done nothing to deserve that title," Emma snaps, then she turns her back on them and pulls me down the hallway.

Stepping outside, I'm so fucking proud of my girl.

CHAPTER 38

EMMA

I slide in behind the steering wheel as Aiden climbs in the passenger seat. Leaning over the handbrake, I bring my hands to his jaw and crush my mouth to his.

There are so many emotions whirling inside of me. Pride, triumph, confidence, and a certainty that I can face my fears and beat them.

And there is immense admiration and gratitude for Aiden.

The man who taught me the meaning of love.

It's not just a four letter word. Love strikes like lightning, unexpected and undeniable. It doesn't come with demands or conditions. Love doesn't break you down, but instead, lifts you up, making you stronger, because you've finally found someone to believe in.

I try to convey all of this in a single kiss, and as I pull back, and I see the same feelings on his face, I whisper, "You're my everything."

Wanting to be alone with Aiden, I've brought us to a secluded spot which overlooks the ocean.

Unsure of what will happen next, I turn in my seat, and ask, "How long are you staying for?"

"Come here," he says, instead of answering my question.

Climbing over to his side of the car, I straddle him, resting my hands against his chest.

My eyes search his for answers, as he places his hands on my sides.

He pulls me closer, until I'm flush with his chest, then says, "I only have a few days before I have to get back to work."

I knew he couldn't stay long, but it still hurts to hear.

"Come back with me, Emma," he says, his eyes pleading with me.

"I wish I could," I whisper as I press my face into the crook of his neck to hide my heartache from him.

"Give me a reason why you can't," he says, as he tilts his head forward, pressing a kiss to my neck.

"I can't afford it. I don't have a visa. I have to find work so I can take care of myself," I list the main reasons.

"Those are all problems I can take care of," he argues.

Lifting my head, I let out a hopeless sigh. "Even if we get a visa, I can't let you pay for the plane ticket. It costs a fortune. And what will I do in Lyman? To apply for a work permit, I need a job."

"Emma," he says earnestly as he frames my face, "stop thinkin' about the financial aspect." Looking deep into my eyes, he declares, "I love you. Forget about all the reasons why we can't be together and focus on why we deserve a future with each other. I want to marry you. I've already applied for a marriage license."

My lips part with surprise when the words leave his mouth.

"You really want to marry me?" I ask, a hopeful smile wavering around my lips.

"This is not how I wanted to propose to you," he says, the corner of his mouth tipping up into that sexy smile I love so much. "Will you marry me, Em? Will you become my wife, and allow me to provide for you, to protect you, to cherish you?"

"I want to say yes with my whole heart, but I have nothing to offer you in return," I admit my fear to him.

"Emma, I just want you. I want you to give me mornings where I can wake up with you in my arms. I want you to give me nights, where I can lose myself in your body. I need to know I'll be comin' home to you after dealing with the worst of the world."

I press a kiss to his parted lips, savoring his words as my heart almost bursts with happiness. "Yes, Aiden," I whisper against his mouth.

Meeting his eyes again, I quickly add, "Though, I'm not sure I'll get used to you providing for everything. I still want to work."

"I'm fine with that but until you find something, let me take care of you," he says.

"Okay," I whisper as I inch closer for another kiss.

Aiden pulls back before I can seal my mouth to his. "So you'll come home with me?"

I nod, a happy smile pulling at my lips. "You're my home, Aiden. Wherever you go, I'll follow."

"Thank fuck, I was about to kidnap you."

My burst of laughter is smothered as Aiden pulls me into his body, showing me just how thankful he is.

CHAPTER 39

AIDEN

I know it's only five A.M. back home, but I phone Zac while Emma's helping Chloe make something for lunch.

He answers after a few rings. "Mornin', how are things that side?"

"Hey, Zac. It got ugly. Damn that mother of hers is a real piece of work."

"Where y'all at now?" he asks.

"We're at Chloe's. I have to find out where the embassy is so we can get Emma's visa sorted." That's the only thing I need to worry about right now.

"So, I was thinkin'," he says. "We have to request Emma to appear as a witness. They have to let her come because she's part of an on-goin' investigation."

389

Everything else fades away but Zac, and what he's telling me.

"Are you tellin' me to fuckin' bring her in?" I ask, making sure I heard him right.

"Do you have a better idea, Aiden?"

No, I don't. I don't have one that will get her into the U.S. tomorrow. Everything else will take time.

"No," I snap, feeling cornered.

"I'll get Jake on it first thing. We'll subpoena Emma as a material witness. I'll email it to you as soon as I have it. I should get it this afternoon. You can get her back here with it. Just keep that in mind," he says.

"Okay. Talk to you later."

Not mentioning my talk with Zac to Emma, I wait until the subpoena comes through just after four.

I walk to where Emma's packing dishes away in the kitchen. "Em, can we take a walk?" I ask.

"Sure." She places the last cup in the cupboard. "Let me just tell Chloe."

Once we're walking down the beach, I say, "I have a way to get you home."

I wait, and she doesn't say anything, her smile doesn't waver.

"I'm going to subpoena you as a witness to testify against Colton and Katia. That way, they have to let you back into the U.S. I didn't want to. The other girls' testimonies were enough to put them away, but this is the only way to get you back on U.S. soil."

"Okay," she says. Just like that with no argument. "Can I ask a favor, Aiden?"

"Anythin'," I say quickly. I'm waiting for the outburst. This means Emma will have to face Colton and Katia in court, and that she'll have to testify. Maybe she doesn't understand.

"Can I see my gran before I go?"

"Of course."

It's surprising how fast things get sorted out when the law gets involved. I can take Emma home. Finally.

It's all I can think about as we're driving to her gran's place. We pull up to a quaint retirement village, and I have to admit that I feel apprehensive about meeting the woman who raised Emma's mother.

THE OCEAN BETWEEN US – Michelle Heard

A petite grey-haired woman with a kind face opens the front door. She looks nothing like I expected.

"I heard what happened, dear," her gran says, and Emma goes straight into her arms. They hold each other. "She's just stubborn, that one. She'll come around, you'll see."

"She can come around all she wants, Gran. I'm finished with her." I can hear the finality in Emma's voice. Then her face lights up again. "I want to introduce you!" She turns to me and holds out her hand. I take a step closer.

This is very different from what went down at her folks' house.

"This is my Aiden."

My heart fucking melts. *Her Aiden.*

"So this is the young fellow." Her gran's sharp eyes give me a once over. "Even better looking in person." She winks at me. "Give me a hug."

"Pleasure to meet you," I say as I lean in to hug Emma's gran. I can see who Emma really takes after. They have the same green eyes.

We go inside, and things get emotional when Emma sits down next to her gran.

"I'm leaving, Gran," Emma whispers as if she's trying to soften the blow.

"It's all good, Emma-dear. My time is almost up, and then you would've been alone with that old hag of a daughter of mine. But now I can rest in peace knowing that you'll be taken care of."

Her gran looks at me. "You *will* take good care of my granddaughter, won't you?"

"Yes, ma'am."

A sad look crosses her features, "Do a better job than I have."

"Why didn't you help Emma? Why did you allow your daughter to abuse her?" I ask, needing to know the answer.

"Abuse breeds abuse," she murmurs as her eyes glaze over with memories. "My husband wasn't a kind man. He liked the bottle too much. By the time he passed away... I guess it all became a way of life. I tried to give Emma all the love I knew she wasn't getting at home."

393

She lifts her life-weary eyes to Emma. "I'm sorry I failed you."

Emma hugs her gran, whispering, "I forgive you."

When the emotion passes between them, her gran points to a cabinet. "Look in that box there, dear."

Emma gets the box her gran points to. It's decorated with butterflies and one big dragonfly. She handles it with care. Her gran opens it with old, shaking hands, and takes a book from it.

"I want you to have this while it's still mine to give to you. It's my most precious possession." She hands it to Emma who has a look of awe on her face. She caresses the book.

"It's your bible," Emma whispers.

"My first one. It gave me the strength to get through this life. Soon, I'll be up there watching over you."

"I'm not saying goodbye," Emma chokes.

I start taking deep breaths as my eyes tear up. This is way too emotional for any man to handle.

"Of course not. It's never goodbye for us. I'll see you again."

Dammit. I watch them hold each other. Emma needed this moment with her gran, and I'm glad I could give it to her.

CHAPTER 40

EMMA

The flight back to Lyman was much better with Aiden than flying alone even though we slept a lot.

I've just unpacked my clothes in the main bedroom and sitting on the bed, I stare at everything around me.

This is my new home... *our home.*

The thought settles warmly in my heart.

Even though Aiden asked me to marry him, I'm not sure if it will happen. He hasn't said anything more on the topic, and I don't want to push him. Especially not with the trial looming over our heads.

I have no idea how I'm going to face Katia and Colton. I'll have to tell Aiden what really happened that week because a courtroom is the last place I want him to hear about it.

Aiden comes into the room, and a broad smile spreads across his face. He places his hands on the bed, caging me in.

"You look so good in my room," he says as he leans in to kiss me.

I wrap my arms around his neck, pulling him down on top of me.

I'll tell him tomorrow. Right now I just want to be with him.

CHAPTER 41

AIDEN

Walking into a home where the woman you love is cooking for you while shaking her sexy ass to a tune she's humming, is a fucking amazing feeling.

I stand and watch her stir something before she switches off the stove, and I can't help but grin like a dumbass. I should go lock my gun and badge away before she sees them, but I want to look at her just a little longer. It's been a month since she moved in and the sight of her in my home never gets old.

Our home.

She wipes down the counter and turns slightly. The look is priceless. She's smiling, a content look on her beautiful face.

"Hey, you," I say, and her face lights up even more when she sees me.

"You're home!" she squeals. She runs to me, almost bouncing with delight. My heart swells with love, and I catch her, pressing her to me.

"I missed you," she whispers into my neck.

I hold her tightly, needing to feel her body melt into mine.

"Ow." The word bursts into my neck and I quickly let go of her. She tries to rub her breast without me seeing, but her eyes are on the side of my chest where the holster is.

Dammit! The gun.

"Ahh… give me a sec." I jog up the stairs to lock it away. I can kick myself for not doing it first.

Opening the safe, I unclasp the holster and place the gun inside. Taking my badge off, I hear Emma behind me.

I glance over my shoulder as I close the safe.

"Can I see your badge?"

I hand it over to her, thinking that I've taken down so many men and women who don't deserve to be called humans. But here I'm standing in front of the woman I love, and *she* has the power to take *me* down.

Her fingers wrap around my badge, and her lashes lower over her eyes as she looks at it.

"Detective Holden," she says, and all my blood flows south. She steps closer to me and puts the badge back in my hand. It's a damn miracle I don't drop it when she leans up to my ear. "Where are your handcuffs?"

"My cuffs?" I ask like an idiot, although I'm already reaching for them behind my back. Holding them up with one finger I ask, "Is this what you're lookin' for?"

She gives me a sexy smirk as she takes them from me.

"On the bed," she demands, and I've got to say, I really like where this is heading.

When I sit down on the bed, she flicks her finger towards the headboard. I move back until my back is resting against the pillows.

Emma climbs onto the bed and straddles me, then taking hold of my shirt, she pulls it off.

As Emma tries to figure out how the cuffs work, I suppress my laugh. She finally fastens one around my left wrist then pushes both my hands up to the headboard, where she loops the cuffs behind a bar before cuffing my right wrist.

Emma bites her bottom lip as her eyes sparkle, then scoots down my legs and begins to unbuckle my belt.

When she has me naked and cuffed to the bed, I ask, "You're enjoyin' this, aren't you?"

"Immensely," she whispers as she pushes her jeans and panties down her legs. Drawing her t-shirt over her head, she quickly unclasps her bra before crawling back up to me.

When her fingers wrap around my cock, my lips part on a harsh breath. My eyes dart down as she positions the head of my cock at her entrance. She sinks down on me drawing a hiss from between my teeth.

Damn, it feels amazing as I take her bare for the first time.

She frames my jaw and crushes her mouth to mine as she starts to swivel her hips, grinding down on my cock.

It's so fucking hot I can't keep still. I wrap my hands around the bar and start to thrust my hips up, needing to bury myself deep inside Emma.

Fuck, this is every man's fantasy, and she's all mine.

CHAPTER 42

EMMA

Lying in Aiden's arms, I open my mouth for what must be the tenth time, only to snap it shut again.

The whole day while he was at work I've been planning how to tell him about Katia and Colton, but every time I try, nothing comes out.

"You keep doing that? What do you want to tell me?" he asks, as he rolls onto his side so he can look at me.

Taking his hand, I weave our fingers together and hold them against my thundering heart.

"With the trial coming up," I begin to say, then swallow hard. "I don't want you to hear what happened to me for the first time in a courtroom."

Pressing his forehead against mine, he says, "How about I go first and tell you about Laurie?"

I nod, grateful that he's willing to share something about himself. It will put me more at ease if I'm not the only one talking about my traumatic experience.

"We weren't even on duty." He takes a deep breath, and I curl my fingers tighter around his. "We'd just finished our shift and were headin' home when we stopped at a gas station. Some kids drove by, and they started shootin' up the gas station sign beside our car," he whispers, but I can hear his sorrow in every syllable. "One hit me. The scar you saw. Laurie was shot twice."

He takes a shuddering breath then his lips set in a grim line.

"I tried so fuckin' hard to stop the bleedin'. Laurie bled out on the scene. Never found the kids, either."

Frantically, I search my mind to find the right words to say to him to ease his pain, but I have nothing. Instead, I press a kiss to his fingers, then keep my mouth against them as I close my eyes.

"Tell me what happened?" he whispers as he pulls one hand free from mine. He curls his body around me, his hand going into my hair.

I press my forehead against his chest as I whisper,

"I saw a doctor when I got back to South Africa. They did tests which came back clean." I suck in a deep breath and push through. "Colton held me down. He had his legs locked over mine so I couldn't close them. That's how I got the bruises you saw."

He wraps his arm tighter around me, his hand fisting in my hair.

"Katia cut my clothes off and then she..." my words trail away as the memory makes me shudder with revulsion.

"Did she force herself on you?" Aiden asks, and thankful that I don't have to say the words, I nod against his chest.

He pulls his other hand free from the death grip I have on it and tucks me entirely under him.

He presses kisses to my shoulder, taking shuddering breaths between each one as his body starts to shake.

"I'm so sorry, Em." His voice is hoarse with tears, and hearing his pain makes my own fall.

We comfort each other with soft touches and gentle kisses, and I know the worst is over. I'm not scared of facing Katia and Colton because I know there's nothing they can do to me.

My biggest fear was Aiden rejecting me, but instead, he loved me.

CHAPTER 43

AIDEN

"Did you ever have a boyfriend?" I ask Emma one night while we're sitting in the den.

She stops reading and glances at me.

"Where did that question come from?" she asks as she closes the book.

"I want to know everythin' about you, even the little things," I say as I pull her into my side.

"I had one," she says, then adds, "When I was twelve."

I burst out laughing.

"Damn, my girl started young," I tease her.

"I'll have you know, he was a real looker." She pokes me in the chest with a slender finger. "Blue eyes one could drown in. I was madly in love with the boy."

I take hold of her hand and tug her closer. My eyes drop to her mouth.

"Who taught you to kiss?"

"You're not going to believe me if I say him, are you?" She wrinkles her nose, and it's fucking cute.

I shake my head. "Not a chance."

"My brother's friend. He was kind enough to teach me how to drive, and he was quite the teacher in the back seat of his car."

Her shoulders start to jerk as she struggles to keep in her laughter.

"He took it upon himself to teach you quite a bit."

"He was really kind and considerate," she bursts out laughing.

"Was he now?" I growl, leaning in.

"Uh-huh." She's all smiles as she leans back playfully. I slip my arm around her to keep her from moving.

"Show me," I whisper.

Her eyes lock with mine. They're sparkling with fun.

"Show you?"

"Yeah, show me how this kind friend taught you."

Her eyes dance between my mouth and my eyes. Then she nods, and she starts to lean closer. At first, her lips are feather-soft against mine. Then I feel her fingers brush against my jaw, tentatively, as if she's asking permission to touch me.

She pulls away slightly, her breath hot before she nips at my bottom lip, sending a streak of lightning right down to my cock. I force myself to sit still, to let her show me this, but then she presses her mouth to mine as her hands slip into my hair.

And I fall.

I'll never stop falling.

Her tongue slips slowly over mine, and I groan, wanting more of her. And then she pulls away and smiles as she walks her sexy ass to the stairs leading up to the books.

"You're gonna read now?" I ask, a little too hoarsely.

She's not going to read now. No way that's fucking happening.

"I was thinking about it. Why?"

She is really enjoying this.

"I was thinking something more along the lines of you and me in the bedroom," I say as I get up.

I stalk towards her, but she darts for the hallway, laughing as she glances over her shoulder.

"But I'm not tired," she teases.

She looks in front of her to check for the stairs, and I go for her. I throw her over my shoulder, and Emma lets out a shriek of laughter.

Racing up the stairs and into our room, I drop her on the bed and pin her arms above her head with one of my hands.

I brush a hand down her side, and she squeals, squirming to get out from under me. I straddle her to keep her in place and moving my hand upwards, towards her arm, she starts to thrash with wild laughter.

"Nooooo, please!" she gasps.

She tries to twist her hips under me.

"It's unfair," she shrieks. "You're stronger. You're-" she screams with laughter as I brush my fingers all the way from her breast to her elbow.

"Sorry, my hand slipped," I tease, "I'm not even ticklin' you. I haven't started."

I start back toward her elbow, and she yells, "Stoop! I'll do anything."

I lie down next to her and pull her hands to my chest where I cover them with one of my own.

"Anythin'?"

"Yes." She's nodding, smiling, laughing. It's perfect.

I brush some of the hair from her face, drinking in her happiness.

"Did you know eagles mate for life?" Her eyes are sparkling from all the laughter.

"Yeah."

"I want to make you laugh. I want to make you happy," I say, and she smiles wide.

"You do make me happy."

I pull the ring from my back pocket and bring it up between us.

"For the rest of your life," I whisper. "I want you to be my eagle, Em?"

She takes a deep breath and stares at the ring with wide eyes.

I'm just about to start worrying when she practically throws herself at me, and her musical laughter fills the air.

"Yes." She presses a kiss to my lips then looks at me with so much love, it makes my heart skip a beat. "I'll be your eagle, Aiden," she whispers, promising herself to me.

CHAPTER 44

AIDEN

When I pick Emma up for the hearing, she gives me a nervous smile.

"You're gonna be fine," I say, taking her hand and kissing her fingers.

"I know. You and Zac will be there. I just want to get this over with."

When we get to the courthouse, Zac comes toward us.

"Mornin' Emma. You ready?" Zac smiles at us.

"Yes." The word is clear, but her smile is stiff. I wish she didn't have to do this.

"We won't be able to sit with you because we were the arrestin' officers," he says, and it's the first time I've wanted to slap him upside the head.

413

I forgot about that.

"Okay," she lets the word out on an anxious breath.

I hold Emma outside the room she has to wait in until they call for her.

"I'll be right there, Em. You'll be able to see me throughout it all." I don't want to let her go, but the proceedings are going to start soon. "I love you."

"I love you most," she says. I kiss her hard, wanting to give her all of my strength.

Walking into the courtroom, I take my place beside Zac.

Waiting for it all to start is excruciating torture. Zac elbows me and tips his head to our left. I glance over my shoulder and see Wyatt and Cole taking a seat in the row behind us. We give each other a chin lift. I haven't talked to Cole since all this shit went down. He told Wyatt that he needed some space from the family.

Then Emma comes in with some of the other girls, and I hate that I can't be at her side.

The proceedings start as soon as they line Colton, Katia, and the rest of the clowns up. Then the judge is announced. As Judge Flo Johnston calls the court to order, I suppress a smile. She's a tough cookie who scowls a lot, but fuck, she's fair.

We listen to the prosecutor's opening statement and a summary of the evidence. The first witness is called up. I lean forward, placing my elbows on my knees and I grimace when both the prosecutor and defense attorney practically tear her apart.

When they call for Emma, I straighten in my seat.

She takes the oath and sits down when instructed to. Everything seems okay until the defense attorney circles in on her like a damn wolf.

"Ms. Bowen, please correct me if I'm wrong, but are you not in a relationship with Detective Aiden Holden?"

"I am," she confirms. I can see where this is going.

"So you knew what you were getting' yourself into?" he asks again.

It all goes to shit right there.

Thirty minutes later he's still going at her. When she starts to cry those silent tears of hers, I lean forward, clasping my hands together, so I don't go flying out of the seat and beat the shit out of the fucker.

The defense attorney is out for blood.

The prosecutor keeps saying words like 'relevance', and 'badgering the witness' which doesn't help at all.

Then Emma snaps. "Nothing you say or throw at me makes what they did right! You can stand there and try and make me look like the bad person all you want, but they kidnapped me." She sucks in a breath. "They held me against my will for a week. For a whole week, that woman," she points to Katia.

Sucking in a shuddering breath, Emma glares at the defense attorney.

I want to get up and take her away, but the second I move, Zac's hand comes down hard on my arm.

"She needs to. Don't," Zac whispers.

"She..." Emma looks like she's going to be sick and it's fucking gutting me.

"Do you need a moment, Miss Bowen?" Judge Flo leans forward, surprising me when she shows compassion.

Emma shakes her head. "No, I need to just get it over with." Emma takes a few quick breaths and then the words just come. "Colton held me down while Katia sexually assaulted me."

It feels as if my heart is breaking all over again. I want Emma down from there. I don't want everyone to hear this.

"By sexual assault, you mean what exactly, Ms. Bowen?" The defense attorney asks.

Emma looks at Katia and Colton and as the seconds tick by, I grow tenser.

"She used a replacement for an erection," her voice has lost all emotion.

The blood drains from my face, and I feel Zac grab hold of my shoulder. Whether it's to keep me still or to offer support, I don't know.

"Katia inserted it into herself and me and proceeded to assault me."

"Was that all Katia Peres did?" The defense attorney asks.

Emma locks eyes with the attorney. "A woman who had no right to touch me, bit me until my skin broke. A woman who I never gave any encouragement to, had sex with me. If you mean whether that's *all*, then yes."

The second they excuse her, she walks right out of the courtroom. Ignoring Zac as he grabs for me, I run after Emma.

Halfway down the hallway, I grab hold of her arm and yank her to my chest. I wrap my arms around her and tucking her head under my chin, I drop kisses to her hair.

"I'm s-sorry." She struggles to catch her breath through the tears as sobs jerk her small frame.

"I'm the one who's sorry, Em." I hold her for a while, apologizing again while I caress her back.

Leaning down, I catch her eyes. "I have to go back in."

"Can I wait here?" She sounds so small.

I give her the car keys. "Sure. My phone's on silent, but call me if you need me. I'll check it every few minutes."

"I'll be fine. Go and work." She stands on her toes, pressing a quick kiss to my mouth before she heads to the car.

Judge Flo scowls at me when I walk back into the courtroom.

Cole and Lily get their chance, and it's just as bad as when Emma was up. My heart can't stand any more of this.

It drags out forever before they call it a day.

I catch Cole outside the courtroom.

"Cole, wait up." He doesn't let go of Lily's hand but instead pulls her close to his side. This is going to suck. "Hi, Lily. I'm Aiden Holden. I'm sorry for your loss," I say before I turn my attention to my cousin. "I am really sorry. It wasn't meant to go down that way."

Cole's jaw clenches tightly, and he looks down at Lily.

"I get it. I would've gone in for Lily, too. Wyatt said you didn't know about her. He explained the whole thing about Emma being taken as well. We heard what happened to her. You heard what happened to us. Shit happens." His arm slips down from Lily's shoulder, and he links his fingers with hers.

Lily hasn't responded to me at all. She looks absolutely devastated.

"But I'm going to need some time," Cole continues. "I only came here because I had to. I'm not ready to do the whole family thing yet. Lily's my priority right now."

I don't hesitate in my reply, "Sure. Take all the time you need."

I watch them walk away, hating that this case has hurt my relationship with my cousin. I know with time we'll get back to how it once was between us, but for now, it sucks.

CHAPTER 45

EMMA

Marriage isn't for the fainthearted.

So we're eloping. Sort of.

Aiden and I decided to have a small wedding. Luckily their pastor has agreed to marry us in his office.

Only Zac, Aiden's parents, and Wyatt will be there with us.

Even though I met Aiden's parents and Wyatt at a lunch, I'm still nervous to see them today. The lunch was a wonderful experience, but I still need to get used to how loving they are as a family. At least I feel safe and secure with Katia and Colton having been imprisoned behind bars.

There's a soft knock at the door. "Hello, darlin'," Mrs. Holden greets me warmly as she comes into the bedroom. "You look gorgeous."

I'm wearing a plain silk dress. Really, nothing spectacular. It got my attention because it has no frills. Long sleeves, tight bodice, then it hangs straight down in pleats.

I feel feminine in it. I have my hair pinned up with butterfly clips. Gran loved butterflies, and I'm wearing them so she'll be with me today.

"Hi, Mrs. Holden," I say, giving her an anxious smile.

"You can't call me that forever, Emma. Either call me Tessa or Mama," she says. "I'd prefer Mama though."

I nod so I don't have to answer this instant.

"Are you ready?" she asks.

"Yes," I smile, but take hold of her hand to hold her back. "Before we go, I'd like to thank you for raising such a wonderful man. Because of you being such a good mother, I'm marrying a great man. I hope I can learn from you one day."

Oh hell, I'm gonna cry before I even get to Aiden.

Mrs. Holden flicks a tear from her cheek. "It's my pleasure, darlin'. You enjoy him. Welcome to the family. I'll be more than happy to be a mama to you."

I see the honesty shining through her grey eyes, the same eyes as Aiden's, and I feel hopeful about my future as her daughter-in-law.

"Mama... uhm..." My cheeks flush, but I push through. Slowly, I lean into her and hug her. Her arms wrap around me, hugging me like I've dreamt Mom would hug me.

"Thank you for taking me to the church, Mama," I whisper.

I'm going to look like a bloody panda because I'm crying happy tears in my mother-in-law's arms.

I pull back, and we both laugh as we quickly fix our make-up.

This is all I ever wanted.

A family.

CHAPTER 46

AIDEN

"Do women have this set rule about makin' a man wait?" I ask Zac when Emma is ten minutes late.

"Laurie was only five minutes late," he grins at me.

Wyatt comes running up the stairs of the church. "She's here!"

"Breathe, Aiden. Blue is not a good skin color," Zac jokes, and I punch him on the arm.

I walk to the stairs with a huge smile on my face. My eyes are glued to the door, then finally Mama appears with Emma at her side.

Fuck, my wife-to-be is beautiful.

Then my heart expands impossibly as Mama presses a kiss to Emma's cheek.

Damn, I'm gonna cry.

Emma lets go and climbs the stairs toward me. She takes my breath away with the dress falling softly around her slender frame.

"Hi," she whispers as she reaches me.

"Hi," I whisper back, no doubt with a dumbass smile on my face. "You look breathtakin'."

"You don't clean up too bad yourself, Detective," she teases as her eyes drift over the charcoal-colored suit I'm wearing. "It matches your eyes."

"Are you ready?" I ask.

"Since the day I met you," she answers.

Taking her hand, I lead her to Pastor Doug's office.

The ceremony begins, and everything goes well until Paster Doug asks, "Does anyone here have any reason why these two should not be joined together in holy matrimony?"

"I do," Emma suddenly says next to me.

I swear my heart stops.

"I mean, I have something I'd like to say to Aiden if that's okay?"

"Of course," Pastor Doug says.

I turn to face Emma, and she has that look in her eyes which makes me feel like I can conquer the world.

I can't swallow past the lump pushing up my throat.

"Aiden," she starts, "Gran once told me that if you give yourself to a person, you give them part of your soul. I'm glad half of my soul is with you. You're my soulmate in every way."

I don't give a damn as a tear rolls down my cheek.

"You have all of my heart, Emma," I whisper with the little voice I have left.

After we say our vows, promising ourselves to each other, Pastor Doug announces, "I give you Mr. and Mrs. Holden."

Not caring about my parents or Pastor Doug, I kiss my wife.

The day after the wedding, I take Emma to Oceans Isle beach for our honeymoon. That's where she gave herself to me, even if it was an epic failure as far as first times go.

Getting out of the car, I take her hand and press a kiss to her ring finger.

426

"Close your eyes for me, please. Just for a few seconds," I say.

I watch her eyes flutter closed and take a second to look at her.

My wife.

I pick her up and carry her into the cottage. Emma lets out a bubble of laughter as she wraps her arms around my neck.

Standing in front of the wall, I say, "You can open them."

"What did you do?"

"Look at the wall, Em."

She turns her head as I lower her feet to the floor. Her lips part as emotion washes over her face, and she steps forward to touch one of the photos.

Mama had to rush to get the photos from our wedding up before we got here. I owe her the biggest bunch of flowers.

"You're a part of a family now," I whisper. A tear rolls down her cheek, and I wipe it away as I frame her face and press a kiss to her lips. "I love you, Em."

"I love you most."

(1 year later…)

Christmas was an experience, but then, every day is an experience with Emma.

We've had a great summer, and Emma has found her happy zone, volunteering at a home for the elderly three times a week. It keeps her busy for now until our daughter is born.

I go looking for Emma, and I find her outside, looking up, at the migrating Monarchs. They migrate up North every year, and sometimes, they pass by. But this year, there seem to be hundreds of them as they form a colorful cloud around Emma.

"Gran, I miss you, too." I hear her whisper, and I stop walking towards her, giving her this moment. "It's never goodbye, Gran. I love you," she says.

I wrap my arms around her, resting my hands on her growing baby bump. She leans back against my chest placing her hands over mine.

"Hey, wife of mine. They sure are pretty," I whisper so I won't disturb the beautiful moment.

She turns in my arms. "You think we can name our baby girl Laurie Margarette Holden? The second name is Gran's name."

"I'd like that a lot. I think Laurie and gran would've liked it too."

Emma rests her cheek against my chest, and we watch the butterflies dance around the yard.

Life with Emma is a dream, and I don't ever want to wake up.

The End

SOUTHERN HEROES SERIES

If you loved The Ocean Between Us, then you'll be happy to know that the series continues with Cole's book in The Girl In The Closet.

Wyatt's book - All The Wasted Time.

Alex's book – The Lies We Tell Ourselves.

Zac's book – We Were Lost.

Aiden's book – The Fire Between Us.

ABOUT THE AUTHOR

Michelle is a Bestselling Romance Author who loves creating stories her readers can get lost in. She loves an alpha hero who is not afraid to fight for his woman.

Want to be up to date with what's happening in Michelle's world? Sign up to receive the latest news on her alpha hero releases, sales, and great giveaways
→ **http://eepurl.com/cUXM_P**

If you enjoyed this book or any book, please consider leaving a review. It's appreciated by authors.

THE OCEAN BETWEEN US – Michelle Heard

ACKNOWLEDGMENTS

Sheldon, you hold my heart in your hands. Thank you for being the light to my darkness. You're not just my son, but my best friend, my soul mate, my past, my present, and my future. I live for you.

Allyson & Leeann, thank you so much for letting me run my crazy ideas by you, and for brainstorming with me.

Elaine, Jennifer, Kelly, Kristine, Laura, Leeann, Morgan, and Sheena thank you for being the godparents of my paper-baby.

Josephine & Sam, thank you for keeping me sane during the cover reveal.

Sybil, thank you for the breathtakingly stunning cover.

Neda, thank you for your badass PR skills, and for always being patient with me.

A special thank you to every blogger and reader that took the time to take part in the cover reveal and release day.

Love,
Michelle.

17498911R00232

Printed in Great Britain
by Amazon